CLAIMED FOR DESTINY

BRENDA JACKSON

CLAIMED FOR DESTINY

ARABESQUE®

Recycling programs
for this product may
not exist in your area.

CLAIMED FOR DESTINY

ISBN-13: 978-0-373-53439-5

Copyright © 2011 by Brenda Streater Jackson

The publisher acknowledges the copyright holder of the individual works as follows:

JARED'S COUNTERFEIT FIANCÉE
Copyright © 2005 by Brenda Streater Jackson

THE CHASE IS ON
Copyright © 2005 by Brenda Streater Jackson

www.kimanipress.com

Printed in U.S.A.

CONTENTS

JARED'S COUNTERFEIT FIANCÉE   9

THE CHASE IS ON   195

THE WESTMORELAND FAMILY

Scott and Delane Westmoreland

John (Evelyn)   James (Sarah)   Corey (Abbie)
                                                                                              Madison

② Dare   ③ Thorn   ④ Stone   ⑤ Storm   ⑦ Chase   ① Delaney
(Shelly)   (Tara)   (Madison)   (Jayla)   (Jessica)   (Jamal)
AJ, Allison   Trace   Rock   Shanna, Johanna Carlton Scott Ari, Arielle

⑥ Jared   ⑪   ⑨   ⑧   ⑭   ⑮
(Dana)   Spencer   Ian   Durango
Jaren   (Chardonnay) (Brooke)   (Savannah)   Quade   Reggie
              Russell   Pierce, Price Sarah   (Cheyenne)   (Olivia)
                                                       Venus, Athena, Troy

⑫   ⑬   ⑩
Clint   Cole   Casey
(Alyssa)   (Patrina)   (McKinnon)
Cain   Emilie, Emery Corey Martin

① Delaney's Desert Sheikh   ⑦ The Chase is On   ⑬ Cole's Red-Hot Pursuit
② A Little Dare   ⑧ The Durango Affair   ⑭ Quade's Babies
③ Thorn's Challenge   ⑨ Ian's Ultimate Gamble   ⑮ Tall, Dark…Westmoreland!
④ Stone Cold Surrender   ⑩ Seduction, Westmoreland Style
⑤ Riding the Storm   ⑪ Spencer's Forbidden Passion
⑥ Jared's Counterfeit Fiancée   ⑫ Taming Clint Westmoreland

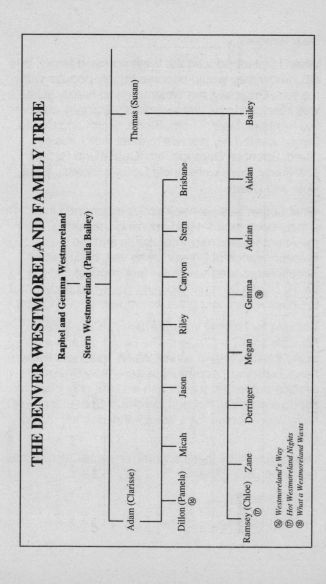

THE DENVER WESTMORELAND FAMILY TREE

Raphel and Gemma Westmoreland

Stern Westmoreland (Paula Bailey)

Thomas (Susan)

Adam (Clarisse)

Dillon (Pamela) ⑯

Stern Westmoreland (Paula Bailey)

Ramsey (Chloe) ⑰   Zane   Micah   Jason   Derringer   Megan   Riley   Canyon   Stern   Brisbane

Gemma ⑱   Adrian   Aidan   Bailey

⑯ *Westmoreland's Way*
⑰ *Hot Westmoreland Nights*
⑱ *What a Westmoreland Wants*

Dear Readers,

When I first introduced the Westmoreland family, little did I know they would become hugely popular with readers. Originally, the Westmoreland Family series was intended to be just six books—Delaney and her five brothers, Dare, Thorn, Stone, Storm and Chase. Later, I wanted my readers to meet their cousins—Jared, Spencer, Durango, Ian, Quade and Reggie. And finally, there were Uncle Corey's triplets—Clint, Cole and Casey.

What began as a six-book series blossomed into a thirty-book series—and counting—featuring the Atlanta-based Westmorelands and the Westmorelands of Denver. I was very happy when Kimani responded to my readers' request that the earlier books be reprinted. And I'm even happier that the reissues are in a great, two-books-in-one format.

Claimed for Destiny includes *Jared's Counterfeit Fiancée* and *The Chase Is On,* books six and seven in the Westmoreland series. When Jared and Dana meet, business becomes pleasure. And Chase and Jessica prove that the kitchen isn't the only place to stir up something hot and delicious. Both stories will have you yearning for a Westmoreland man of your own.

I hope you enjoy these special romances as much as I enjoyed writing them.

Happy reading!

Brenda Jackson

JARED'S
COUNTERFEIT FIANCÉE

In whom are hid all treasures
of wisdom and knowledge.
—*Colossians* 2:3 KJV

To my husband, the love of my life
and my best friend, Gerald Jackson, Sr.

To everyone who wants to meet those
Westmoreland men, this book is for you!

Prologue

Jared Westmoreland glanced up from the legal document he'd been reading when he heard a commotion outside of his office door.

He heard his secretary say, "Wait a minute, miss. You just can't barge into Mr. Westmoreland's office unannounced," moments before his door flew open and a gorgeous but angry woman stormed in.

Jared's heart rate quickened and his pulse accelerated. He forced back the blatant desire that rushed through him as he walked from behind his desk. The woman was absolutely stunning. Even her apparent anger didn't detract from her beauty. In one smooth glance, he took in a mass of dark brown curls that framed her face and the smooth, creamy texture of her skin—the color of rich mahogany. Then there were her beautiful dark brown eyes with perfectly arched brows, a delectable pair of lips and rounded cheeks with dimples that not even her anger could hide. A sleek, curvy body in a pair of slacks and a tailored blouse completed the vision of beauty.

"Mr. Westmoreland, I tried to stop her but she—"

"That's all right, Jeannie," Jared said to his secretary, who had raced in behind the woman.

"Do you want me to call security?"

"No, I don't think that will be necessary."

Jeannie Tillman, who'd worked for him for over five years, didn't look too convinced. "Are you sure?"

He stared at the seething woman who was standing with both hands on her hips, glaring at him. "Yes, I'm sure." Jeannie gave him a hesitant nod and turned to leave, closing the door behind her.

Jared turned his full attention to his beautiful intruder. He was fairly certain that she was not a client since he didn't forget a beautiful face. In fact, he was sure he'd never met her before.

Dana Rollins met Jared's stare and tried to keep her intense reaction to him from showing. She had heard about Jared Westmoreland, Atlanta's hotshot, millionaire attorney. Now she was seeing him for herself and it seemed that all she'd heard was true. He was definitely the stuff dreams were made of. A sharp dresser, all the way down to his expensive-looking leather shoes, he was tall, with a body that was well built. Solid as a rock. He had coffee-colored skin, dark brown eyes, a solid jaw, straight nose and close-cut black hair. They were handsome features on a sensual face; the kind that would definitely make her do a double take. But she couldn't dwell on how sexy he looked. She was here for business and nothing more.

"I'm sure there's a reason why you barged into my office, Miss..."

"Rollins," she supplied sharply. His words reminded her of what that business was. "And yes, there is a reason. This!" she said, pulling an envelope out of her purse. "I received this certified letter from you less than an hour ago demanding that I return my engagement ring to Luther. I tried calling him but was told he's out of town so I immediately came here to get an explanation."

Jared took the letter from her and looked at it. The assessment didn't take long. He glanced back at her. "I gather you have a problem with returning the ring, Miss Rollins?" he asked.

"Of course I do. Luther decided he wasn't ready to give up his single status and called off our wedding a week before it was to take place. Besides the embarrassment and humiliation of everything—explaining things to my friends and returning shower gifts—I was left with all the wedding expenses. And to pour salt on the wound, I received that letter from your firm."

Jared inhaled deeply. Evidently she hadn't yet realized that Luther Cord had done her a favor. "Miss Rollins, I suggest you consult your own attorney to verify what I'm telling you, but my client has every right to ask for the engagement ring back. An engagement ring represents a conditional gift. The proposition is that the condition is marriage and not a willingness to marry.

Thus if the engagement is broken, for whatever reason, the expectation is that the ring is returned, just as you returned the wedding presents and shower gifts," he said.

He watched as she crossed her arms over her chest and the angry frown on her lips deepened and turned rebellious. "I refuse to give it back. It's the principle of the thing."

Jared shook his head thinking that principle had nothing to do with it. The law was the law. "Unfortunately, Miss Rollins, you're faced with a losing battle and a very costly one. Do you want to add a bunch of legal fees to everything else right now?"

He knew the mention of finances would help make her think straight. And knowing he had her thinking in the right direction, he pressed forward. "I know what you're going through must be painful, but my advice to you is to try and put this episode behind you and move on. You're a beautiful woman, and I believe there's a man out there who's truly worthy of you. Evidently Luther Cord isn't. Perhaps you should count your blessings."

Jared knew his words weren't what she wanted to hear but he wanted to be as honest with her as he could. There was only so much he could say, considering the fact that Luther Cord was his client. In fact, he had said too much already. But for some reason he wanted to help end her heartache as soon as possible.

Moments passed and Dana didn't say anything, but he could tell she was thinking about what he'd said. Then he watched as she pulled a small white box from her purse and handed it to him.

He met her gaze when she said softly, "I appreciate your advice and although it's a bitter pill to swallow, I'll return the ring."

He flipped it open and saw the dazzling diamond solitaire before placing the small box on his desk. "You're doing the right thing, Miss Rollins."

She nodded and extended her hand to him. "The last thing I need is to get into more debt. Luther isn't worth it."

He accepted her hand, liking the way it fit neatly into his. "I hope things work out for you," he said with complete sincerity.

Dana gazed intently into his eyes and smiled appreciatively. Although she hadn't wanted to hear what he'd said, she couldn't help but be grateful for his honesty. In her experience, compassion and kindness were two emotions attorneys seldom possessed. "Somehow they will. I know I interrupted your work by barging in here the way I did and I apologize," she said.

"You didn't interrupt anything," Jared said smoothly. "And as for my advice, consider it a favor."

The smile that touched her lips widened. "Thanks. Maybe I'll be able to return the favor some day. I owe you one."

As he released her hand and watched her turn and walk out of his office, Jared thought to himself that Dana Rollins was as sensual as a woman could get.

One

A month later

Jared Westmoreland was having one hell of a morning.

It began with the message his mother had left on his answering machine last night, reminding him that his father's and his uncle's birthdays fell on Easter Sunday this year and requesting that he set an example for his five brothers by bringing a date to the huge dinner party she and his aunt Evelyn had planned.

His cousin Storm's recent wedding had made his mother, Sarah, take stock and realize that her six sons had yet to show serious interest in any woman. And of course, since he was the eldest, she felt he should be the first and had every intention of prodding him in the right direction. It didn't matter that he and his brothers were successful and enjoyed being single. She felt that the only way any of them could truly be happy was to find that special woman and tie the knot. The only one who wasn't experiencing the heat was his brother Spencer, whose fiancée Lynette, had died in a drowning accident three years ago.

Jared rose from his chair and walked over to the window. To add to the annoyance of his mother's call, he had arrived at work an hour later than usual because of traffic. And as if things couldn't get any worse, he had just received a phone call from entertainer Sylvester Brewster, who wanted to file for a divorce—from wife number three. Sylvester was good for business, but it was hard to watch him involve himself in relationships that didn't last.

When Jared heard the buzzer sounding on his desk, he turned around and sighed heavily, wondering if the morning could get any worse. Crossing the room he picked up the phone. "Yes, Jeannie?"

"Mr. Westmoreland, your mother is on the line."

Jared shook his head. Yes, his morning could get worse. It just did. "Go ahead and put her through."

A few moments later after hearing the connection, he said. "Hi, Mom."

"Did you get my message, Jared?"

Jared raised his gaze to the ceiling before saying. "Yes, I got it."

"Good. Then I'll be setting an extra plate out for dinner next Sunday."

Jared wanted to tell her in a nice, respectable way that if she set out the plate there was a strong chance it would sit there empty. But before he could get the words out, his mother quickly added, "Remember, you're the oldest and I expect you to set an example. Besides, you're not getting any younger."

She made it seem as if he was fifty-seven instead of thirty-seven. Besides, his mother knew how he felt about the institution of marriage. He was a divorce attorney for heaven's sake. He ended marriages, not put them together. He'd handled enough divorce cases to know that marriage wasn't all it was cracked up to be. People got married and then a lot of them eventually got divorced. It was a vicious cycle; one that made him money, but sickened him at the same time. Although there were long-lasting marriages in the Westmoreland family, he considered them exceptions and not the norm. It would be just his luck to have the first failed marriage in the family and he had no intention of becoming a statistic.

"Jared, are you listening?"

He sighed. When she used that tone, he had no other choice but to listen. "Yes, but has it occurred to you that Durango, Ian, Spencer, Quade, Reggie and I like being single?" he asked respectfully.

"And has it ever occurred to any of you that your father and I aren't getting any younger and we'd love to have grandchildren while we're still of sound mind to enjoy them?"

Jared shook his head. First, she was trying to shove marriage down their throats and now she was hinting at grandchildren. But he was smart enough to know that the last thing he needed was to butt heads with caring, stubborn Sarah Westmoreland. He would rather face an uncompromising judge in the courtroom than oppose his mother. It was an uphill battle that he just didn't have the energy for right now.

"I'll see what I can do," he finally said.

"Thanks, Son. That's all I ask."

"Really, Dana, I wish you would think about going with us."

Dana Rollins glanced up at Cybil Franklin, who stood in the middle of her office with a determined frown on her face. Cybil was Dana's best friend from high school and the primary reason she had relocated from Tennessee to Atlanta three years ago to take a position at Kessler Industries as a landscape architect.

"Thanks, Cybil, but I'm sure you've heard the saying that three's a crowd. I don't think going with you and Ben to North Carolina this weekend is a good idea."

Cybil rolled her eyes. "It's just a camping trip to the mountains. I feel awful knowing you'll be spending Easter alone."

Leaning back in the chair behind her desk, Dana smiled easily. "Hey, I'm a twenty-seven-year-old woman who can take care of herself. I'll be fine and I have no problem spending Easter alone." *It will be just like every other year since Mom and Dad died.*

None of the holidays were the same anymore since her parents had been killed in a car accident on their way to her college graduation five years earlier. Since she had no other family, their deaths had left her truly alone. She'd thought all that had changed when she met Luther. They began dating in early spring and after six months, he had asked her to marry him.

"It's times like these when I'm tempted to find

Luther Cord and kill him," Cybil said angrily. "When I think of what he did to you, I get so mad."

Dana smiled softly, no longer able to muster up anger when she thought about Luther. He had paid her an unexpected visit last week to tell her that he was moving to California. He told her that his decision not to marry had nothing to do with her, that he'd come to terms with his sexual preference, and that in his own way he loved her, but not in the way a husband is supposed to love his wife. At first she had been shocked, but then she'd acknowledged that the signs had all been there. She couldn't, or hadn't wanted to see them. Dana hadn't told anyone about Luther's confession, not even Cybil.

Dana turned her attention back to her friend. "I told you that I'd be fine. It won't be the first or the last holiday that I spend alone."

"I know but I wish that—"

"Cybil, let it go. You need to get out of here if you're meeting Ben for lunch," she said, trying to propel her out the door.

"Okay, but call me soon?"

As soon as Cybil left, Dana released a huge sigh.

Since her breakup with Luther, Dana put all of her time and energy into her job. Work wasn't a substitute for having a family and a personal life, but it did take her mind off her loneliness.

She glanced at the calendar on her desk. It was hard to believe next week was Easter already. Her parents would make every holiday special and even while in college she enjoyed going home during spring break to spend Easter with them. She remembered their last

Easter together. They had gone to sunrise church service and later they had feasted on the delicious dinner her mother had prepared, not knowing it would be the last holiday meal they would share together.

She sighed deeply, not wanting to relinquish the memories just yet but knowing that she had to. Somehow she would get through another holiday without her parents. She had no other choice.

"What would you like to order, sir?"

Jared studied the huge menu posted on the wall behind the counter and made his decision. "Umm, give me a ham and cheese all the way on whole wheat, an order of French fries and a glass of sweetened tea."

"All right. Your order will be ready in a minute."

Jared nodded then glanced around. Usually he met clients for lunch at restaurants that served the finest cuisine; and at other times he would order in and eat lunch at his office. But he had decided to take advantage of how beautiful a day it was and walk the block from his office to the deli.

The place was crowded and he hoped that he would be able to find a seat by the time his lunch was ready. He was even willing to share a table or booth with someone if the person didn't have a problem with it.

As his eyes scanned the crowded restaurant, he tried to find someone sitting alone. Abruptly his gaze stopped on a familiar-looking woman at a booth, who was reading a book while leisurely munching on a French fry. A memory suddenly flared in his mind, jump-started his senses and instantly stirred heat within him.

Dana Rollins.

It had been a month since she had stormed into his office, but he vividly recalled the impact she'd made on his male senses when she'd barged in that day. He felt blood race through his veins, reminding him that he'd been so busy at work, he hadn't been with a woman in over eight months.

He was accustomed to beautiful, gorgeous women, but there was something intrinsically special about Dana Rollins. He hadn't been this attracted to a woman since heaven knows when. Now it seemed he was making up for lost time.

"Sir, your order is ready."

Jared turned and took the tray loaded with his food from the man behind the counter. "Thanks." He then glanced back over at Dana Rollins and after making a quick decision, he crossed the room to where she sat.

She was so absorbed in her book that she didn't notice him standing next to her. She was leaning forward with both her elbows on the table while holding the book in front of her, so that the neckline of her blouse gapped open enough for him to get a generous glimpse of her cleavage. He liked what he saw—firm, full breasts.

Knowing he couldn't stand there and continue to ogle her, he cleared his throat. "Miss Rollins?"

She quickly glanced up and recognized him. He watched her shimmering bronze lips tilt into a smile guaranteed to turn him on. "Mr. Westmoreland, it's good to see you again."

Her dimpled smile made him acutely aware of just how beautiful she was. "It's good seeing you again, too. It's rather crowded in here and I saw you sitting alone and wondered if perhaps I could join you?"

Her smile widened into a grin. "Yes, of course," she said, placing her book down on the table, making sure not to lose her spot.

"Thanks," he said, sliding into the seat across from her in the booth. "How have you been?"

Her lashes fluttered downward before sweeping up with her gaze to meet his. "I've been fine and have done what you suggested and moved on."

Jared nodded. "I'm glad to hear it, Miss Rollins."

Her smile widened. "Please call me Dana."

He chuckled. "Only if you call me Jared."

After saying grace, he took a sip of his drink then proceeded to put ketchup on his fries. He glanced her way and smiled. "So what are you reading?"

She took a sip of her drink then picked up the book and held it up. "A book of poems by Maya Angelou. She's a wonderful poet and I love reading her work. It can be so uplifting."

He nodded. He had read several of her poems himself. Dana met his gaze. "Do you read a lot, Jared?"

He shrugged broad shoulders under an expensive suit. "The only pleasure reading I have time for these days is my cousin's novels. He writes under the pen name Rock Mason."

Her eyes lit up and showed her surprise. "You're related to Rock Mason?"

Jared laughed. "Yes. His real name is Stone Westmoreland."

Dana smiled. "Wow. I've read all of his books. He's a gifted writer."

Jared chuckled. "I'll make sure I tell him you said that when I see him again. He and his wife, Madison, are in Texas visiting cousins we have there, but they'll be back for our fathers' birthdays next weekend."

"Your fathers' birthdays?"

He smiled. "Our fathers are fraternal twins and they turn sixty this year. Since their birthdays fall on Easter Sunday, our mothers are hosting one huge celebration."

"Sounds like all of you will have a wonderful time."

He chuckled. "We usually do when we all get together. The Westmoreland family is big. What about you? Are you from a large family?"

He watched sadness appear in her eyes. "I don't have any family. I was an only child and my parents were killed five years ago in an auto accident en route to my college graduation."

"I'm sorry."

She met his gaze and saw the sincerity of his words. "Thank you. It was hard for me, but I got through it. Since my parents didn't have any siblings, and their parents are deceased, I don't have a family."

He watched as she caught her lower lip between her teeth as if to keep it from trembling with the remembered pain. "What are your plans for Easter Sunday?" he couldn't help but ask.

"I don't have any. I'll go to a sunrise service at church and will probably spend the rest of the day at home relaxing and reading."

He lifted an eyebrow. "What about dinner?"

She shrugged. "I'll pull out a microwave dinner and enjoy the day that way."

Jared tried shifting his attention back to his food but couldn't fully concentrate on what he was eating. Because of his large family, he had grown up loving the holidays and even looked forward to them, although lately his mother's interfering had tempered his anticipation.

An idea suddenly popped into Jared's head. His mother was expecting him to bring someone to dinner so why not Dana? When his mother and his aunt Evelyn got together, the two women cooked up a storm. That had to be better than a microwave dinner. "How would you like to join me for Easter dinner at my parents' home?" He could tell that his invitation surprised her.

"You're inviting me to dinner at your parents' place?"

"Yes."

She shook her head, as if still not understanding. "But, why? We barely know each other."

Jared knew he had to level with her. "It just so happens that you can help me out of a jam."

Dana lifted a brow. "What kind of jam?"

"My mother is obsessed. Lately, a number of my cousins have gotten married and since none of her six sons are rushing to follow suit, she's taken it upon herself to prod us along. I'm the oldest so I'm feeling the heat more than the others. She expects me to set an example by bringing someone to dinner. And since I recall you owe me a favor, I figured now's the time to collect."

Dana blinked and then she released a deep sigh. Jared could tell she had forgotten about her promise. "But I'm sure there're plenty of women you've dated who would love going to dinner with you at your parents' home," she implored.

Jared nodded as he continued to smile. "Yes, but if I take any of them they might get the wrong impression and think that I'm actually interested in a serious relationship. Besides, my mother and aunt are good cooks. All you'll have to do is show up with me, endure the likes of my family and join in with the birthday festivities. I understand it's a lot to ask, but I'd really appreciate it if you'd come. It will definitely get Mom off my back."

Jared watched as she nervously gnawed her bottom lip. He had presented the situation just as it was.

Dana met his gaze. She had felt that pull between them, that physical attraction, so to consider being in Jared's company for any reason wasn't a good idea. But, she did owe him a favor and she'd always been taught to keep her word. "And it's just this one time?"

"Yes, just this one time," he assured her. "But to pull this off, we'll need a convincing story. I think it would be a good idea if I called you one day this week to discuss answers to the questions I have a feeling my family will ask."

Dana frowned. "What kind of questions?"

Jared grinned. "Oh, the usual, like how long have we known each other? When and how we met? How serious are things between us? And there's a strong chance my mother might get downright personal and want to know if you've moved in with me yet, whether you're capable of producing babies and if so, how many you're willing to have."

Dana blinked, then laughed out loud. Jared thought it was a beautiful sound; and in all honesty, the deep rumble in her throat was a blatant turn-on.

"You aren't serious, are you?" she asked, bringing her laughter under control.

He chuckled. "Unfortunately, I am. Just wait until you meet my mother for yourself. Marrying off one of her sons seems to be her number-one priority."

Dana raised an arched brow. "And marriage is something you have an aversion to?"

"Yes. I handle enough divorce cases to know that most marriages don't last."

He watched as she sat back in her chair with a thoughtful expression on her face. "So will you be my date that day?"

Dana considered Jared's invitation. After a few moments she nodded her agreement.

Jared smiled, pleased with the turn of events. "Thanks, Dana. I appreciate you helping me out of this jam. You don't know how much it means to be able to get my mother off my back."

Two

Dana glanced down at her watch. Jared was coming to pick her up at any moment and she was a nervous wreck.

They had talked on the phone earlier in the week to get prepared for his family's inquisition. Just hearing his voice had sent sensuous chills all through her body and reminded her that she was definitely a woman, something she had forgotten since her breakup with Luther.

That reminder came with a mixture of empowerment and restraint. The last thing she needed was to test emotional waters that were best left uncharted. All she had to do was remember what had happened with Luther to know that, woman or not, the last thing she wanted was to become vulnerable to any man again.

Dana almost jumped when she heard the sound of her doorbell. She inhaled deeply and reminded herself that she probably wouldn't see Jared again after today so there was no reason for her to come unglued. She released a sigh of relief and opened the door.

Jared gazed at Dana and quickly pulled in a deep breath. If he thought that she was gorgeous before, today she had surpassed his memories. He'd always had a healthy sex drive, but seeing her standing in the doorway with all that glorious hair spread over her shoulders and wearing a pair of jeans that hugged her curvy figure and a pretty knit top, had him wondering how he would get through the day.

"Hi, Jared, please come in."

"Thanks. You look nice."

She smiled and stepped back as he entered and closed the door behind him. "Thank you. I just need to grab my purse," she said, walking off toward a room he assumed was her bedroom.

He was glad for the extra time to pull himself together. The woman was sexy and feminine all rolled into one.

Trying to distract himself, he glanced around her living room. It was nicely decorated in bright colors and with upscale furnishings. He felt something rubbing against his leg and looked down and smiled. "Hey, where did you come from?" he asked, leaning down and picking up a beautiful black cat.

"I'm ready now," Dana said, reentering the room. She smiled when she saw him holding her cat. "I see you've met Tom."

Jared chuckled. "Oh, that's his name?"

"Yes. I've had him for a couple of years, since he was a kitten. Now he's spoiled rotten but great company."

"He's a handsome fellow," Jared said as he continued to pet the animal.

"Shh, don't say that too loud. He's conceited enough already," Dana whispered.

Jared smiled as he placed Tom back on the floor. When he straightened back to his full height he met Dana's gaze. Desire shot all the way through him and with an effort he swallowed. "Ready?" he asked.

"Yes, I'm ready."

"Welcome to our home, Dana. I'm so glad that Jared brought you."

Dana suddenly found herself swept into strong arms as a woman who she figured to be Jared's mother gave her a gigantic hug. She had expected a nice welcome but certainly not this outpouring of affection.

"Thanks for having me," Dana said once the woman released her. She glanced up at Jared. Their gazes met and held. His expression was unreadable and she couldn't help wondering what he was thinking.

Dana noticed a sudden thickness in her throat when she remembered how she'd felt when Jared had arrived at her place, exactly at noon. The only thing she could think was that even dressed in jeans and a pullover shirt he looked polished, suave, debonair and sensual.

"You two can give each other that dreamy-eyed look later," Sarah Westmoreland said, beaming. "Come on in, everyone is anxious to meet Dana."

Jared shook his head, catching himself and regaining his concentration. The last thing he wanted was for his mother to get any ideas that Dana was more than just a dinner date. "I take it that we're the last to arrive," he said, placing his hand at the small of Dana's back while his mother led them through the foyer.

"Quade isn't here but he called to say that he's on his way."

Jared nodded. His brother Quade was involved in security activities for the Secret Service and often missed family gatherings because of it. But it wasn't from lack of trying to be present. Like all Westmorelands, Quade enjoyed family get-togethers.

Jared could hear voices coming from the living room and took another look at Dana. He had intended it to be a quick look but even in the daylight, the soft glow from the crystal chandelier overhead seemed to enhance her beauty. There was something about the shape of her mouth—he wondered how it would feel under his when he...

"My goodness, Jared, will you stop staring at Dana like that!" his mother scolded in a chuckling voice.

Damn. He hadn't realized he'd been staring again. He kept forgetting just how observant his mother was; her eyes missed nothing. His mother was smiling and for the first time he wondered if perhaps he had made a mistake in inviting Dana. If his mother noticed his attention to her, he could just imagine what the other family members would think. That meant he had to keep his cool and not appear so taken with her.

"It's about time you got here."

Jared's head jerked around and he frowned. His brother Durango, the man who thought all women were made for his pleasure unless they had another man's stamp on them, was talking to Jared, but looking at Dana.

"Durango," Jared acknowledged when his brother came to join them.

Durango nodded but his gaze went straight back to Dana. "And who is this beautiful creature?" he asked smoothly, as a smile touched both corners of his mouth.

"This is Jared's girl. And she's off-limits to you, so behave," Sarah Westmoreland spoke up.

Jared's girl. Jared rubbed the back of his neck, feeling the heat already.

"Are you sure that you don't want any more birthday cake, Dana?"

Dana smiled at Sarah. "Thanks for asking but I don't think I can eat a single thing more. All the food was wonderful, Mrs. Westmoreland."

Dana was completely overwhelmed when Jared had escorted her into the living room and introduced her to his family. The house had been decorated with birthday streamers and balloons from corner to corner. It didn't take long to see that the Westmorelands weren't just a clan but a whole whopping village. The love and warmth between them was easy to see and feel.

There were Jared's male cousins, Dare, Thorn, Stone, Chase, Storm, Clint and Cole. They all favored each other and it was easy to tell they were kin. There were few women in the Westmoreland family: Jared's cousin Delaney who was married to a Middle East sheikh, a tall, dark, handsome man; his cousin Casey who lived in Texas and was sister to Clint and Cole, as well as Shelly, Tara, Madison and Jayla, the wives of Dare, Thorn, Stone and Storm. She also met Jared's uncle Corey and his wife, Abby.

She had never seen so many relatives gathered in one place before, and for a moment a part of her had felt a tinge of jealousy that some people had such a huge family while others had none. But that bout of jealousy soon dissolved when she saw just how friendly and down-to-earth everyone was. At first they had been curious because Jared had never brought a woman to any family function before, but eventually they began to treat her like one of the family, without hesitation, but with a few questions that she felt she effectively answered to satisfy their curiosity. When Jared's brother Quade arrived, all of the attention had momentarily shifted off her, but now it was back on her again.

Jayla was pregnant with twins and the women invited Dana to join them on a shopping trip they had planned for next weekend to help select items for the babies' nursery. Since Dana knew Jared intended for this to be the last time she socialized with his family, she declined, coming up with an excuse about all the errands she had to do Saturday morning, but had thanked them for the invitation.

She glanced over to where Jared stood talking to his brothers and cousins and her heart thumped an unsteady beat just watching him. As if he felt her looking at him, he cocked his head in her direction and their gazes connected. Goose bumps skittered along her arms and she expelled a long, silent breath before breaking eye contact with him.

Needing to distract herself, she glanced out of the window. Jared's parents' home sat on three acres of land and the huge, two-story, Southern style structure was simply stunning. A huge window provided a view of a lake. It was late afternoon and getting dark, which was a stark indication that Easter was almost over.

"I need to talk to you privately for a moment," Jared whispered softly in her ear.

She sucked in a sharp breath. She hadn't heard him approach and the warmth of his breath touched her neck and the faint spicy aroma of his aftershave made her skin tingle.

She wondered what he had to talk to her about and knew his family wondered, as well, when he took her hand and guided her into the kitchen, closing the door behind them.

He leaned against the kitchen counter and for a moment they stared at each other, not saying anything. Then he cleared his throat. "I should have given you this earlier at your apartment when I picked you up but I forgot." Jared knew he could have waited until he returned her home, but for some reason he wanted to get her alone, even if only for a few minutes. "Luther Cord sent a special delivery to me on Friday with instructions that I give you this. After arriving in California he evidently had a change of heart and decided he wanted you to keep it."

Dana raised a curious brow as she watched Jared reach into his pocket to pull out a small white box. She immediately knew what it was. "My engagement ring?" she asked, startled.

Jared saw the surprised, but pleased look on her face

and couldn't help but smile. "Yes, it's for you," he said, handing the small box to her.

"I knew it! I just knew she was the one!"

Jared jerked his head around when his mother burst through the kitchen door. Her face was all aglow.

"I happened to be passing by the door and heard the words engagement ring. Oh, Jared, you have made me so proud and happy," his mother exclaimed between bouts of laughter and tears of joy. She then hugged Dana. "Welcome to the family."

Jared's head began spinning when it became crystal clear what his mother had assumed. He was just about to open his mouth to set her straight when the kitchen door flew open again and his entire family poured in.

"What's going on?" Jared's father asked when he saw his wife in tears.

Again Jared opened his mouth to speak but his mother's voice drowned out any words he was about to say. "Jared and Dana. They just got engaged! He gave her a ring! Oh, I am so happy. I can't believe that one of my sons is finally settling down and getting married."

Jared and Dana suddenly became swamped with words of congratulation and well wishing. He glanced over at Dana and saw she was as shocked with the way things were escalating as he was. He reached over and gently squeezed her hand, hoping that he was assuring her that he would straighten things out. He knew that he should do so now but couldn't recall the last time he'd seen his mother this happy.

Sarah Westmoreland began crying again. "You have

really made me happy today, Jared. Who would have thought that of all my sons you would have a change of heart about marriage? But I could feel the love flowing between the two of you when I opened the door and saw you standing there together."

Dana glanced over at Jared. She read the message in his eyes that clearly said: *Trust me, I'll get us out of this mess, but for now, please let my mother have her moment of happiness.* She gave him a silent nod to let him know she understood what he was asking. She inhaled deeply. Of all the misunderstandings she'd heard of, this one was definitely a doozy.

"Dana and I are leaving," Jared said, taking Dana's hand and leading her out of the kitchen.

"But—but we haven't celebrated your good news," his mother called out when he headed for the door.

He turned to look at his relatives, wanting to tell them that they wouldn't be celebrating it, either. They had followed the couple to the door and were crowded around them. He frowned at the "glad it's you and not me" look on the faces of the other single Westmoreland men. "I'll see everyone tomorrow," he told his family.

Then without saying another word and holding Dana's hand firmly in his, he walked out of his parents' house, closing the door behind him.

"I'm sorry about what happened back there," Jared said. Talk about the wrong information getting blown out of proportion. "I just couldn't tell my mother the truth. She was so happy."

Dana nodded. "I understand."

Jared lifted his head and gazed over at Dana, met her gaze and something about the way she was looking back at him told him that she really did understand. "Thank you."

She smiled. "You don't have to thank me. This was a special day for your family. I saw how happy your mother was when she'd thought we'd gotten engaged."

Jared nodded, grateful for her understanding. "I'll talk to her tomorrow and straighten things out," he said quietly.

"All right."

Satisfied, Jared put his car in gear and backed out of his parents' driveway. At the first traffic light they came to, he glanced over and noticed the engagement ring was on Dana's finger. He frowned, remembering his mother's insistence that she put it on. For some reason he didn't like seeing her wearing Luther Cord's ring. "Now that you have the ring back what are you going to do with it?" he asked, trying to keep his voice neutral.

Dana glanced over at him before looking down at the ring. "What I had planned to do all along. Hock it and use the money to pay off the remaining wedding expenses. I'm surprised Luther returned it to me."

Jared wasn't surprised. During the last conversation he'd had with Cord, he had suggested that he do the decent thing and relieve some of the financial burden breaking the engagement had placed on Dana. He had strongly recommended that although he wasn't legally obligated to do so, he should consider letting her keep the ring. Evidently the man had taken his advice.

When the traffic light changed, Jared glanced over at Dana. Her eyes were closed and her head was back against the headrest. He couldn't stop the smile that touched his lips. No doubt this had been a tiring day for her. He was used to his huge family, but a stranger might be overwhelmed.

"Considering everything, do you regret going to my parents' home for dinner?" he couldn't help but ask.

Although she didn't open her eyes, a smile touched her lips. "No, I had a wonderful time, Jared. Being around your family and seeing your closeness, brought back so many memories of how close I was to my parents and how they used to make every holiday so special for me." She opened her eyes, tilted her head to him and smiled. "I really appreciate you sharing your friendly, loving pack with me today."

The warm look Dana gave him sent heated sensations down Jared's spine. She might have enjoyed spending time with his family, but he could admit that he had actually enjoyed spending the day with her, as well. She was a charming person to be around and, unlike a lot of his other dates, Dana had not demanded his complete attention, by clinging to him or refusing to let him out of her sight.

He had watched how easily she had blended in with his family and how quickly she had won them over. He could see why his mother thought he had fallen for her.

Jared's hand tightened on the steering wheel. Thinking he was falling for her was one thing, but actually believing that he was engaged to her was another. How could his mother assume such a thing? She knew how he felt about marriage. Did she actually believe one woman could make him change his whole thought process on something he felt so strongly about?

Moments later he pulled into Dana's driveway and brought the car to a stop. He glanced over at her and saw that she had fallen asleep. He hated waking her but knew that he had to. So as not to startle her, he leaned over and softly whispered, "Dana, you're home."

He watched as her eyes slowly opened, then of its own accord his gaze latched on to her lips, full, luscious, tempting. He would give anything to know how they tasted.

"I think I'd better walk you to the door," he said, fighting the urge to pull her into his arms and kiss her.

He watched as she took a deep breath and nodded. "All right."

Opening the door he got out of the car and walked around to open the door for her; then together they walked to her door. She turned to face him. "Thanks again, Jared, for such a beautiful day. It was special."

He nodded. He wanted to say that she was special, too, but knew that he couldn't. This was their only time together and he had to accept that. "Thanks for being my date. I'll talk to my mother tomorrow."

"Okay."

He watched as she put her key in the door and moments later she turned to him. She hesitated for a moment, then asked, "Would you like to come in for a drink?"

He suddenly decided that he wanted to go in, but not for the drink she was offering. He wanted to do something he'd been thinking of all day. "Yes, I'd like that."

He followed her inside, but when she headed toward the kitchen he placed his hand on her arm. "I can't think of a better way for this day to end than this," he said softly, before leaning down and gently capturing her mouth with his, needing to taste her as much as he needed to breathe.

Shivers of profound pleasure shot through every part of Dana's body the moment their lips touched and her eyelids automatically fluttered shut. When Jared's tongue slipped into her mouth, tasting of the sweet tea he had sipped earlier, she shuddered as a delicious shiver ran up her spine.

Sensations she had never felt before consumed her and when she felt his hands wrap around her middle, pulling her close to the fit of his hard body, she could have melted right where she stood. His assault of her mouth was deliberate, sensuous, unhurried. It was meant to tantalize and awaken every part of her and it did.

Then he deepened the kiss, taking it to another level as he continued to take her mouth slowly, thoroughly, passionately. A part of her wanted to pull back, but he was right. This was the perfect way to end the day. They had been attracted to each other from the first and to pretend otherwise would be a complete waste of time. And since this was the last time they'd spend together, they could at least have this moment.

So she hung in and continued to let him kiss her, finding exquisite pleasure in every moment that he did so. Then he changed the rhythm of their kiss as his tongue played seek and retreat with hers, making a whimper rumble from deep within her throat.

Heat throbbed within Jared as he continued to kiss Dana. Initially, he had meant for the kiss to be nothing more than a way of saying goodbye, to satisfy his curiosity and hunger, but the moment he tasted her sweetness he was helpless to do anything but sink in and savor.

He made sure his kiss was gentle but thorough as he relentlessly explored her mouth. His tongue dueled with hers in a slow sensuous motion and when she wound her arms around his neck and arched her body to the hard length of his, he was consumed with hot waves of desire. There was something about her that had his senses pulsating. Never before had he been this driven to devour anyone.

Moments later with a fevered moan, he lifted his mouth away from hers although he continued to track her lips with his tongue. "You're beautiful in every way that a woman can be, Dana," he whispered roughly against her ear, burying his face in her neck and placing a kiss there.

His compliment touched Dana's very core. No one had ever said such a thing to her. "Thank you."

"Don't thank me. It's the truth," he said, releasing her slowly and taking a step back. "And I want to thank you again for helping me out today."

"I want to thank you, as well. Like I said, your family is wonderful."

He nodded. There would be no reason to see her after today. He tried racking his brain for some excuse to drop by, but couldn't find one. He ran a frustrated hand across the back of his neck. No woman had ever had him this reluctant to say goodbye. He glanced around the room, stalling for time. "Where's Tom?" he asked, trying to prolong the time by even an additional second if he could.

"He's probably in my bed."

Damn lucky cat. Jared met her gaze and knew he should leave before he did something really crazy such as grabbing her and starting to kiss her again. "Goodbye, Dana."

"Goodbye, Jared."

"Take care of yourself." And with those final words he turned, opened the door and walked out of the house.

Three

Around ten the next morning, Jared walked into his parents' home. His nine o'clock court appointment had gotten canceled, which afforded him the opportunity to visit his mother and straighten out yesterday's misunderstanding.

"Mom! Dad!" he called out while walking through the living room to the kitchen.

"I'm out back," was his father's reply.

Jared opened the kitchen door and stepped onto the sun deck his father had built last year. He saw him busy at work putting a coat of polish on his classic Ford Mustang. "Good morning, Dad."

"Morning, son. What a nice surprise to see you on a Monday morning."

"I had a canceled court hearing this morning. Where is everyone?"

"Durango stayed over at Stone's place last night and Ian and Spencer are having breakfast with their cousins at Chase's Place. Quade had to fly out first thing this morning to return to D.C. and Reggie, I imagine went to work."

Jared nodded and glanced around. "I need to talk to Mom. Is she upstairs?"

His father sighed deeply. "No, she had a doctor's appointment this morning."

Jared frowned. "A doctor's appointment? Is anything wrong?"

His father shrugged. "I hope not, but you know your mother. If something is wrong then I'll be the last to know. She thinks if she tells me anything I'd worry myself to death. I wouldn't know about her appointment today if I hadn't heard the message the doctor's office left on the answering machine reminding her of it. Appears they found another lump during her checkup last week."

Jared's frown deepened. Three years ago his mother had been diagnosed with breast cancer and had undergone a series of chemo and radiation treatments before being given a clean bill of health.

"Mom's car is in the driveway so how did she get to the doctor's?"

"I offered to drive her but she had already made arrangements for your aunt Evelyn to take her. You know those two. They have been best friends for years."

Jared nodded. Everyone in the Westmoreland family knew how the two women who had been best friends since high school had ended up marrying the Westmoreland twins, becoming sisters-in-law. "Do you think it's anything serious?" he asked.

He couldn't help but remember how things were the last time. The cancer treatments had made his mother sicker than he'd ever remembered her being. He, his brothers and his dad had made the mistake of hovering over her as if she was an invalid. That hadn't helped matters, which was probably the reason she hadn't mentioned this doctor's appointment to any of them. They would have all shown up at the doctor's office with her today.

"To be honest, Jared, I was beginning to get concerned. I could tell she was worried, although she tried pretending that she wasn't. But then all that changed yesterday."

Jared raised a brow. "Yesterday? What happened yesterday?"

"You made her one extremely happy woman when you and Dana announced your engagement."

Jared opened his mouth to say that he and Dana hadn't exactly announced anything. His mother had assumed the wrong thing and jumped to conclusions.

"I think your engagement actually gave her a new lease on life, a determination to handle whatever it is the doctor is going to tell her today and for that I'm grateful. You know how depressed she got the last time she had to undergo all those treatments. If that's the verdict again, and God knows I hope it's not, she'll be more of a fighter because she knows she has an important day to look forward to."

"What day?"

"The day you and Dana will marry," James Westmoreland said, smiling. "That's all she talked about last night and this morning. She likes Dana and thinks she'll make you a fine wife. So do I. You selected well, Jared, and your timing could not have been better. If there's a chance your mother's cancer has returned and she has to undergo more treatments, she'll do whatever she has to do to retain her health to help plan your wedding."

"My wedding?"

"Yes, your wedding. Thanks, Son, for giving your mother a reason to fight whatever we might be up against. She'll be able to handle anything now since she knows one of her sons is finally getting married and will eventually give her a grandchild."

Jared stood in stunned silence. One thing was clear—he couldn't tell his mother the truth about Dana now.

Dana glanced through her peephole and raised an arched brow. She and Jared had said their goodbyes yesterday, so why was he standing on her front porch at six o'clock in the afternoon?

She swallowed the knot in her throat and tried to stop the rapid beating of her heart. It didn't take much for her to remember the kiss they'd shared, a kiss she had thought about most of the day. Instead of concentrating on her work, her mind had been filled with memories of Jared Westmoreland and how well he could kiss, not wanting to think about what else he was probably an expert at doing.

She continued to study him through the peephole. He was dressed in his business suit, which meant he had probably come straight from the office. He looked coolly reserved, in control and professional. Yet at the same time he also looked devastatingly male, incredibly sexy and he was affecting her in that man-woman kind of way. Swallowing hard, she blew out a slow breath and told herself to get a grip as she opened the door.

"Jared?" She sounded breathless, even to her own ears and could only imagine how she might have sounded to his. And the way he was looking at her with those dark, intense eyes wasn't helping.

"Dana, I hate to bother you but I need to talk with you about something important."

Her eyes widened. Whatever he had to say sounded serious. "All right."

She stepped aside to let him in and closed the door behind him. "Can I get you something to drink?" she asked, leading him to her living room.

"No, I'm fine," Jared said, but feeling anything but fine. His conversation with his father had thrown a monkey wrench into what he'd planned to tell his mother. Out of the corner of his eye Jared saw Tom race from where he had been near the sofa to the vicinity of the kitchen.

Jared took the seat Dana offered him on the sofa and watched as she sat in the chair across from him. With everything on his mind, the last thing he needed was to notice the skirt and blouse she was wearing. But he hadn't been able to look away when she sat down and he caught a glimpse of thigh that her short skirt revealed. Nor could he dismiss the way her blouse hugged her breasts.

"Jared? You said you had something important you needed to discuss with me."

Her words reminded him of the reason he was there and he met her curious gaze. "I went to see my mother this morning to clear up the misunderstanding, but things didn't go the way I had intended. She wasn't home so I talked to my dad instead."

Dana nodded. "And you told him the truth."

"No."

"Oh?" Dana said, confused.

"There seems to be a problem," Jared said, knowing that he needed to tell her everything. He decided to start at the beginning.

"Three years ago my mother was diagnosed with breast cancer. The lump was removed and she went through eight weeks of both chemo and radiation. She had good days and bad days and my father, brothers and I saw just what a remarkable woman she was."

The sincerity in Jared's words touched Dana. She could imagine what Jared, his brothers and father had gone through. After spending time with his family yesterday, it was easy to see just how much Sarah Westmoreland was adored by everyone.

"Anyway," Jared said, reclaiming Dana's attention, "I talked to Dad this morning and before I could tell him the truth about us, that there really wasn't an 'us,' he told me that the doctors found another lump in my mother's breast and if it's malignant, we might be talking about cancer treatments again."

"Oh, no," Dana whispered and immediately moved from her chair to sit next to Jared on the sofa. She reached out and touched his arm. "I'm sorry to hear that, Jared," she said in all sincerity.

He slowly stood and shoved his hands into his pockets. Her touch had elicited sensations throughout his body, sensations he didn't want to deal with right now. He had to stay focused.

"So am I," he said slowly. "However, knowing my mother, she will handle this like the fighter that she is. But there's something I can do to make the fight a little easier for her."

"What?"

Jared met her gaze. "It's a crazy idea but at the moment I'd do anything for my mother, including lie."

Dana frowned, wondering what he would lie about. "Jared, what do you need to lie about?" she asked, rising from her seat to come stand in front of him.

His jaw muscles tightened and he briefly glanced away. When he met her gaze again, his eyes were intense and her breath caught at the tormented look she saw lodged there.

"Jared, what do you need to lie about?" she asked again.

He hesitated for a moment then said, "Us. My father made me realize just how happy my mother is, believing that I've finally decided to settle down and get married. Considering everything right now, I don't want to take that happiness away from her."

Reeling in confusion, Dana felt the need to take a step back. "What are you saying?" she asked, not sure she was following him.

"I have a proposal for you," he said, holding her gaze.

Dana swallowed. "What kind of a proposal?"

He gave her a not-so-easy smile. "That we continue to pretend we're engaged for a little while longer...for my mother's sake."

It would have been easier, Dana thought, if she had been sitting down instead of standing up. Nevertheless, the impact of Jared's words slammed into her.

She stared at him, looked for some sort of teasing glint in his gaze that indicated he was joking. But all she saw was an expression that said he was dead serious. Her mouth went dry and her heart began hammering in her chest. "Pretend we're engaged?" she finally found her voice to ask.

"Yes."

She inhaled slowly, deeply. "B-but we can't do that."

For several seconds he just looked at her. His shoulders straight, his gaze intent, clear. "Yes, we can. I never realized how much seeing at least one of her sons settling down meant to Mom. Now I do and I will do whatever I can to make her happy."

"Even get married?"

He frowned. "I hope I don't have to go that far, Dana. I think her believing I'm engaged will help at least until the worst part is over."

"And then?"

"Then I tell her things didn't work out between us and that we broke our engagement. It happens."

Deciding that standing wouldn't work, Dana sank back onto the sofa. "Trust me, I know all about broken engagements, Jared."

He sighed deeply. "I'm sorry. I know it's a lot to

ask of you, considering your broken engagement with Luther, but I don't know what else to do."

The warmth in his gaze touched her. She wet her lips and leaned back in her seat, trying to absorb everything he'd told her. She couldn't help but admire him for his willingness to be a sacrificial lamb. He had no intention of ever getting married and had made that fact very clear. Knowing that, she was sure he didn't want to get involved in any of the trappings that led to marriage, either pretended or otherwise. Yet, for the love he had for his mother he would do what he felt he had to.

She lifted her chin and rubbed nervous hands against her skirt. "If I went along with you on this, Jared, just what would you expect of me?"

Jared moved to sit in the chair across from her. He was glad she was at least considering his proposal. "I've never been engaged before but you have. How were things with you and Cord?"

Dana sighed. "In the beginning I could actually see us spending the rest of our lives together. But now I have to admit that I wanted to marry him for all the wrong reasons. Love had nothing to do with it. He was handsome, successful—"

"And gay."

Dana raised a surprised eyebrow. "You knew?"

Jared shrugged. "I wasn't absolutely certain until I met you. The first thing that crossed my mind when you walked into my office was that no straight man in his right mind would let you slip through his fingers."

Dana couldn't help but smile at the compliment.

"Thanks. I had no idea about Luther's sexual preference until recently. He came to see me and told me the truth. I can only appreciate that he broke our engagement when he did."

Jared nodded. "The two of you dated for over a year and you had no idea?"

Dana shook her head. "Not even a clue, although I realized afterward that the signs were all there but I ignored them."

Jared's brow furrowed. "What signs?"

Dana met his gaze. "Sex for instance."

A knot formed in Jared's throat. Silence grew between them—rather awkwardly, then he asked in a strained voice, "Sex?"

"Yes, sex. We decided that we wouldn't sleep together until after we were married."

Jared nodded. "Soo." He drew the word out, as if his mind was befuddled. "Whose idea was that?"

Dana bit her lip before answering. "It was Luther's idea and of course I went along with it since sex is overrated."

Jared's gaze was puzzled. It wasn't overrated in his book and he wondered how she could think such a thing. "Is it?"

"Yes."

She had him curious and he couldn't resist asking for clarification. "Why would you think that?"

She shrugged. "I'm not a virgin, Jared. I've had sex before and frankly I've never experienced anything worth losing sleep over."

He wondered who the men were who had disappointed her? He met her gaze, locked on it. "Maybe you haven't done it with the right person."

His softly decreed words spurred a hot little quiver that moved down the length of Dana's spine before blossoming out to every part of her body. She couldn't help wondering if a tumble between the sheets with him would make her think differently, then decided it was something she would never know. But still the thought caused a warm pool of heat to form in her belly.

She cleared her throat, needing to regain control of her senses. "Trust me, twice was enough. I can possibly understand the blunder in college, but I was involved with someone a few years ago and my opinion hasn't changed."

He leaned back in his chair, surprised that she was able to dismiss such a profound intimate act from her life just like that. "A few years ago? How far back was that?"

"Three years, closer to four."

Jared raised a dark eyebrow. "Are you saying that you haven't slept with a man in almost four years?" he asked, not sure if he had heard her correctly.

Dana lifted her chin, wondering how they had gotten on such a personal subject, but decided to answer anyway. "Yes, that's just what I'm saying."

Deciding she had given him enough information about herself, she said, "So tell me what things you expect us to do during this pretended engagement?"

He watched as she licked her lips again and wished it were his tongue at work instead of her own. And if that wasn't bad enough she crossed her legs and his gaze moved down the length of them, catching sight of the thigh he'd gotten a glimpse of earlier. His gut clenched when he thought of licking those legs and thighs.

Damn! He couldn't help but curse his bad luck. He was still way too attracted to her and the last thing he needed was a reason to spend more time in her company. In this situation, his mother's needs came before his own. But boy did he have needs and the enormity of those needs was hitting home—in this case right below his belt. He shifted in his seat to relieve the strain he felt behind his zipper. He could definitely use some sexual playtime and would've loved to suggest a purely physical relationship, with no emotions involved. But after her broken engagement, the last thing he wanted to do was take advantage of the situation by suggesting such a thing.

He cleared his throat. "What kinds of things did you and Cord do together?" He gave her a lopsided grin. "You've already told me about one particular activity the two of you didn't do."

Dana smoothed down her skirt. He watched as she then rolled one shoulder, which made his gaze move from her legs to her breasts. Suddenly he felt tension in his fingers. He would give just about anything to cross the room, lift her top, unhook her bra—if she was wearing one—and take his fingertips and graze her flesh before taking his mouth and latching on to a nipple and sucking—

"Luther and I went out a lot," she finally said, snatching back his focus. "We attended concerts, plays and parties. He was a sales representative with his company and often had to do a lot of socializing."

For several seconds Jared looked at her, thinking because of his clientele he often did a lot of socializing, as well. However, recently he'd cut back because of his workload. "We can do those same things. However, my mother is big on family gatherings and would expect us to also attend any. Can you handle that?"

Dana thought about how much she had enjoyed herself yesterday, almost too much. "Yes, I can handle that. Like I told you yesterday I think you have a wonderful family. But I'd hate deceiving them."

"It's for a good reason." A grin turned up the corners of his lips. "And I'd like to think that a pretended engagement with me wouldn't be so bad. I'm a pretty decent fellow."

Decency was the last thing on Dana's mind at the moment although she knew it shouldn't be. Heat was curling in her stomach just from staring at him. "How long do you think this pretended engagement will have to last?"

"That will depend on my mother's condition. If this is a false alarm, then we're only looking at a couple of weeks. But if we're looking at treatments, the last time they lasted for eight weeks. Will that be too long for you?"

Dana sighed. Any length of time would be too long as far as she was concerned. "No, umm, that would be fine."

Jared hated the uncertainty, the wariness he saw in her eyes but knew those emotions mirrored his own. He swallowed hard as he stood, shoving his hands in his pockets. "So, you're willing to keep on pretending to be my fiancée?"

Several tense minutes passed before Dana answered. She knew she might be asking for trouble, considering how attracted she was to him. But under the circumstances, there was no way she could turn him down. "Yes."

A relieved smile touched Jared's lips. He crossed the room and taking her hand he pulled her from her seat. "Thanks, Dana. Now I'm the one who's in your debt."

Having Jared in her debt stirred strange sensations in Dana's belly. She licked her dry lips, tried to smile and said teasingly, "That's okay. I won't demand anything that I don't think you'll be able to deliver." As far as she was concerned that left the options pretty wide-open.

Jared's gaze was drawn to Dana's lips; lips that were still moist from the recent sweep of her tongue. They stood so close that all he had to do was lean down and capture what he wanted most in his mouth and feast on it.

"So what's first?"

Her question made him lift a dark brow. He was about to say that a tongue-sucking kiss wouldn't be so bad, but changed his mind. "What's first?"

She smiled and he wondered if she knew what he'd been thinking, since his gaze was still glued to her lips. "Will your family need to see us together again anytime soon?"

He inhaled slowly. It's a good thing she'd asked. He had almost forgotten. "Yes. My brothers are remaining in town until Sunday, except for Quade. He had to get back to D.C. and flew out this morning. The folks are planning a cookout on Saturday evening."

Dana nodded. After spending time with Jared's family she knew his brother Quade worked for the Secret Service; Durango was a park ranger who lived in Montana; Ian was a ship's captain whose luxurious riverboat cruised the Mississippi River and whose home was in Memphis, and Spencer was a financial advisor, who lived in the quaint and quiet community of Sausalito, California. Jared and his youngest brother, Reggie, were the only ones living in the Atlanta area.

"Do they know what's going on with your mother's health?" she asked.

Jared shook his head. "No, and knowing Mom she'll tell us as little as possible and only what she thinks we need to know. It's her way of protecting us. But I'm going to tell them what I do know. We're meeting for dinner at Chase's Place in an hour, and I'll call Quade with details later tonight."

"Will you tell them the truth about us?"

Jared shook his head. "No. The less people who know the better. I won't take a chance on one of them letting something slip. I don't want to give my mother any reason not to think our engagement isn't the real thing."

Dana nodded. Suddenly, she remembered something. "The ring!"

Jared frowned. "What about it?" His gaze went to her left hand. He had noticed earlier that she wasn't wearing it.

"I don't have it anymore. I took it to a jeweler during my lunch hour. I needed the money to pay off some bills."

Jared rubbed the back of his neck. Although he hadn't much cared for seeing Cord's ring back on her finger, that ring symbolized their engagement. "Where did you take it?"

"Garbella Jewelers. Do you think they still have it?"

Jared inhaled as he checked his watch. Garbella was a well-known jeweler that was frequented by a lot of high-profile individuals. "Even if they do, chances are the shop is closed now. I'll check with them first thing tomorrow. If they still have it, I'll get it back."

"And if they don't?"

Jared inhaled again. "Then I'll get you another one."

"B-but your family saw *that* ring. They will think it's odd for me to start wearing a different one."

Jared nodded, knowing that was true. "Then I'll have to think of a good reason to tell them why I changed it."

Dana nodded. Whatever reason he came up with would have to be good. "All right."

He checked his watch again. "I need to leave if I'm going to be on time to meet my brothers for dinner."

Dana focused on putting one foot in front of the other as she walked him to the door. Concentrating on him was too mind-boggling.

They stopped when they reached her door. She lifted her gaze to his. His eyes appeared darker, the same color they had become right before he'd kissed her yesterday.

"I'll call you tomorrow," he said huskily. "Will there be a problem with me calling you at work?"

"No, there won't be a problem. Wait, I'll give you my business card."

Jared watched as she quickly crossed the room to a table, tempted to let out a low whistle. Heat flared through him as his gaze wandered down her hips, thighs and legs. He took a deep breath and released it. Dana looked particularly sexy in her short skirt. She definitely had all the right body parts for it.

"This has all of my contact information," she said, returning to where he was standing.

He took the card from her and felt her shiver when their hands touched. "Thanks."

She cleared her throat when he didn't make a move to leave. "Is there anything else, Jared?"

Her question made him realize that, yes, there definitely was something else on his mind. "It would be a good idea to seal our agreement and I think this way is more appropriate than a handshake."

Before she could gather her next breath, he leaned down, slanted his mouth across hers and captured her lips in his, tasting her the way he had wanted to since entering her home. He heard her purr, felt her nipples tighten against his chest, all the way through his jacket, which only made him intensify his hold on her mouth as his tongue continued to devour her.

His heart missed a beat with every stroke of his tongue and the multitude of sensations he encountered while kissing her washed over him, short-circuiting whatever functioning brain cells he needed in order to think straight. As if they had a mind of their own, his fingers inched downward to touch her thigh and to trace his fingertips along the hem of the short shirt that had been driving him mad for the past half hour. A warning flared in his mind that this woman was pure, unadulterated temptation.

He released her slowly and fought to control his breathing, his desire and his lust. The only word he could think of was—wow! Seducing Dana Rollins was not part of his proposal but...

"Do you think that was wise?" she asked in a low whisper.

His gaze went to her lips, lips that were still moist from his kiss. He liked the sight of them and a smile touched the corners of his mouth. "Yes, in all honesty, I think that was the smartest thing I've done all day."

Jared glanced around Chase's Place as he sipped his drink. The meeting with his brothers had gone rather well and everyone was in agreement that they wouldn't hover over their mother as they had the last time. They'd also agreed that Jared's engagement had been perfect timing, although they were glad it was him and not them.

"You okay?"

He glanced up and stared into the dark eyes of his cousin Dare. He and Dare were only months apart in age and had always shared a rather close relationship. "Yes, I'm fine, considering everything."

Dare took the chair across from him. "Durango told me and Chase what's going on with Aunt Sarah. You know the family is here if you need us for anything, but I know things are going to be fine."

Jared nodded as he rubbed a hand down his face. "God, I hope so. I don't even know how Mom's appointment went today. I stopped by earlier but it was like getting blood out of a turnip. The only thing she wanted to talk about was my engagement."

Dare chuckled. "Well, you have to admit that has given the family something to talk about. Who would have thought that you of all people would decide to finally tie the knot?"

Jared frowned. "It's just an engagement, Dare."

Dare nodded. "Yes, but unless you know something that I don't, most engagements are the prelude to a wedding. You'll be marrying Dana eventually."

Jared took another sip of his drink as he met Dare's gaze over the rim of his glass. One thing he'd learned as a successful attorney was knowing whom he could trust to keep their mouths closed and whom he couldn't.

"The engagement isn't real."

Dare straightened in his chair. "Excuse me?"

Jared spent the next ten minutes telling Dare the entire story, including how he and Dana had originally met.

"Damn, a pretended engagement. You know what happened when Shelly and I tried pretending a courtship. It became the real thing," Dare said, remembering that time.

Jared stared at Dare. "That won't happen to me. You know how I feel about marriage."

Dare chuckled. "Yeah, and you know how I felt

about it, too. But I can't imagine not having Shelly in my life now."

"The two of you had a history. And then there was AJ."

Dare nodded when he thought of the son he hadn't known about until Shelly had returned to town after having been gone ten years. "But even with all that, Shelly and I had to get reacquainted, find ourselves all over again. It was only then that we discovered that we still loved each other."

Jared snorted. "At work I see marriage at its ugliest—when two people who'd vowed to love each other till death do them part, face each other in a judge's chamber with hatred in their eyes, wanting to strip the other bare of anything and everything."

He chuckled before continuing. "The man I'm representing in court tomorrow is fighting his soon-to-be ex-wife for custody of the dog."

Dare shook his head sadly. "Don't let what you see in your profession discolor your opinion of marriage, Jared."

Jared sighed deeply. "It already has, Dare. This thing with Dana is for Mom's sake and there's no way I'm going to forget it."

Four

Dana glanced up from her desk and smiled when Cybil walked in. "Good morning."

"Umm, I don't know how good it is when you find out your best friend has been keeping secrets."

Dana raised an arched brow. "Excuse me?"

Cybil frowned as she crossed the room to stand in front of Dana's desk. "I don't know whether you're excused or not. News of your engagement made the society column today," she said, waving a section of the *Atlanta Constitution* in front of Dana's eyes.

"What!" Dana snatched the paper from Cybil to read the article. "I didn't know."

Cybil lifted a confused brow as she crossed her arms over her chest. "What didn't you know? That you're engaged to one of Atlanta's most eligible bachelors or that news of it would appear in today's paper?"

Hearing the hurt in her best friend's voice, Dana lifted her gaze from the article to meet Cybil's gaze. "I can explain."

"Do tell."

Sighing deeply, Dana stood and crossed the room to close her door. She turned to Cybil. "You better sit for this."

It took a full twenty minutes to explain everything. It would have taken less time had her best friend not interrupted every five minutes to ask so many questions.

"Boy, this is unreal. The entire office is buzzing. I hope Jared gets you a different engagement ring. People will have a lot to say if they see you wearing the same ring Luther gave you."

Dana blinked. Jeez. She hadn't thought of that since she hadn't expected news of their engagement going public.

"Who do you think tipped off the papers?" Cybil asked.

"I'm not sure but it really doesn't matter at this point." Dana knew it had to have been someone in Jared's family, probably his mother. The article had been nicely written, letting all Atlanta know that one of the city's most sought-after bachelors had gotten engaged to Dana Rollins over the Easter weekend. "I wonder if Jared has seen it."

Cybil smiled that little knowing smile that meant her mind was churning and usually in the wrong direction. "My guess is that he has." She chuckled. "I can assure you that everyone in this office has."

Dana looked at her with a concerned expression on

her face. "What are they saying?" She knew if anyone knew about the office gossip it was Cybil. Not that she participated in it but everyone knew that her two staff members, Mary Bonner and Helen Fisher, were Kessler Industries' biggest gossips.

"They're perplexed since no one noticed a ring on your finger. But I think most of them are happy for you considering your breakup with Luther. They've gone from pitying you to envying you, especially since you've snagged the handsome and wealthy Jared Westmoreland."

Cybil's smile suddenly faded before she continued. "But, once you and Jared break this engagement everyone will go back to feeling sorry for you again and wondering how you could let two good men get away." She met Dana's gaze. "I have a feeling I'm not going to like the way this will turn out, Dana."

Dana wasn't all that crazy about how things were going to turn out, either, but it was too late now. She had given Jared her word. She opened her mouth to tell Cybil not to worry, that in the end things would work out okay when the phone on her desk rang.

Grateful for a moment's reprieve she reached over and picked it up. "Hello?"

"Good morning, Dana."

Dana couldn't help the flutter that suddenly went through her midsection upon hearing the husky, sexy sound of Jared's voice. It would not have been so bad if she didn't also remember their kiss yesterday, not to mention the feel of his hand on her thigh. His kisses were getting bolder, hotter and more earth-shattering.

"Good morning, Jared." She glanced over at Cybil then quickly looked away when she saw how intently her friend was watching her.

"Have you seen this morning's paper?" he asked.

She considered his question and glanced over at Cybil again. This time she gave her a pointed look, one that requested privacy. However, Cybil just sat there, ignoring her request.

Dana sighed after giving Cybil a mean look and answered Jared's question. "Yes, I've seen it."

"I apologize for not letting you know about it, but I didn't know myself until I read it this morning. It seems my mother's happiness is getting the best of her."

"Yes, it appears that way, doesn't it," she responded, not knowing what else she could say. From his tone he didn't seem upset. In fact there appeared to be an underlying tenderness and warmth in his voice. Or was she just imagining things?

"Will you have lunch with me?" he asked.

"Lunch?"

"Yes, at Jenzen's."

Dana's eyes widened. Jenzen's was an exclusive restaurant in North Atlanta. She'd heard that reservations had to be made well in advance, oftentimes weeks. It was certainly not someplace that she frequented.

"Lunch is fine. Do you want me to meet you there?" she asked. She hated admitting it but she was looking forward to having lunch with him and a part of her chafed at the thought of that.

"No, I'll come pick you up. Is eleven-thirty okay?"

She checked her watch. She had a meeting that

would be ending a few minutes before then. "Yes, that will be fine. I'll be standing in front of the building."

"Okay. I'm looking forward to seeing you again, Dana."

Dana hung up the phone, closed her eyes and bowed her head wondering how Jared could set off so many emotions within her. Emotions she'd never felt before.

"You okay?"

Dana snatched her head up. She had forgotten Cybil was still in her office. "Yes, I'm fine. That was Jared."

Cybil smiled. "So I heard." She then stood. "Enjoy lunch but promise me one thing."

"What?"

"That you won't get yourself in too deep. I saw the expression on your face when you heard Jared's voice."

"And?"

"And I don't want to see you get hurt again."

Dana waved her hand in the air, dismissing Cybil's concerns. "Hey, I know the score between me and Jared. I'm merely doing him a favor."

"Some favor. I've seen him before and he's a hottie, every woman's fantasy. How far do you plan to take this pretended engagement? Will the two of you get intimate?"

Dana swallowed. "Intimate?"

Cybil grinned. "Yeah, you know, sleep together. Share the same pillow. Bump and grind. Have orgasms."

The scenario that suddenly played out in Dana's

mind had her heart beating so fast she thought she would pass out. "Of course not!"

"Are you sure about that?"

Before Dana could respond Cybil opened the door and walked out.

Jared gazed across his desk at Sylvester Brewster, hating to admit that he hadn't looked forward to their meeting.

At twenty-eight, Sylvester was a well-known recording artist who toured the country performing songs that consistently hit the number-one spot on any billboard charts.

Unfortunately, in addition to his blockbuster hit records, Sylvester had this serious problem of wife-boredom. The man changed wives like he changed shirts, but one thing was always certain, when he cast one off to take on another he was extremely generous with the alimony.

Jared sighed deeply. It seemed Brewster was ready to dump the third Mrs. Brewster for wife number four. The only glitch in his plans was that his current wife wanted more alimony than Sylvester was willing to give her, which had his client fuming.

"I don't want to give her one penny more, Jared. Baby or no baby."

Jared lifted a brow. This was the first he'd heard of a baby. "Your wife is pregnant?"

"She says she is and could well be, but it makes no difference since it's not mine."

Jared's brow inched even higher. "Do you know that for certain?"

"Yes," Sylvester said with a frustrated sigh. Then lowering his voice as if the office might possibly be bugged, he whispered. "I'm sterile, man. As sterile as a new hospital on opening day. It's the result of a childhood illness. So if Jackie's claiming she's pregnant with my child then it's not mine."

Jared sighed deeply. "If what you're saying is true, that won't be hard to prove with a paternity test."

"It is true and nobody is going to try to lay a claim that I'm their baby's daddy."

Jared watched Sylvester pace around the room. "Should I be surprised if you remarry within hours of your divorce being final?" he asked, knowing that was usually the norm.

Sylvester stopped his pacing and met Jared's gaze and he actually saw deep hurt in the man's eyes. "No. I loved Jackie and wasn't involved with anyone else. With her there was never a dull moment, man, always excitement. She was something else. For the first time in my life I fell in love and look what happens. And that's what makes it so bad. Jackie refuses to level with me even after I told her I was sterile and there was no way that baby was mine. Now she's claiming that I'm the one who's lying." In anger, he hit his fist on the desk. "Women can't be trusted, man. I'll never marry again."

Jared was silent for several moments before he nodded, although not for one minute did he believe Brewster would keep that promise. Marriage was an addiction to Brewster, one Jared was glad he didn't have.

"I'll contact Jackie's attorney next week. I'm sorry

things have come to this because I thought the two of you made a nice couple. But if you're certain she's been unfaithful then—"

"I'm certain. I don't have the name of the man she was involved with but there was an affair. Her pregnancy is proof enough."

Half an hour later, Jared had completed dictating information into his recorder for his secretary to transcribe. Standing, he walked over to the window and looked out. This was another morning that wasn't going well. First off the bat, while drinking his coffee and reading his newspaper, he had come across the article announcing his engagement to Dana.

Then he had arrived at Garbella Jewelers as soon as their doors had opened only to find that they had already sold Cord's ring. He had ended up purchasing another ring and was racking his brain for an excuse to give his family as to why Dana would no longer be wearing the original one. In his opinion, the only saving grace was that the one he'd purchased had a diamond that was twice as large and was closer to what he imagined Dana might like.

He sighed as he checked his watch. It was time to leave if he wanted to pick Dana up for lunch on time.

Dana.

She was becoming a major problem. He didn't consider his proposal a business arrangement. Otherwise he would have drawn up formal documents between them. She was merely doing him a favor. They had exchanged favors before so he knew she wouldn't go back on her word. But there were factors thrown in the equation that he hadn't counted on.

Like his strong attraction to her. And the dreams he'd been having.

Last night he had actually dreamed about her legs and thighs, in addition to other parts of her that he hadn't seen. In his dream, he had gotten all the way under that skirt she'd been wearing yesterday, first caressing the soft skin of her inner thigh before letting his fingers slide inside her damp heat. And then there were the kisses they had shared. His mouth tingled just remembering the taste of her on his tongue. Just thinking about her body parts and their kiss made his arousal thicken against his zipper.

For the life of him he couldn't understand this unusual brand of sexual chemistry. It wasn't as if he didn't come into contact with beautiful women. He'd once dated a former Miss Georgia for heaven's sakes. So what was there about Dana Rollins that had him counting the minutes, the seconds before he would see her again?

He hated admitting it, but the women he'd dated in the past were usually self-centered, aggressive and accustomed to getting their own way. But not Dana. She was strong-willed, but although he had witnessed her explosive temper the first day they'd met, he knew she was a kind person. She had cared enough about his mother's welfare to go along with his outrageous proposal of a fake engagement.

And speaking of his mother, Sarah Westmoreland definitely liked Dana. Yesterday she had gone so far as to suggest they have a short engagement and a June wedding. He had immediately burst a hole in her bubble by letting her know that was out of the question. But still, seeing the look of happiness on his mother's face made him realize that no matter what, this pretense of an engagement with Dana was worth it.

Jared rubbed the top of his head as he remembered his conversation with Dare last night. He'd meant what he told his cousin. Nothing, and he meant nothing, would develop between him and Dana, no matter how attracted he was to her. It wouldn't be the first time he was attracted to a woman and it wouldn't be the last.

His meeting with Sylvester had reaffirmed his conviction that marriage wasn't all that it was cracked up to be and he intended to enjoy his remaining days on this earth as a single man.

Whatever pep talk he'd given himself an hour earlier stood on shaky ground when lust took control of his body. A jolt of sexual awareness raced up his spine when he pulled up and saw Dana standing in front of her office building.

She was the model of professionalism with her upswept hairdo and two-piece navy-blue powerhouse suit. Her knee-length skirt was longer than the one she'd been wearing yesterday, thank goodness. He wasn't sure he'd been able to resist putting his hands on her bare thighs again.

She opened the car door and slipped inside. "Hi, Jared."

He swallowed. The air was suddenly charged with sexual energy. "Dana."

He watched as she snapped her seat belt in place and tried not to notice how her skirt inched up a little, exposing those thighs and long, shapely legs he had dreamed about. He breathed in the scent of her, a womanly fragrance that was just another sexy detail for his fantasies.

"Were you waiting long?" he asked, adjusting his sunglasses and trying to control the rapid beat of his pulse.

She smiled as she pressed back against the car's leather interior, unintentionally showing more leg and thigh. His heartbeat raced right along with his pulse. "No, I walked out a few minutes ago. Your timing was excellent."

His grip tightened on the steering wheel as he eased into traffic. There were cars everywhere, and he needed to focus on his driving and not on how firm Dana's breasts looked against her blouse. And heaven forbid he thought about her mouth and how it had parted under his yesterday, inviting him to deepen their kiss.

"Were you able to get the ring?"

He allowed his gaze to travel over to her when he came to a traffic light. "No. They had already sold it so I had to buy another one." He watched as that sexy mouth twisted into a frown.

"What will we tell your family?"

"That I liked this one better." Jared sighed deeply. That was the truth. He still didn't understand why it bothered him to see Cord's ring on her finger. Probably because he knew the whole story and felt she'd deserved better.

He glanced over at her again and watched as she pursed those same sexy lips and saw the frown lines appear between her prettily arched eyebrows. "It's going to have to sound convincing when you tell them that," she said.

He chuckled as he shifted his gaze from her to stare straight ahead. "I'm an attorney, remember. My job is to be able to convince people."

A grin spread over her face. "Yes, you're right. Sorry, I forgot." She was quiet for a few moments then said, "It was for the best anyway."

He lifted a brow. "What was?"

"Getting a different ring. That article in the newspaper this morning has my office buzzing and of course everyone wanted to see my ring. It didn't occur to me that had I kept Luther's ring they would have remembered it."

Jared blew out a breath. That hadn't occurred to him, either. "What did you tell them?"

"That it was being sized."

He nodded. "Sorry you were put in a sticky situation like that."

She shrugged. "No problem. I just hadn't expected that announcement to appear in the papers. I thought I only had to pretend this engagement for your family, not all Atlanta."

"Will that cause you problems?" he asked, seeing how deep the extent of their deceit was going.

"No, not as long as it doesn't cause you any problems."

Jared's forehead furrowed in confusion. "What kind of problems?" The car came to a stop at another traffic light and he glanced over at her.

"Your livelihood. You're one of Atlanta's most eligible bachelors. Being engaged takes you off the market for a while."

One corner of his mouth curved slightly. Being engaged would definitely change his life, but only temporarily. "Umm, I guess it does, but only for a short while." He held her gaze, studied it, looking for something, anything that would indicate she wished otherwise.

He let out a slow breath when he didn't see anything. He was glad that she understood that nothing could and would develop between them. Those hot and heavy kisses hadn't meant a thing and he didn't want her to get lust confused with love. Not that he thought that she would. But still, he had to be certain they were on the same page.

Their engagement was a game and nothing more.

Dana was very much aware of the man who sat across from her in the exclusive restaurant, and had been since he had picked her up for lunch. The twenty-minute ride had been taxing when all she could do was remember what Cybil had asked about their physical relationship.

The thought that Jared might expect them to become intimate was confusing and something she knew they should discuss. But she hadn't been able to bring it up. During the drive they had talked about several things but had played it safe and avoided mentioning their engagement. Instead they had discussed the weather, the new movies that had come out over the Easter weekend and Georgia's recent elections.

She wasn't surprised to learn that he lived in Country

Club of the South, an affluent subdivision in North Atlanta, in the suburbs of Alpharetta. The houses were priced in the millions and a number of celebrities and sport entertainers lived there.

"You're quiet."

Dana glanced up and met Jared's dark gaze. He had been watching her. Something flickered in the depths of those eyes that made her catch her breath, made something unbearably hot flow through her veins. She picked up her coffee cup to break eye contact. Cybil had warned her not to get in too deep and she had assured her friend that she wouldn't. When she said it she had been sure, confident, but now all that assuredness was skating on thin ice. Jared Westmoreland was not a man to take lightly. He had made it clear in the car that their arrangement was temporary. She was smart enough to read between the lines. He'd been letting her know that he was not a man to whom any woman should give her heart. "Umm, I was just thinking about things," she finally said.

"Are you thinking of changing your mind about this?" he asked quietly.

She looked up and met his gaze again. Although she couldn't read his expression she really didn't have to. She knew how much keeping his mother happy meant to him and she couldn't help but admire the lengths he would go to for her. "No, I'm not, but there's something I think we do need to discuss," she said softly.

He nodded. "All right. What would you like to talk about?"

Dana sighed deeply. Even now she felt it, the hot, sultry passion that radiated between them, that was always there whenever they were together. It was that passion, the sexual chemistry, the strong attraction that let her know she was walking on dangerous ground with him.

"Our kisses," she said, almost in a whisper. But the sudden intensity of his expression let her know he had heard her.

"Our kisses?"

She looked down at her coffee cup again when she saw the desire that darkened his eyes. After pulling in a deep breath she met his eyes again. "Yes."

He tilted his head at an angle that seemed to make his gaze focus in on her. Only on her. "What about our kisses, Dana?"

Her palms were beginning to feel sweaty and her insides felt like molten liquid with his question. She wished she could respond by stating that she wanted more of them, but knew that would definitely be a wrong answer. She could barely handle the ones she had gotten so far.

She cleared her throat. "I—I don't want them to lead to other things."

He stared at her a moment then asked, "Does your definition of *other things* include what you and Cord never got around to doing?"

She bit her lip and tried not to look at him. "Yes."

After a brief pause he said, "Dana?"

The way he said her name only forced her to look at him. "Yes?"

"Why does the thought of making love to me bother you?" he asked softly.

She felt a tiny pull in the pit of her stomach at the

silky timbre in his voice. The thought of making love to him didn't bother her but it did keep her constantly off balance and made her imagine some wild and purely wicked things. It also had her conscious of her sexual state more so than ever.

She hadn't slept with a man in almost four years. That fact hadn't bothered her before. It had seldom crossed her mind. Now it did. She was experiencing wants and desires for the first time and had a feeling that a sexual experience with Jared would obliterate her long-standing belief that sex was highly overrated. She knew to ask for a purely platonic relationship would not be realistic. After all, she was a woman and he was a man unlike any other she'd ever known. He had a way of making her feel attractive, wanted and desired.

The silence between them had stretched long enough and she knew that he deserved an answer. "It doesn't bother me, Jared. It confuses me."

He didn't say anything for a long moment, and then he said, "Although I want to share a physical relationship with you, would it help to give you my word that I won't push you into doing anything you aren't ready for?"

She frowned. "That's just it, Jared. How will I know when I'm ready for anything? All of this is rather new to me."

"You'll know, Dana. You'll know better than anyone," he said softly. "I'd be telling a lie if I said I didn't want you. Even now, I want you so bad I ache with the thought of having you. I'm not Luther Cord. But since our engagement is not the real thing, I won't expect or assume anything. How far we take things will always be up to you."

"Thank you."

A warm shudder of awareness passed through them as well as an understanding and acceptance of their predicament. Jared recognized the depth of desire in her eyes although he knew she did not.

A part of him wanted to curse the two fools that had made her think that lovemaking wasn't worth losing sleep over. There was no doubt in his mind that if he ever made love to her, sleep wouldn't be involved. just constant pleasure, gratification and enjoyment all night long.

"And as far as the kisses," he said. "They can be dangerous but necessary. Engaged couples do kiss, so a certain degree of open affection will be expected. And although we don't have to kiss when we're alone, I enjoy kissing you and hope you enjoy kissing me, as well. But if you prefer that—"

"Kissing is fine," she interrupted. "Now that we have an understanding. Like you said earlier in the car, our pretended engagement is only temporary."

The drive back to her job was done mostly in silence. There really wasn't a whole lot left to be said. They understood each other and the situation they were in.

"Here's the new ring," he said, when he parked the car in front of her office building and she'd unsnapped her seat belt.

She accepted the gray velvet box and opened it up. He heard the gasp that escaped her lips and watched as she blinked then blew out a long whistle. "Wow!" She quickly looked over at him. "Don't you think this is a bit too much?" She took it out of the box and slipped it on her finger. It was a perfect fit.

Jared's mouth tilted into a smile. For some reason he liked seeing that ring on her finger instead of the one Luther had given her. "No. If I'm going to convince my family there was a good reason for me to change rings then seeing is believing. I'll just tell them that I saw this one and thought it would look better on your hand. They'll buy that story."

Dana nodded. Anyone would. Jared hadn't just given her a ring, he had given her a rock. It had to be the most beautiful ring she had ever seen and the design was unique. She knew it most have cost him a fortune. Of course she'd return it when their fake engagement was over. She held her hand out in front of her. "It's simply beautiful, Jared."

Smiling at her, Jared reached out and captured her hand in his and brought it up to his lips. "I'm glad you like it."

Dana swallowed when he released her hand. Jared kissing her hand had been totally unexpected and she felt a sizzle all the way to her toes.

"Now I have a question for you," he said quietly before she could gather her wits.

"What?"

"Are those two people friends of yours? They have been standing there and staring at us ever since I pulled up."

Dana followed his gaze and saw Mary Bonner and Helen Fisher standing at the entrance of the building, pretending to be engaged in deep conversation.

"They're co-workers, not friends, and two of the biggest gossips in the building."

A mischievous glint appeared in Jared's eyes. "Then how about if we gave them something to gossip about."

Dana smiled. She knew where he was coming from although she also knew his plan included another kiss. But they had said at lunch that engaged couples were expected to publicly display a certain degree of affection. And if she was totally honest, she wanted to feel his lips against hers again. "Okay."

Dana's breath hitched when Jared reached over and nearly pulled her out of the seat into his lap and captured her mouth with his. Her body respond instinctively. The kiss was soft, gentle, slow and hot. It was also thorough—so methodically complete that she felt blood race all the way down to her toes. Kiss number three was everything the last two had been and more. He was making her concentrate on his taste and the slow buildup of desire that was flowing through her. His tongue tangled with hers and she felt desire and urgency consuming him and overtaking her, as well. His hard shaft was pressed against her stomach and she knew for him to have gotten that aroused meant they were definitely putting on a show.

He slowly pulled back and she placed her hands against his muscled chest as she tried to restore her breathing to a normal pattern. Her insides felt like mush and heat, and an intensity she had never felt before settled smack between her legs.

"So…do you think that worked?" he asked, lowering

his head to lightly taste the sides of her mouth while placing her back in her seat.

His breath was warm, his tongue moist and her control was steadily slipping. "Yes," she said, barely able to get the single word out. "I'm sure they won't be able to stop talking about us."

Five

Lanterns furnished a translucent glow to the West-morelands' backyard. Chairs and tables were assembled in front of the lake and an area had been cleared for dancing. There was the mouthwatering smell of ribs and chicken cooking over charcoal, and a huge tent covered a number of tables that were loaded with all kinds of delectable foods.

In addition to Jared's brothers and cousins, former classmates and friends had been invited to the cookout. Dana sighed as she glanced around. She had been introduced to everyone as Jared's fiancée and when asked when the wedding would take place she would smile and say they hadn't set a date, but doubted it would be anytime that year.

"I can certainly see why Jared preferred this ring," Madison was saying, pulling Dana's attention back to the conversation around her. Jared had been right. His family had accepted the reason he'd given about the change in rings without question.

"It certainly makes a statement, doesn't it?" Tara inserted. "It's such a beautiful ring. The other one was really nice but this one is more like Jared."

Dana was about to ask Tara what she meant when Jared's mother appeared by her side smiling. "Are you enjoying yourself, Dana?"

Dana returned the older woman's smile. "Yes, and thanks for inviting me."

"No thanks needed. You're family now."

Dana nodded. She hated deceiving the older woman.

"You've been Jared's best-kept secret. Not once did he let on that he was seeing anyone seriously, in fact I assumed the opposite. For the longest time he claimed that he would never marry. That just goes to show what can happen when a person falls in love. And it's plain to see that he's fallen hard," Sarah added, chuckling. "He hasn't taken his eyes off you all evening. I've never seen him this attentive to anyone before, and I'm supremely happy about it."

The thought crossed Dana's mind that continuing that "supreme happiness" was the only reason Jared had propositioned her to take part in this sham of an engagement. She wondered why that had her feeling oddly let down.

"What do you think of Jared's theater room?" Jayla asked a few minutes later when the topic had switched from Dana and Jared to the movies that were now playing at the theaters.

Dana looked puzzled, not knowing what Jayla was talking about but knowing it was something that she should. "His theater room?"

Shelly grinned. "You mean he hasn't told you about all the remodeling he's done? When was the last time you were over at his place?"

Dana didn't know what to say. To say that she had never been to Jared's house would definitely seem odd. She opened her mouth to make something up when suddenly Jared materialized by her side. He leaned over and kissed whatever lie she was about to fabricate off her lips.

"Come dance with me, sweetheart." He glanced over at his mother and his female cousins. "Excuse us for a moment," he said before leading Dana off to the makeshift dance floor.

Taking her into his arms he looked down at her. Holding her close, he liked the feel of her breasts against his chest and the perfect fit of her body against his. "Was my rescue quick enough?" he asked, smiling and searching her face. He wished they were alone so he could end the torture and kiss her the way he'd thought of doing all evening. "I was on my way over to get you when I heard Jayla's question about my theater room."

Dana tilted her face up, and chuckled quietly. "Yes, you were quick enough. It would have seemed awfully odd for me not to know about your house. Is there something I should know about this room so when the next person asks I can be prepared?"

Jared lightly skimmed his fingers down her bare arm. He felt her shiver and liked the fact that he had caused it. But then, she was causing things to happen to him as well—like the unbearable ache that was building in his groin. He wanted her, and with their bodies so close, there was no way she wasn't aware of his aroused state. "I like watching old movies and I've installed a state-of-the-art home theater system, the latest in plasma technology. The sound system is three times clearer than in a movie theater." In truth, he didn't want to talk about his theater room. What he really wanted to do was nudge Dana's body even closer to his, latch on to her mouth, ignore everyone around them as he kissed her crazy.

Dana smiled up at him. "Umm, I'm impressed."

It was on the tip of his tongue to tell her that besides being impressed she was also hot. Her heat was burning him, further arousing him and making him want her even more. He had to give her a lot of credit. She knew how to make a statement in anything and everything she put on her body. Tonight she was wearing a V-neck green dress that stopped just above her knees. The way the dress hugged her curves showed just what a small waist and well-toned bottom she had. Her outfit had been murdering his senses ever since he had picked her up and was still killing them. He stifled a groan. Dana Rollins was subtle, but provocatively sexy.

"I think it's time you visited my home so you won't be left in the lurch again. I'd love to fix dinner for you at my place," he said, leaning down and caressing her lips with his. He looked for any reason to kiss her and didn't mind performing for an audience. At least that's what he tried to convince himself. But he knew he wasn't performing, liking the feel of her mouth against his. He couldn't wait to get her alone.

She gave a soft laugh as she gazed up at him. "Can you cook?"

He grinned. He was on a low simmer even now. "Yes. So what about this weekend?"

Her smile faltered. "I'll be going away this weekend, to Brunswick. Saturday is my mother's birthday and I want to put flowers on her grave."

His gaze focused on her eyes and he saw that the sparkle had gone. He had also heard the sadness in her voice and knew going back to where her parents were buried would be hard on her. "My thoughts will be with you this weekend," he said softly. He pulled her close against him. Moments later he asked, "What about dinner at my place the week after you return?"

She looked up at him and smiled. Knowing he would be thinking of her this weekend touched her. "I'd love to," she said just as the music ended.

It was close to one in the morning when Jared returned Dana to her home. Although it was late she invited him in for coffee and, not surprisingly, he accepted. They had shared several slow dances, and each time she had been fully aware of his aroused state, and just as certain he had been aware of hers. At one point, he had guided her to a darkened area of the yard and had been seconds away from kissing her when Durango had cut in. She had seen the murderous look in Jared's eyes, but his brother had merely laughed it off. But now she was home, he was here with her and they were alone.

As soon as the door closed behind him, he pulled her into his arms and she went willingly, wanting his kiss as much as he wanted to give it. The mating of their mouths seemed endless, his tongue was torture of the most brazen kind.

Lust ignited within Jared with the way Dana's body seemed to dissolve into his, and at that moment he had to touch her, taste her, further stroke the heat building between them. He stroked his palms over her shoulders and upper arms, hearing the sound of her whimpering and moaning in his mouth. He continued to kiss her hungrily, greedily, needing her taste as much as he needed his next breath. And she clung to him, kissing him in return, sending him more over the edge than he already was.

Moments later he pulled back before he was tempted to sweep Dana into his arms, take her into the bedroom and make love to her all night long.

He met her gaze. Saw the heated look in her eyes and his entire body immediately reacted. Leaning forward he kissed the bare skin of her neck, liking the way it tasted, tempted to taste her all over. Beneath his tongue he felt her shiver, felt himself get harder and knew if he didn't stop what he was doing, temptation would get the best of him.

But he didn't want to stop. He wanted her with an intensity that almost took his breath away and had him working on minimum control and very little else.

With much effort he leaned away to look at her. He would give anything to take that dress off her body and get her naked. Then he would take his hands and cup her breasts and after driving her wild with his tongue

on her nipples he would get on his knees and kiss a
path all the way down her body until he reached—

"Jared?"

Her soft whisper interrupted his thoughts. "Yes?" he
responded, his voice husky, thick with sexual need.

"I think you should leave now."

He took a deep breath, losing his calm as he'd lost
his control. He knew that asking him to leave was her
way of letting him know that she wasn't ready for the
bedroom yet, and if they continued at this pace he
would definitely take her there. He heard her words but
still a part of him—that part that wanted her, needed
her—felt inclined to push.

"You want me, Dana. I can see it in your eyes. I can
hear it in your breathing. I can taste it in your kiss. Why
deny what you want?"

She placed her fingers to his lips. "Yes, I want you,
but I can't become involved in a meaningless affair,
Jared. As soon as your mother is given a clean bill of
health you'll be ready to break this fake engagement
and walk away. Do you deny that?"

She stared at him, waiting for an answer, and he
gave her the only one that he could give. "No, I don't
deny it."

"Then Counselor, not giving in to my desires is the
right thing," she said, taking a step back away from
him.

He frowned. "I can't give you more, Dana," he said,
annoyed with the circumstances surrounding them.

"And I haven't asked you to give me more, Jared.
But then you shouldn't expect me to give you more
than I can, either."

Exasperated, he rubbed a hand down his face. "Why make things complicated?" he asked, clearly frustrated.

"That's the last thing I want. In fact I'm trying not to complicate things. If I thought for one minute that I could handle an affair with you then we would be in my bedroom right now, getting it on. But I can't," she said feeling just as frustrated as she knew he was.

Jared sighed and reached out and pulled her tensed body into his arms. "Look, I'm sorry. I didn't mean to push, especially when I said that I wouldn't. But I want you in a way that I shouldn't. I don't think I've ever wanted a woman as much as I want you."

Jared was consumed by a need to do nothing but hold her. He didn't know how long he could hang on with their pretense but knew he had to see it through. Somehow he needed to build an immunity against the wants and desires that overtook him whenever he was within ten feet of her.

Moments later, he pulled back and looked at her. "I'll be out of town this week and won't be returning until late Friday night. When are you leaving town?"

"Early Saturday morning. It's about a seven-hour drive because I like to take the scenic route and spend the night on one of the Sea Islands."

He draped an arm casually around her shoulders. "Which one?"

"Jekyll Island. It's beautiful and close to Brunswick. My parents used to take me camping there each year."

"When will you be back?"

"Probably late Sunday evening."

Jared nodded. If she was leaving early Saturday morning that meant he wouldn't see her again until she returned. He leaned down and gently kissed her once more. And now since they were alone, he nudged her body closer, liking the feel of his palms on her backside. He felt the tips of her breasts harden against his chest and reacted by pressing his erection low against her belly. The sensations spreading through him were relentless and fierce, and he plunged his tongue even deeper into her mouth, tasting her, devouring her, driving them both crazy with desire. "Miss me while I'm gone," he whispered, when he finally released her mouth. He knew he had to leave. If he stayed one minute longer, he wouldn't be able to control his actions. "Goodnight, Dana."

He then opened the door, stepped out and closed it quietly behind him.

Dana sighed deeply and leaned back against the door, missing Jared already. She had to be realistic about her pretended engagement or else she would fall head over heels in love with him. And that was something she could not and would not let happen.

Two hours later Jared was in his bed wide awake, flat on his back and staring up at the ceiling. Maybe he was moving too fast with Dana and should slow down. He had a reputation for being an in-control kind of guy, but lately he'd been losing control whenever it came to her.

He wished there was some way he could close his mind and thoughts to wanting and desiring her so much but was finding it impossible. He never intended for their pretended engagement to lead to a brief affair. It was hard getting his mind back in focus, and nearly impossible to remember that their relationship wasn't real.

Even his brothers and cousins had teased him relentlessly tonight about how hard he had fallen for her. And on top of that, his father had taken him aside and asked if he was sure he could wait another year for a wedding.

Jeez. Was it blatantly obvious to everyone just how much he wanted her? And for a while tonight, while introducing her to neighbors and friends, he had actually considered Dana his.

His.

His heart slammed against his ribs at the thought of anything so foolish. He'd never considered a woman his because he didn't want any woman to consider him hers. He was only interested in the physical side of a relationship and not the emotional. He had enough of emotional entanglements with the cases he handled.

Crossing the room to his dresser, he opened a drawer and pulled out a pair of swimming trunks. Removing his pajamas bottoms he eased the trunks over his still aroused body thinking that a swim in the pool might cool him off and help calm his mind.

It was almost dawn when Jared returned to his bedroom. His body was exhausted but his mind still swam with thoughts of Dana.

The next few days were busy for Dana. The buzz around the office about her engagement had settled down, however, word had quickly spread about the rock she was wearing on her finger. More than once, a curious co-worker had stopped by her office to get a look at it. Tara had been right. Jared certainly knew how to make a statement. It was just too bad the statement he was making was not true.

On Tuesday morning, she got an unexpected call from Jared's mother.

"Mrs. Westmoreland, this is a pleasant surprise," she said smiling, and meaning every word. The more she was around the older woman, the more she liked her, mainly because she reminded her a lot of her own mother—friendly, outgoing and devoted to her family.

"Dana, how are you dear? I was wondering if you could join me for lunch at Chase's Place?"

Dana lifted an eyebrow as she checked her watch. "Sure. Would noon be fine?"

"It would be perfect. Do you know how to get there or do you need directions?"

Dana chuckled. "Yes, I know how to get there. It's a favorite for a lot of my co-workers. I've even eaten there a couple of times myself. The food is fantastic."

"Yes it is. Chase still uses some of the Westmoreland family's secret recipes."

A few hours later as Dana drove to Chase's Place, she couldn't help but think about Jared. He had left a message on her answering machine last night to let her know where he'd gone, which was definitely information a fiancée should know should anyone ask. He'd even left the number where he could be reached should she need him.

But she didn't need him.

Unfortunately, she had to remind herself of that very thing pretty often these days. She shouldn't make more of what was going on between them than there really was. Even he had admitted that when this sham was no longer needed he would walk away without a backwards glance.

So why don't you just enjoy whatever moments you have with him? an inner voice screamed. *Why does there have to be regrets after goodbyes? You may not want to fall in love with him but you're halfway there already. Admit it.*

A lump formed in Dana's throat. She refused to admit anything. Hadn't she learned a cruel lesson about depending on others for her happiness? First there was the loss of her parents and then Matt and Luther, two men who had walked into her life and then walked out…just like Jared intended to do.

She'd known the score going in so, unlike the others, when he did his disappearing act she would be ready.

Dana saw Jared's mother sitting at a table the moment she entered the restaurant. She thought Sarah Westmoreland was a beautiful woman at fifty-seven with short black hair she wore in an Afro. She had dark brown eyes, dimples in both cheeks and a medium-size figure. Her smile was always gracious and sincere and Dana knew she wouldn't just be a mother-in-law to her sons' wives, she'd be like a second mother.

"Mrs. Westmoreland," Dana said as she approached the table.

"Dana, it's good seeing you again," the older woman said, standing and giving her a huge hug. From the first,

Dana had decided that Jared's mother was a warm, loving person. And there was so much excitement in the older woman's voice on seeing her that no one would think they had just seen each other on Saturday, which was only three days ago.

"And it's good seeing you, as well," Dana responded, thinking she could get used to all the love and affection the woman generated.

Once they took their seats Mrs. Westmoreland smiled and said, "How are things going at work? Jared mentioned you're a landscape architect. That sounds like a real interesting profession."

Dana smiled. "It is. My parents owned a nursery so I got interested in trees, plants and shrubs fairly early in life." She paused while the waitress gave them glasses of water and their menus. Then she continued. "A lot of people don't understand the involvement of a landscape architect whenever a building is constructed. My job is to make sure the outside area is not only functional but also beautiful and compatible with the natural environment."

Sarah Westmoreland nodded. A sad look then appeared in her eyes. "Jared told me about your parents' passing. That must have been devastating for you."

Dana nodded. "Yes, it was. I was the only child and was very close to my parents. Their deaths left me without any family."

Sarah smiled warmly as she reached out and covered Dana's hand. "Well, all that's changed. Like I told you the other night, the Westmorelands are your family now and I want you to feel like a part of us."

"Thanks." Dana felt a deep lump in her throat. She

hated deceiving Jared's family, although she knew it was being done for a good reason. Dana looked down to study her menu. There was no way she could look at Mrs. Westmoreland right now.

"So, dear, have your heard from Jared since he's been gone?"

Dana glanced up. At least her answer wouldn't be a total lie. There was no reason Mrs. Westmoreland needed to know that, although Jared had called, she hadn't actually spoken with him. "Yes, he called last night."

"I'm sure that he's missing you."

Dana smiled. She doubted Jared was missing her but she definitely was missing him, although she didn't want to. She spent her days trying not to think about him, but found herself doing it anyway.

Dana took another sip of her water and decided to shift the topic off her and Jared. "So, how have you been?" she asked the older woman.

Sarah smiled. "I'm fine. I'm sure Jared told you that I had breast cancer a few years ago and that recently the doctor found another lump. But there's a chance it's nothing more than fatty tissue. I'm having it removed in two weeks and then we'll know the results. Whatever it is, I'll deal with it. I'd be the first to admit chemo and radiation were hard on me, but if I have to go through them again, then I will. I'm a fighter, Dana. My family gives me a lot to fight for. And I'm looking forward to the day when I become a grandmother," she said excitedly. "Jared told me that the two of you wanted children."

Dana inwardly thought that that was a lot for Jared

to have said, considering they had never discussed children, not that they really planned on having any together.

At that moment the waitress walked up to take their orders and Dana was grateful for her timely arrival. A pretended engagement was bad enough. The last thing she needed to think about was having Jared's baby.

Six

On Wednesday evening after feeding Tom, Dana curled up in her favorite chair to read and relax. It had been a hectic day. One of her clients had been difficult, upset that the city's ordinances would keep him from constructing a huge man-made waterfall on the property where he planned to erect his company's building.

Not wanting to think about the problems that had plagued her that day any longer, she switched her thoughts to the lunch she'd shared with Jared's mother yesterday. Afterward she felt a special bond toward the woman that she shouldn't feel and didn't deserve. She wondered what his family would think when they ended their engagement, which just might be two weeks from now if his mother's test indicated her lump was benign.

She glanced up from her book when she heard the sound of the doorbell. It was barely six o'clock and she wasn't expecting anyone. Cybil and Ben had decided to take the week off to visit his brother in Tennessee.

The moment she glanced out of the peephole, her heart stopped. It was Jared. She hadn't expected him back until late Friday. Taking a deep breath she slowly opened the door. "Jared, you're back."

He leaned in the doorway, and they stared at each other for a moment before he said, "Yes, I finished up earlier than expected but I haven't made it home yet. I thought I would drop by here first."

Dana was curious why he would come by her place before going home. The only thing she could think of was that maybe he'd heard about her having lunch with his mother and wanted an update. But then he could have called her to get that information. She cocked her head and looked at him. He stood in front of her door with such a strong, manly presence, she barely found her voice to say, "Come on in."

Jared sighed deeply as soon as he walked into Dana's home and the door closed behind him. Her expression had indicated that she was surprised that he had come straight from the airport. Hell, he was surprised himself. He had missed her like crazy and the only thing he could think of was that when the plane landed he had to see her.

He looked at her, thinking that the late-afternoon sun that shone through the living-room window seemed to make Dana all aglow. He could only stand there and stare at her, thinking just how beautiful she looked while wearing a pair of shorts and a T-shirt that said

I'm Yours. Boy did he wish. Every fiber in his body stirred at the thought.

Being alone with her was causing his brain to short-circuit and he felt heat slowly move around in his belly. He breathed in her womanly scent and watched all the questions that were forming in the depths of her dark eyes.

"Did you miss me?" he finally asked. Needing to know. Wanting to know. Hoping like hell that she did and at the same time not understanding why he cared if she had or hadn't.

Dana tried shoving aside the shiver that raced up her body. Yes, she had missed him. Damn him for asking. It didn't take much to recall what happened the last time they were together, in this very same room—the heated kiss that had had her tasting him for days afterward. She could lie to him and say that she hadn't missed him or she could tell the truth.

But first, before she would admit to anything, she had a question of her own. "Did *you* miss me?"

Slow amusement lit the depths of Jared's dark eyes at the way Dana had turned the tables so he would be answering her question instead of her answering his. He smiled. She was about to get an answer he doubted she was ready for. But she *had* asked.

"Oh, yeah, I missed you. I thought about you every day, although I didn't want to. I also dreamed about you every night, and in those dreams I did all those things that you aren't ready for me to do. I made you realize how wonderful it can be when two people—the right two people—make love."

He crossed his arms over his chest and after a short

moment of silence he said, "Okay, I've answered your question so how about answering mine. Did you miss me?"

They stood facing each other, both intently aware that something had shifted between them. They were doing more than wavering on the edge; they were hanging on for dear life. The chemistry between them was more powerful than ever, explosive, and deliriously potent. At that very moment, Dana wondered what could be the worst thing to happen if she told him she *had* missed him, *and* with the same intensity he'd claimed and so vividly stated.

She had also dreamed about him each night and each time he had invaded her sleep he had made love to her. In the deep unconsciousness of her mind she had easily and willingly given everything to him and he had pleasured her in ways she could only imagine. She had felt safe in knowing that when she awoke, she could face reality. But a secret part of her yearned to see how close her dreams were to the real thing. Could he actually make her reach an orgasm that many times? Even reaching one would be a first for her.

"Dana?"

He reclaimed her attention. "Yes?"

"I asked if you missed me," he said softly.

Yes, he had. And she would try to answer him, although not in the same depth that he'd done. "Yes, I missed you. And I dreamed about you, too." She watched as his nostrils flared and she heard his quick intake of breath.

He slowly uncrossed his arms. "And in these dreams…"

Dana tilted her head and looked at him. "That's for me to know."

A smile touched the corners of his lips as he took a couple of steps toward her. "And for me to find out?"

She held his gaze. "I doubt that you can."

Jared lifted a dark eyebrow and Dana immediately knew her mistake. She had given him a challenge.

She couldn't help but let her gaze lower to his fly and felt herself stirred by what she saw. He was an unashamed, very aroused man. She swallowed deeply and snatched her gaze back to his face. She tried desperately to remember the last conversation they'd had here in this house. Hadn't it been a mere five days ago? But for the life of her, her mind was getting fuzzy, heated and filled with more desire than she could handle.

"I thought we decided not to complicate things," she said, trying to hold on to her sanity as much as she could.

Another smile curved his lips. "Finding out just what kind of dreams you had is the most uncomplicated thing I'll ever do. Uncomplicated and very satisfying for the both of us."

Dana saw the look of intent in his eyes and took a step back. She folded her arms beneath her breasts. "I won't sleep with you, Jared."

She saw him lift another eyebrow as he regarded her. She realized too late that she had made another mistake because she had intentionally given him another challenge.

"And I told you, Dana, that I won't push you into doing anything you aren't ready for."

She frowned slightly. "And what do you think you're doing now if not pushing."

He lifted a shoulder in a shrug. "Making an attempt to destroy your theory that sex is overrated. But, I don't have to sleep with you to do that."

"You don't?"

"No."

Dana swallowed, saw the intensity in his gaze. She believed him. Now she understood why he was one of the most successful attorneys in Atlanta. "You're smooth," she decided to say, meaning every word. He was using every weapon at his disposal to break down her defenses. There was the huskiness of his voice, the look of heated desire in his eyes and his very obviously aroused body. Even his stance was provocatively sexy.

"I'm also thorough, Dana."

She swallowed again and wondered why on earth was he making this difficult? But then another part of her couldn't help but be curious. Could he really prove that sex wasn't overrated without sleeping with her? What would he do to prove it? Just thinking about what approach he might use stirred her up. Boy, was she tempted to find out. And his penetrating stare wasn't helping matters. He was definitely rattling her resolve and kicking good common sense straight out the window.

"You once asked me how you would know when you were ready for me, Dana," he said softly, reclaiming her attention—not that he'd fully lost it. "You might not be ready to sleep with me but I think you're ready for this. What do you think?"

Dana sighed. How could she know if she was ready for *this,* when she didn't have a clue what *this* entailed. But she did know that whatever it was, it would be something she would regret not experiencing if she sent him away.

Her gaze swept over him thoroughly one more time before she made her decision. "I think you might be right."

He nodded slowly. "It's your call."

There was considerable silence. Then finally, Dana retraced the distance between them and stood before him, met his gaze, held it. Everything inside of her stirred with heated lust. "Then I'm making it."

Jared smiled. He liked everything about her—her smile, her body, her mind. He shook his head. Forget about what he liked. It was time to focus on what he wanted. Dana Rollins was one hell of a seductive woman.

And he wanted her.

He had told her they wouldn't sleep together, but he intended to drive her as far over the edge as she could go. "Do you trust me, Dana?"

She nodded, realizing what he was asking and why he was asking it. She stared deeply into his eyes when she answered. "Yes, I trust you."

"Good." And then without wasting any more time, he swept her into his arms and quickly moved in the direction of her bedroom.

"But—but you said we wouldn't sleep together."

He gazed down at her. "We're not. We're going to play a game."

She clutched the front of his jacket to hold on to since he was walking so fast. "A game?"

"Yeah. My version of Red Light, Green Light."

"Oh."

Jared smiled thinking of the possibilities as he placed her on her bed. He was glad Tom was nowhere around, and just to make sure the cat didn't show up later, Jared walked over to the bedroom door and closed it.

He sighed when he turned back to Dana and saw the look of uncertainty in her eyes. He had to remain composed for both their sakes. "Do you want to change your mind about this?" he asked softly, respecting her doubts and fears. It wasn't about taking care of his body's needs but rather, introducing her to how wonderful things could be between a man and a woman.

She met his gaze as she settled back in the bed. He tried not to concentrate on her legs and thighs and was finding it near impossible not to. "No, I don't want to change my mind, Jared."

"Are you sure?"

She nodded. "Yes."

He moved away from the door and came to stand by the foot of the bed. "Then let me tell you about this game," he said, removing his jacket and tossing it on a chair in her room. "The light will always be green, letting me know it's okay to move forward. But at any time you feel rushed, overwhelmed or want me to stop, all you have to say is red light. Understand?"

She slowly nodded, although at the moment the only thing she fully understood was that he looked good standing at the foot of her bed, especially in his extremely aroused state. She wondered what he would be getting out of this since they wouldn't be sleeping together.

He must have read the questions in her eyes. "This isn't about me, Dana. It's about you. I can handle things and how I do so is only for me to know."

"And for me to find out?"

Jared laughed. The first real good laugh he'd had in a long time. "Yes, maybe one day."

He moved slowly toward the bed and braced one knee on the mattress. He pulled her into his arms and whispered, "Green light." Bending his head he captured her lips. The moment his tongue slid inside her mouth, heat consumed him in a way it never had before. It was hard to believe that he could want a woman this badly, with this much intensity and desire. He kissed her the same way he had dreamed about and was thrilled that she was returning his kiss with equal fire, with an urgency that only made him want her even more.

Suddenly, she broke off their kiss. "Red light," she said breathlessly, barely able to get the words out.

He stopped kissing her and met her gaze. "I needed to breathe," she explained. He didn't say anything but continued to look at her. He watched as she took slow uneven breaths and licked her lips. Moments later she said softly, "Green light."

He was ready. He captured her mouth again in his and pulled her up against his erection, wanting her to not only see but to feel what she did to him. He palmed her bottom, and then moved his hand to stroke her thighs. He slowly shifted his hand to the area between her legs, wanting to touch her and not intending for a pair of shorts to stand in his way.

He pulled back. "Red light," he said and smiled when he heard Dana whimper in protest. He met her gaze. "May I remove your shorts and T-shirt?"

Dana stared at him for a moment, melted under his seductive gaze and whispered, "Green light."

Jared's breathing almost stopped. She had given him the go-ahead and he intended to take it to the max. Leaning toward her, he whipped the T-shirt over her head and tossed it across the room, leaving her in a black lace bra. His mouth itched, his tongue thickened at the thought of how her breasts might look. Whether he got to find out or not would be her decision. But he was a man who was used to compromising. If she wanted to keep her scrap-of-nothing bra on, he could taste her breasts without taking anything off.

He shifted his attention to her shorts, reached out and when she lifted her hips he slowly eased them down her legs to reveal black lace panties. He'd never appreciated black lace so much until now. He tossed her shorts aside to join her T-shirt. Then on his knees he leaned over her and gently lifted her bra to uncover her breasts. Dana whimpered, but didn't protest. At that moment he couldn't have looked away even if someone yelled "Fire." He had to actually fight to control his breathing. She had the most beautiful, luscious pair of breasts he had ever seen on a woman. They were full and firm.

He met her gaze. She was looking at him just as hard as he was looking at her. "The light still green?" he asked softly, in a shuddering breath.

"Yes."

One day he would show her his undying gratitude. But for now…he reached out and cupped her breasts, tracing a fingertip around the dark tip of her nipple, first one and then the other. He heard her sharp intake of breath and it heated him more. Leaning over he captured a nipple gently between his teeth and holding it captive he used his tongue to make her as hot as he was.

Dana curled her hand into a fist as feelings she had never encountered before slammed through her. She could barely stay on the bed, with the sensations Jared was evoking heightening her gratification to a level of pleasure she hadn't thought existed. He was taking one breast, and then the other, tugging at a nipple drawing them into his mouth, torturing them with his tongue.

She closed her eyes, feeling herself being pulled under the most sensual haze ever. A moan escaped her throat. She heard it and knew he heard it, as well. But he didn't stop doing what he was doing. She had dreamed about him doing this to her but her dreams weren't anything like the real thing.

When she felt him release her nipples she opened her eyes and met his heated gaze. "Light's still green?" he asked huskily.

She nodded. She couldn't speak. "Then lie back for me," he requested softly.

She did what he asked and her stomach clenched when he began tracing a trail of kisses from her breasts all the way to her navel. And if that wasn't bad enough, she felt his fingers easing inside her panties, setting off a deep throb between her legs. Any thoughts of resisting were forgotten. She had given him the green light to do as he pleased; and it seemed his most fervent desire was pleasing her.

Jared felt her heat. He smelled her scent and his erection got harder, increased in length. He ignored the tremendous ache in his groin as he forced his mind to concentrate on Dana. He eased his finger inside her panties and found her wet heat.

He let his fingertips have their way and Dana automatically parted her legs for him. Then he went to work, stroking her back and forth, over and over again, glorying in the sounds of her moans, the sensuous catch in her breath, her purrs, the way she groaned his name.

Without missing a beat with his fingers, he eased his mouth away from her navel and back to her lips, nipping at them, tracing his tongue from corner to corner. And then he went into her mouth with an urgency that was earth-shattering, increasing the stroking of his fingers, feeling her getting wetter, hotter, slicker. She couldn't stay still and wiggled her bottom and pushed up against his fingers.

"Jared!"

And then it happened. He felt it and continued what he was doing but lifted his head to look at her. He thought that she was beautiful while having an orgasm and knew at that moment he would want to see her in the throes of passion for the rest of his days.

For the rest of his days. He blinked, quickly pushed that thought away and wondered what craziness would make him even think such a thing. Dana had no place in his future. No woman did. But knowing that couldn't keep him from reaching out and pulling her into his arms and kissing the sweet taste of sweat from her forehead as her spasms slowly subsided.

He felt his erection throbbing and he fought back his own need for release. This was her time and as far as he was concerned, it was only the beginning. One day his time would come. Meanwhile…

He brought his head down and captured her mouth. Needing the taste of her with an urgency that he didn't quite understand. The kiss was quick, hard and deeply satisfying. She sighed into his mouth and his groin tightened at the feelings it stirred.

"How about going out with me tomorrow night," he whispered close to her ear moments later when she lay curled in his arms while he held her. In the back of his mind he could still hear her cry out her response to what he'd done to her.

Dana gazed up at him. How on earth could he think of tomorrow when she was still sensually stirred up from what had happened today? She hadn't known such pure hot pleasure existed and all with the use of his fingers. She didn't want to think about what would happen if they were to actually make love. In her mind she would die a slow death, several times over.

"Tomorrow?" she said, barely getting the word out.

"Yes, tomorrow. We can go out to eat, take in a movie and then afterward walk around Stone Mountain. Anywhere that doesn't have a bed. You, lady, are too much temptation. I can only take so much."

She shifted in his arms and gazed up at him. Maybe it was her hormones talking, but when it came to Jared, she wanted to take all he had to give and not think of the consequences. "Okay, wherever you want to go is fine. I'll let you decide."

He nodded and she watched as he eased from the bed to stand. He still had his shirt and pants on and looked as rumpled as she felt. She then remembered something very important. "That was my first you know."

He glanced over at her and raised an eyebrow. "Your first what?"

She hesitated, not knowing exactly what to say or how she should say it. But as he waited for her response she knew she had to tell him of his gift to her. "My first orgasm."

He gazed at her. Shocked. When it wore off, he dropped back down on the bed and pulled her into his arms, made her look at him. "I'm glad you shared your first with me," he said huskily, meaning every word.

She smiled. "Me, too."

Jared leaned over and kissed her again, and she felt his desire but also a tenderness that overwhelmed her. He slowly pulled back, stood and crossed the room to get her shorts and T-shirt. Coming back over to the bed he took the time to redress her. He didn't say anything and neither did she.

When her clothes were back in place she looked up at him. He reached out and slid a slow finger across her cheek. "I'll call you tomorrow."

"Okay." She then remembered she needed to tell him something else. She sat up straight and pushed the hair out of her face. "I had lunch with your mom yesterday."

He startled. "You did?"

"Yes. She called and invited me to have lunch with her at Chase's Place. She's so nice, Jared, and I really hate lying to her even though I know why we're doing it."

He nodded and fixed dark eyes on her. "Don't worry about it. Things will work out."

She gave him a shaky smile. "I hope you're right." But a part of Dana wondered how things could possibly work out when the one thing that she hadn't wanted to happen was happening anyway.

She was falling in love with Jared Westmoreland.

Seven

"What do you mean there's a possibility the child is mine?" Sylvester Brewster shot to his feet.

Jared slid the documents out of the envelope and across the table as he met the man's shocked gaze. "What I'm saying is that according to this medical report, based on the physical that you took last week, you're not sterile. In fact you have a very high sperm count."

Sylvester sank back into his chair. "B-but what about that childhood disease?"

"According to Dr. Frye, you may have had a low sperm count at one time but there's no indication you were ever sterile and nothing is documented in your medical history."

Sylvester shook his head, squeezed his eyes shut. "This doesn't make sense, Jared."

"You were misinformed. Whatever doctor told your parents you were sterile evidently misdiagnosed your condition. And since you are capable of producing children, there's a strong possibility that your wife's child is yours…just like she claimed."

Sylvester dropped his head on Jared's desk with a solid thump. "Damn, Jared, you don't know what all I said to her, all the things I accused her of."

Jared nodded. He could just imagine. "All that medical report does is indicate you aren't sterile. It doesn't prove the child is definitely yours. The next step is to order an amniocentesis."

Sylvester lifted his head. "A what?"

"An amniocentesis. It's a test that's done to the mother, generally during the fourteenth to twenty-fourth week of pregnancy to determine the paternity of an unborn child. We can have the results back in two weeks."

"No."

Jared lifted a brow. "No?"

"No. I've humiliated her enough. Did you see the tabloids this morning, man? Someone leaked my accusations to the papers and it's all in the news. Jackie is never going to forgive me for not trusting her."

Jared knew that was a very strong possibility. That very morning, he had spoken to Jackie Brewster's attorney, who had informed him that his client was hurt and upset, but would be more than happy to undergo a paternity testing. Once it's proven that Sylvester *was* her baby's father, she planned to sue him for every cent he had for publicly humiliating her.

Jared met the man's stare. "I suggest you don't make

decisions about anything today. Take the report home and read it and then let's meet one day next week to discuss how we're going to proceed."

"I don't want a divorce, Jared. I want my wife back. I was wrong. I should have trusted her. I love her and I owe her a huge apology."

It was on the tip of Jared's tongue to remind Sylvester that two weeks ago, when he was certain he was sterile, he'd been singing a totally different tune. "Yes, that might be the case but I doubt a reconciliation is what Mrs. Brewster has on her mind right now. According to her attorney, she doesn't want to see or talk to you. As your attorney, I suggest you don't try to contact her until we've determined our next course of action."

Thirty minutes later, Jared was standing at the window in his office looking out. Sylvester had gotten himself in a real mess this time. The love he had for his wife had gotten overshadowed with mistrust. Was there any hope of the marriage surviving? For Sylvester's sake, he hoped so.

Jared sighed deeply as he switched his thoughts from Sylvester's problems to his own. He could sum up his troubles with one name.

Dana.

There were very few times in his life when he'd been faced with a situation that he couldn't figure out or adequately handle. And this was one of those times. Frustrated and annoyed, he drew in a deep breath. What had happened between them yesterday had touched him in a way that it shouldn't have. And what was so extraordinary about it was that they hadn't made love.

Yet he had shared something with her that he hadn't ever shared with another woman.

While in that bed kissing her, touching her, he had felt as if she was the only woman he could ever want. The only woman that he wanted in his lifetime. Damn, but this pretended engagement was going to his head, zapping him of common sense and confusing the hell out of him.

It hadn't been easy to leave her last night and before he'd left he had sat on the bed and pulled her into his arms. For the longest time she had sat curled up in his lap with neither of them saying anything. The only sound that had intruded on their moment had been the soft meowing of Tom at the bedroom door. Even now, just thinking about her made his chest tighten with a need he wasn't used to.

He glanced down at his watch. He would be picking her up at six for dinner. And the only thing he could think about was seeing her again and kissing her with the desperation he felt. Dana Rollins was definitely getting under his skin.

"Would you like some more wine?"

"No, thank you, Jared." Dana bit down softly on her lip and tried not to stare at him. Every time their gazes met she felt a tiny pull at her heart.

"Are you ready for your trip this weekend?"

She met his gaze and forced a smile. "Yes, I'm ready. Since it's not a long trip, a lot of packing isn't necessary."

"I'd like to go with you."

Dana's eyes widened in surprise. "Why?"

Jared shrugged as he sank back in his chair. That was a good question since he had just made the decision. "I don't like the idea of you driving so many hours alone."

Dana couldn't help but appreciate his concerns. "It's something I do every year, Jared. And when my father's birthday comes around in September I'll be doing it again. No big deal."

Jared frowned. To him it was a big deal. "You shared my father's birthday with me and I want to be there to share your mother's birthday with you."

Dana glanced down at her wineglass. How could she not fall in love with him when he said something like that? She slowly lifted her head and met his gaze. "Thanks, Jared, but that's not necessary."

He smiled. "It is to me." He leaned closer over the table. "Besides, it's been years since I've been to Jekyll Island and I'd like to go there again."

Dana inhaled deeply. The part of her that was fighting what she was feeling for Jared wanted to tell him to find another time to go, that she needed time alone, time away from him, but she couldn't say that. She decided to use another approach. "I don't think it's a good idea for us to go out of town together, Jared."

"Why? Because of last night?"

Dana felt a jolt to her body at the memories, something she'd tried to downplay all day. She had played Red Light, Green Light, many times as a child but never like that and never with a playmate like Jared. He gave the game a whole new meaning. "That, among other things," she finally said softly. *And please don't ask me what those other things are,* she silently screamed. *I don't want you to know that I'm falling in love with you.*

"I know your thoughts on us sleeping together, Dana. You've been pretty clear on that and I think I've been straightforward in saying that I won't push you into doing anything you're not ready for. But this isn't about us sharing a bed."

Dana met his gaze. "Then what's it about, Jared?"

His eyes held hers. "It's about me being with you and enjoying your company. I like talking to you."

Dana knew he was holding something back. She had been around him enough to know when something was bothering him. She could feel it. "Is there something else? Is everything all right with your mother, Jared?"

He stared at her for a moment and after taking a deep breath he said, "I spoke with Dad earlier today and he said that Mom got a call from the hospital. There was a cancellation and they were able to schedule her outpatient surgery for next week instead of waiting two weeks."

Dana nodded. "That's good news, isn't it?"

Jared heaved a long sigh. "Yes, but…"

She waited for him to finish. When he hesitated she asked, "But what?"

He dragged a hand over the back of his neck, seemingly frustrated. "But nothing. I guess I'm just remembering how it was the last time."

Dana understood and reached out, took his hand in hers and held it tight. A part of her was glad she was here with him and that he was sharing his innermost fears with her. "All we can do is hope and pray for the best, Jared. And I know you, your father and your brothers appreciate and love your mother. Your willingness to pretend to be engaged just to make her happy proves how much you care."

Dana let go of his hand and sat back, hoping she'd said something to make him feel better. She could tell he was worried but a part of her believed Sarah West-moreland would come through this just fine.

"How did your parents meet?" she decided to ask, wanting him to dwell on happier memories.

She watched the corners of his lips turn up into a smile. "My mother and Aunt Evelyn were best friends growing up in Birmingham, Alabama. When they grad-uated from high school, Aunt Evelyn came to Atlanta to visit her aunt. During her first week here she went on a church outing and met Uncle John. She wrote back to my mom telling her she had fallen in love and asking her to come to Atlanta to be her maid of honor. She'd only known her new groom a little more than a week!"

Jared gave her a lopsided grin. "My mother, being the levelheaded person that she is, caught a bus that same day and arrived in town to talk some sense into Aunt Evelyn. She didn't think love at first sight was possible."

Dana chuckled. She could just imagine his mother doing that. "What happened next?"

Jared smiled. "She got to town, met John's twin brother, James, and fell for him just as hard as Aunt Evelyn had fallen for my uncle. My parents got married within a couple of weeks of my aunt and uncle's wedding."

A smile softened Dana's lips. "That's a beautiful love story."

Jared shrugged as he took a sip of his drink. "Yes, it is, isn't it?" It had been a long time since he had thought about how his parents had gotten together. They had met and fallen in love immediately. They hadn't thought about any of the ups and downs they would face. They had simply loved each other and had wanted to be together. To them that was all that had mattered.

Sighing deeply, Jared glanced down at his watch. "Are you ready to leave? Tonight is a nice night to walk around the park. Would you like to do that?"

"I'd love to." Dana met his gaze, suddenly understanding his need to get away for a few days and making a quick decision. "I'd love your company this weekend if you're serious about going with me to Brunswick."

He smiled warmly. "I am."

She returned his smile. "Good."

Over an hour later Jared returned to Dana's home and walked her to the door. She turned and looked at him.

"I enjoyed being with you tonight, Dana," he said, taking her hands in his.

Jared's words, spoken in a soft husky voice, immediately reclaimed Dana's attention. And his touch sent all kinds of sensations escalating through her body. "I enjoyed being with you tonight, as well," she said honestly. "Would you like to come in for something to drink?"

He shook his head. "No, it's late and I'd better go."

Dana let out the breath she'd been holding. A part of her was glad he had turned down her invitation but then another part was disappointed. She wanted to be alone with him. She wanted him to kiss her again. And more.

She gazed up at him. "Then I guess we need to say good night."

He gently tugged on her hand, pulling her from the shaft of light shining down on them from the porch light to a darkened area of the porch. She saw the kiss coming, wanted it and moaned with pleasure the moment their mouths touched. Intense heat, overwhelming pleasure shot through her as his tongue masterfully mated with hers. She could only stand there and grip his solid shoulders for support as he took her to another world, feasting on her lips as if they were a meal he had to savor.

When he finally released her mouth she had to rest her head on his chest while she caught her breath. Jared Westmoreland could incite passion with a mere touch, a kiss, a look. And she had felt his solid hard erection pressing against her, through the material of her skirt. He was as aroused and as she was.

"Go into the house, Dana," he whispered against her lips after slowly releasing her. He took a step back.

She swallowed. His voice sounded hoarse, husky, and sexy. "Good night, Jared," she said and turned to unlock the door.

"Good night. I'm playing pool with my cousins and Reggie tomorrow night, but I'll be by early Saturday to pick you up. Is seven o'clock a good time?"

She turned to him and wished she hadn't. He had stepped back into the light and stood tall and looked handsome. His coat jacket was slung over his shoulder and held in place by his fingertips. The pose was unforgettably sexy.

She cleared her throat. "Yes, seven will be fine. I'll be packed and ready to go."

"All right."

Giving him one last look, Dana opened the door and slipped inside. She leaned against the closed door when she heard him walk away, and then moments later the sound of his car leaving.

It was only then that she was able to slow down the beating of her heart and breathe easy again. How would she ever survive a weekend alone with Jared Westmoreland?

Jared stood next to Dana and watched as she placed the bouquet of fresh flowers on her mother's grave.

When he had picked her up bright and early she had been friendly and perky, the complete opposite of him first thing in the morning. He could be a bear until he downed at least two cups of coffee. But she had opened the door all smiles, packed and ready to go.

During the drive they had talked about a number of things including early memories of the time she'd spent in Brunswick, backyard cookouts with her parents, going to church together as a family on Sundays and how she would greet her father at the door whenever he'd come home from work.

They stopped once for lunch, but otherwise they had driven straight to town. Once there they had found a florist shop to purchase the flowers and had then driven to the cemetery.

He had considered remaining in the car, letting her have her private moments, but a part of him wanted to be with her, to stand beside her and let her know that he was there and that he cared. After a few moments of silence she straightened and automatically, as if it was the most natural thing to do, she leaned up against him and he offered her the support she needed.

He wrapped his arms around her shoulders and held her close to him. "You okay?" he asked softly.

She tried to smile and the effort made Jared's throat tighten when he saw the tears in her eyes. "Yes, I'm fine. It's just harder this year more than ever because today would have been their thirtieth wedding anniversary. They got married on my mother's birthday."

Dana gazed up at him through misty eyes. "Mom always reminded Dad that she should get two gifts that day instead of one, and of course he always came through. They loved each other very much, Jared. In a way I think if they had to die it was better for them to go together. I can't imagine my father living a normal life without my mother or vice versa. They had dated since high school and were so close, so connected. But the beauty of it all was that they never made me feel like I was an outsider. Dad used to say that I was the greatest gift of their love."

Jared nodded, knowing she needed to talk, get her feelings and emotions out. He was jarred into the realization that some marriages endured. Her parents' had. So had his parents' and his aunt and uncle's marriage. For a long moment they didn't say anything, they just stood there, needing the silence. He admired her ability to do this, to come here twice a year and face the pain of her loss with the poise and grace he had come to associate with her. He couldn't imagine getting a call, saying that both his parents were gone—unexpectedly, just like that. And if that were to happen, at least he had his brothers, the entire Westmoreland family. Dana had no one.

But today she had him and he wanted her to know that. He reached for her hand, linking their fingers. He was glad he had come, pleased that he was with her in this place, sharing such a personal and private moment. It meant a lot to him that it was his shoulder she was leaning on, his hand she was holding. And for the very first time in his life he felt he was in danger.

Danger of losing his heart.

"Thanks, Jared."

He tipped his head and looked at her. "You don't have to thank me, Dana. At the moment, I can't think of any place I'd rather be than here with you." And he meant it. "Ready to go?"

"Yes, I'm ready."

Back in the car, Jared headed toward Jekyll Island. His secretary had made hotel reservations for them. If Jeannie had thought it odd that he'd told her to get two separate rooms she hadn't said anything.

He glanced over at Dana. "Are you hungry?"

She shook her head. "No, in fact I think I'm beat and going to take a nap when we get to the hotel and check in."

He smiled. She might feel tired, but she didn't look it. She looked great dressed in a pair of slacks and top.

He spared her another quick glance. There hadn't been one time he'd seen her that he hadn't gotten turned on by what she was wearing.

Jared could see them in one bed, in each other's arms doing a number of things, and taking a nap wasn't one of them.

Dana woke up from her dream with a start, her breathing uneven, a wave of heat slowly building and touching her in her most intimate places. She closed her eyes to recapture the moments when she had imagined Jared in bed with her, naked with his arms around her, holding her, and his aroused body pressed intimately against her pelvis, sending her over the edge as he tried to connect with her.

She had felt the dampness of his skin, the perfection of his muscles as they clenched beneath her palms and the texture of his chest hair rubbing against her breasts, hardening the tips.

She had experienced all those things. But only in her dream.

Dana pulled herself up in bed and inhaled deeply as she pushed her hair from her face. She'd known she was a goner when he had walked her to her hotel-room door. After saying that he hoped she enjoyed her nap, he had lifted her palm to his lips and placed a kiss at her wrist. And it hadn't been your typical wrist kissing. His hot, wet tongue had slid over her wrist and then he had gently sucked the area, leaving a mark. His mark.

She glanced down at her wrist. She still felt the heat. She then looked across the room at the closed door that separated his room from hers—a shield, a barrier, a connecting door. But if it were to open…

She wondered if he was there. Had he taken a nap, as well? Had he dreamed of her as she had dreamed of him?

Slipping out of bed she stood and decided it was time to take part in some sort of physical pleasure. The other night Jared had shown her just what her body had been missing. He had given her a taste of what pleasures were out there if she decided to indulge.

Visiting her parents' graves had made her realize just how unpredictable life could be. You could be here today and gone tomorrow. Life held no guarantees, there were no promises. There were no forevers.

There was only the moment. And you had to seize it to get what you wanted, capture it, slow it down and take advantage of it, make every second count.

Jared had always been honest with her, totally upfront. She knew how he felt about serious involvements. And she knew that no matter what, he had no intentions of changing his mind about that. Next week, if things worked out with his mother, he would walk away, just as surely as there was a sun shining in the sky. But dammit, she refused to let go without at least having something to look back on and remember from their time together.

She turned when she heard the gentle knock on the connecting door. Tightening the belt of her silk robe, she crossed the room and slowly opened it. Jared was there. She inhaled gently, breathing in the manly scent of him. He stood tall, handsome, hot and sexy. His features were sharp; the eyes that were holding hers were keen. She felt her heart beat violently at such profound sexiness.

Regardless of whether Jared was dressed as a million-dollar businessman or wearing faded jeans and a chambray shirt, as he was now, he looked like a man any woman would want both in and out of her bed. The man any woman would want to strip her naked, kiss her senseless and make love to her with an all-consuming passion.

And the man a woman would want to give her heart to on a silver platter.

Suddenly, she knew she was no longer falling in love with him. She *had* fallen in love with him. She loved him with every sense of her being, with every ounce of blood flowing fast and furious through her veins, with the breaths she was now taking—slow and uneven. Over the past couple of weeks she had seen more than a glimpse of him. She had gotten to know him as a man of high intelligence and intense integrity. He had proven it that day when she had shown up at his office, spitting fire and mad as hell. Luther had been his client, yet he had gone beyond what some would consider ethically proper and had given her off-the-record advice to save herself from further embarrassment, humiliation and financial ruin. And for that she truly appreciated him.

She also appreciated the way he showed her that sex wasn't overrated, and that with the right person it could be a definitely satisfying and gratifying experience. And even now, here, today, he had come to Brunswick with her. He had stood beside her and had given her his shoulder to lean on when the pain of losing her parents had resurfaced.

"I hope I didn't wake you from your nap, Dana."

She swallowed deeply as she stared up at him. "No, I'm awake." *In more ways than one,* she thought. "Did you sleep?"

He smiled, and his smile sent sensations oozing through the pit of her stomach. "No, I found that I couldn't sleep after all and decided to catch a tennis match on television."

He glanced beyond her and she knew his eyes lit on her rumpled bed. He returned his gaze to her. "Do you find the accommodations acceptable?" he asked softly.

Dana couldn't stop the smile that touched her lips. The accommodations were more than acceptable. He had made reservations at one of the most expensive hotels on the beach, right on the ocean, connecting suites with balconies facing the water. She had offered to share the cost but he refused to talk about it. "Everything is wonderful, Jared. Thank you. I hadn't expected such extravagance."

Jared nodded. He knew she hadn't and that was one of the things that made her so special and unique. Because of his success other women had expected certain luxuries. Dana expected nothing but in his opinion she deserved everything.

He considered how sexy she looked now, wearing a leopard-print robe that was destined to bring out the beast in any man. It hadn't helped matters when he had glanced over and saw her bed with the messed-up covers and tangled sheets.

"Would you like to take a walk on the beach before dinner?" he decided to ask. "We can either eat in the restaurant downstairs or, if you prefer, we can dine in our rooms."

Dana lowered her gaze and quickly made her decision—about a number of things. She tipped her chin up and met his gaze. "I'd love to take a walk on the beach and if you don't mind I'd prefer if we ate here."

"All right."

She continued to hold his gaze and in the dark depths of his eyes she knew that he recognized that something had changed. Something elemental and deep. She also knew he would keep his word. He would take things slow, be patient and let her take the lead. He wouldn't push, he wouldn't pressure, but he would be ready whenever she was. And when he pounced, there would be no stopping him. God, she hoped not. She wanted it all. Everything he had to give. And she knew when it happened there was no going back. Their time together was limited. The moments would be short. But she intended to make the most of them, and when he walked away, she would have special memories to last a lifetime.

"I guess I'd better let you get dressed then," he said, breaking into her thoughts.

She smiled at him. "Yes, I think you'd better if we want to take that walk while there's still a lot of day-light."

He nodded. Then slowly he leaned down and captured her lips. It was a slow, drugging kiss, gentle, tender. Whether he was kissing her this way or devouring her mouth, it didn't matter. He still knew how to rob her of her senses and want to make her scream out for more.

He slowly released her lips but kept his attention glued to them as she took her tongue and licked her mouth. She heard his sharp intake of breath, saw his guts clench and knew he was walking the same tight-rope that she was.

"I'll knock on the door when I'm ready," she whispered, and when he nodded and took a step back, she gently closed the door and leaned against it. Throwing an arm over her eyes she inhaled deeply. What a kiss! Her already hot body had gone up another degree. The man was a master at seduction but she wouldn't have him any other way.

A smile touched her just-kissed lips. Jared was an excellent teacher. And although she knew there were more lessons to be learned, he had given her enough tutoring for what she needed to do.

At that moment the only thing she could think of was her plans to take on Jared Westmoreland.

Eight

If Jared didn't know any better he would swear Dana was trying to drive him mad. Mad with desire.

He doubted very seriously if he could hold on to his sanity, as well as his control, much longer. At any moment he would snap and Dana would drive him to reach across the table, snatch her into his arms and have her for dessert. *Dana Delight* would definitely be a mouthwatering temptation, a delectable treat.

The seduction started when she had knocked on the connecting door to let him know she was ready to go walking on the beach. He had been literally blown away by her outfit, a pair of denim shorts and a white halter top. He had seen halter tops before but never this enticing. He'd been tempted to untie the damn thing and set her breasts free. And he didn't want to think about how sensual her flat stomach looked totally bare, showing off the navel he'd grown so fond of a few days ago.

They had held hands while walking along the beach, enjoying the sunset and the ocean. They had talked about a lot of things. The weather, the economy, books they had read and exotic foods they had eaten. The conversation then shifted to the Westmoreland family and how they looked forward to the birth of Storm and Jayla's twins in a few months. Dana listened, hearing the excitement in Jared's voice. She felt a tinge of sadness that she wouldn't be around to share in the excitement since she would be out of the picture by then, out of Jared's life. At some point, he must have realized it, too. She glanced up, saw him staring at her and the intensity in his gaze gave her pause. The twins were a stark reminder that the two of them didn't have a future together. During the remainder of their walk, conversation ceased. They were caught up in their own private thoughts—thoughts they preferred not to share with each other.

When they returned to the hotel, they reluctantly went their separate ways to dress for dinner and within an hour's time, the food had been wheeled into Jared's suite. Even he would admit it was a night of romance with the candles burning on the table and the soft music playing in the background, compliments of the hotel's management. Evidently Jeannie had mentioned when she'd made reservations that they were a recently engaged couple and the hotel staff wanted to be remembered, in case they were undecided as to where they would spend their honeymoon.

A honeymoon that would never take place.

For the second time that day, Jared felt numb, his feelings paralyzed. All he could think about was that he and Dana didn't have a future together. He forced himself to get a grip and refused to dwell on that now. All he wanted to think about was the woman sitting across from him, who was slowly sipping her champagne—another compliment of the hotel—as she watched him through beautiful dark eyes.

His body's temperature rose a few degrees. All during dinner he had been turned on by everything she did. Even watching as she opened her mouth to eat her food had stirred a flame of arousal within him. She had a pair of sensuous lips and every time she used them he felt his loins burning.

He couldn't help but wonder what she was thinking. She hadn't been talkative and the attorney in him, the one whose senses were sharp and mind alert, was waiting patiently for her to say something. Anything that would give him an indication of what was going on inside her head.

Since the suspense was killing him, he decided to just ask. "A penny for your thoughts."

Dana placed her glass down on the table. An intimate smile played at the edges of her mouth. "I was just thinking about you and how grateful I am that you came and how much I enjoy your company."

"I enjoy yours, as well."

And he really meant it. He had dined with other women but this was the first time he had felt so totally comfortable. So at ease with a beautiful woman that he both liked and desired.

"You mentioned earlier that you wanted to talk to

me about a party that Thorn and Tara are giving," Dana said, recapturing his attention.

He fixed his gaze on her, looking fully into her eyes. "The weekend after Mother's Day is Thorn and Tara's first wedding anniversary. They're planning a huge celebration and I wanted to make sure you're free to attend with me that Friday night."

Dana's smile faltered. "But that's two weeks after your mother's surgery."

Jared nodded. "Yes. Is there a problem with that?"

She thought there was. "I assumed that if things were fine with your mother's surgery that we wouldn't…"

When it became apparent that she was having difficulty completing her statement, Jared reached across the table and took her hand in his. "That we wouldn't what?" he asked softly.

"Be seeing each other again, that you'd end things, break our engagement."

Jared stared into dark brown questioning eyes as he thought for a moment. Although he understood what she was saying and agreed that at one time he had thought breaking up with her as soon as possible was best for all concerned, there were a few things he felt they should take into account.

"My family, especially my mother, will find it rather odd that we broke our engagement so soon after her surgery. I think we should at least wait a couple of weeks before dropping the bomb on them." *And I don't know how I'll let you go.*

Dana couldn't see putting off the inevitable. "We're going to have to end things sooner or later, Jared. We can't continue to deceive everyone."

Jared stared at the hand he was holding then slowly released it. "I guess you're right. If things work out and my mother won't need any further treatments, then maybe the night of Thorn and Tara's party should be the last time we see each other. Agreed?"

Dana tipped up her chin and held his gaze. "Yes. Agreed." She knew that meant they had only three weeks left to spend together. Already she felt a deep pain in her heart but refused to let it ruin her evening.

"Dinner was wonderful," she said dabbing at her mouth with a napkin.

Heat flared within Jared. He would have been more than willing to wipe away any lingering crumbs from around her lips with his tongue.

He reached up and loosened the top button of his shirt. For dinner he had dressed casually, wearing a pair of khaki slacks and a black collared shirt. Dana was wearing a beautiful printed dress that had an endless slit up the side. That dress had nearly driven him crazy before she had finally taken a seat for dinner.

Moments later, his gut clenched. It seemed she was about to drive him crazy all over again. "I like the view from the balcony," she said, taking her glass and walking over to the double French doors.

"Yes. Gorgeous." He liked the view, as well, but he wasn't talking about what was on the other side of those French doors. The view he was feasting his eyes on was right in this very room.

"I bet it's simply beautiful at night," she said softly, turning around and meeting his gaze, looking at him with something akin to desire in her eyes. He shook his head wondering if that's what he actually saw or what he wanted to see.

"I bet it is, too," he managed to say as his gaze did a long, slow slide down the length of her body. "If you stick around for a while, I'm sure we'll see just how beautiful it is. It won't be long before it's completely dark."

A smile creased the corners of her eyes. "Can you imagine standing out there under those stars?"

It was on the tip of his tongue to say he would rather be lying down under those stars and making love to her. He picked up his own glass and slowly walked over to her. When he came to a stop in front of her, a thick silence hung over them as he held her gaze, watched her uneven breathing and smelled her scent.

Aroused.

He was an experienced man. A man who knew women. And he would recognize that scent anywhere, especially with Dana. It was the same scent he'd drowned in that night they played Red Light, Green Light. The same one that had almost driven him over the edge while watching her first orgasm. If there was any way he could bottle that scent he would. Tonight it mingled with the fragrance of the seductive perfume she was wearing and the combination was a very passion-stirring force.

"Let's make a toast."

Her words broke the silence and his deep concentration. "And what would you like us to toast, Dana?" he asked huskily. Intense desire was mounting within him. It wouldn't take much for him to drop to his knees, lift her dress and go straight to the source of that scent. Both his fingers and his tongue itched to—

"I propose that we toast life."

He met her gaze as his mind was jerked back to attention. "Life?"

"Yes. It can be taken from you in a second, a minute, at any place, anytime. That's why you should live life to the fullest. Enjoy it. Appreciate it. Because when it's gone, it's over. And there's nothing you can do about it."

Jared considered her words. *Life*. He couldn't help but think of how different his had been since she had walked into it. Stormed into it was a better word. In a span of less than eight weeks, he had met her, introduced her to his family and given them the definite impression they were engaged, had purchased a very costly ring for her—one he intended for her to keep—and had spent the last couple of weeks pretending to be a man very much in love. To say that Dana Rollins hadn't affected his life would be an understatement.

"Okay, we'll toast to life," he said, lifting his glass to connect with hers. They took a sip of their champagne.

"Umm, want to have some fun?" she asked, holding his gaze over the rim of her glass.

Jared lifted a brow. "What kind of fun?"

A smile turned up her lips. "I'd like to play a game," she said softly.

"A game?"

"Yes. A game of hide-and-seek. I hide, you find me."

Jared smiled. He liked the thought of doing that. "And what happens when I find you?"

She returned his smile. "That depends."

"On what?"

"Where I'm found."

Jared downplayed the possibilities as he glanced around the room. "There aren't many places you can hide."

She grinned. "Oh, between my room and yours I'm sure there's a few."

Jared was tempted to tell her that hiding from him wouldn't do any good since her scent would give her away. When it came to her, his nose was like radar.

"All right. So what do you want me to do?" he asked, more than willing to play this game she'd suggested.

"Leave the room for about ten minutes. When you come back, the suite will be totally dark, and remember I'll be either hiding in my suite or yours."

Jared nodded. This was the second game they had played together, and for someone who usually lived a structured life, he was enjoying letting go and being adventurous with Dana.

He began walking toward the door. "Ten minutes. That's all I'm giving you. Then I'll be back, whether you're ready or not."

Dana watched as he gave her one last stomach-churning smile before opening the door, walking out of it and closing it behind him. She slowly crossed the room and dropped down on the floral-printed sofa and kicked off her sandals. She inhaled deeply and smiled seductively.

She would definitely be ready when he returned.

* * *

Jared returned ten minutes later. Ten minutes on the nose and not one second more.

He opened his door and stepped into the darkened room. He couldn't help but be amused as he switched on a light. Dana must have figured her scent would give her away so she had liberally sprayed his suite with the perfume she'd been wearing.

He glanced around the room and noticed her sandals were by his sofa. Evidently she had kicked them off there. He walked over and picked one up. They were pretty and boy did she have small feet, sexy feet. He placed the shoe back down and glanced at the sofa. It seemed her shoes weren't the only thing she had left behind. He picked up the scarf she'd worn around her waist.

He glanced around, his ears on alert. The door connecting their suites was open. He crossed the room to go into hers. It was dark and he turned on a lamp. His gaze looked around, nothing looked amiss, and there wasn't a sound to be heard. And the scent of her perfume was in this room, as well. He walked out of the bedroom to the sitting area. He looked down in front of the sofa and blinked. There in a pool on the floor was her dress.

His breath caught exactly the same moment his arousal thickened. This was definitely one hell of a game she was playing. He hadn't expected it to take this turn so quickly, but he wasn't complaining. He had told her that he would leave it up to her to let him know if and when she was ready to take their relationship to another level. This was her way of letting him know she was ready.

Now it was his job to find her.

He was the hunter and would find his prey. With a determined purpose he walked across the room to the small kitchen that had a breakfast bar and table. He opened a closet door and found it empty.

He then retraced his steps back to her bedroom and went to check out her bathroom. He found it almost empty. A red lace bra was hanging from a light in the ceiling. He reached up and pulled it down.

He was getting hot.

Walking back to her room he got on his knees and looked under the huge king-size bed and found nothing. He looked in the closet and came up empty. He opened the French doors and walked out on the balcony. It was bare.

Frustration, added to intense arousal, wasn't a good thing. The pressure of his erection against his pants was almost killing him. When he found Dana she would pay dearly for this torture. He walked back through the connecting door into his suite and glanced around. The bedroom door was closed and he distinctly remembered it being open when he'd left.

An enticing possibility flooded his mind, made his body harden even more as he slowly crossed the room. He glanced down the moment he reached for the doorknob and saw red lace. Leaning down he picked it up. It wasn't much, barely a scrap, but he definitely knew what it was and where it came from.

Bringing the item to his nose he inhaled Dana's scent, a different one than the perfume. It was a womanly scent that was all hers. Privately. Exclusively. Deciding that she definitely wouldn't need it anymore tonight, he slipped her thong into his back pocket. Slowly opening the bedroom door, he walked into darkness and closed the door behind him.

Dana held her breath. Jared had finally found her. Not that she had done a good job at hiding. She thought she had made it easy for him but evidently she hadn't.

She had known the exact moment he had returned and had heard every step he'd taken around the room. She'd known when he had searched her suite and when he had returned to his own. And now he was here, in his bedroom, and she was in his bed, totally naked and waiting for him.

Her mind was made up, her decision final, with no regrets. When he walked away she would have reminders of this night. They would be memories that would last her a lifetime because she knew whatever he did, Jared never did anything halfway. He was meticulously thorough and methodically efficient.

"I know you're in here, Dana," he whispered huskily in the darkened room. "And ready or not, here I come."

She heard his footsteps, slow, yet determined. She heard the sound of his breathing, quick and uneven. She almost held her breath when he came closer and closer to the bed. She felt his presence and smelled his masculine scent.

And when he switched on the lamp, bathing the room with a soft translucent glow, their gazes connected. Held. Then slowly, his gaze drifted from her face and moved downward to the sheet that covered her nude body. Then it moved back up to her face. It was a while before he spoke.

"I found you," he said in a raspy voice that was so husky it stirred heat all over her skin. "So what do I get?"

She paused a moment before saying, "Anything you want."

A hint of a smile touched his lips. Intense desire darkened his eyes. "Anything?"

"Yes, *anything*."

He continued to hold her gaze. "Are you sure?" he asked moments later.

"Positive."

His sensuous smile deepened. "And you're ready?" he asked, wanting to be doubly sure that she was. Once he began making love to her, he would be hard-pressed to stop. Unable to help himself he reached out and pushed away a strand of hair that had fallen in her face. He needed to touch her, connect with her on any level.

"Yes, I'm ready."

"With no regrets?"

She inhaled slowly. Knowing what he was asking and why. Nothing had changed. Sooner or later, possibly even sooner, depending on the results of his mother's surgery, he would be walking out of her life. She knew it. Had accepted it. And would be prepared when it happened.

But she wanted to seize the moment. Celebrate life.

With him. "There won't be any regrets, Jared. I knew the score going into this game."

She then slowly eased up, letting the sheet fall away, hearing his sharp intake of breath when it did so. Getting on her knees she brushed her hand against his chest and moved slowly downward to feel the hard planes of his stomach. "Are we going to talk all night or are we going to get on with what we've wanted for quite a while?"

He reached out and traced a path around her nipple with his finger, teasing the darkened tip. "And what is it that you think we've wanted?"

"Some of each other."

"Some?"

Her lips smiled with warm confidence. "Okay, I stand corrected. *All* of each other."

Without giving her the chance to draw her next breath, Jared pulled her into his arms and covered her mouth with his, igniting an explosion of passion between them. He kissed her with hungry intensity. It seemed as if a dam had burst, emotions were flooding and there was no one around to fix it.

Dana's arms came around him and held on, taking everything he had to give and wondering how she had denied herself for so long. Jared was a special man who had always treated her like a lady. And for that she would always be eternally grateful.

He slowly released her and stepped back. Her legs trembled from the impact of his kiss. He continued to hold her gaze, looking at her with virile intensity, as he unbuckled his belt. She felt heat pouring into her stomach and drifting downward between her legs as she began catching fire from his flame.

"Tonight I'm going to do all those things I've been dreaming of doing to you," Jared said, his voice a thin whisper and full of sexual need. "I want to see you reach a climax again, several of them, over and over. But this time, you won't be alone. I'll be there with you, joining in and sharing the pleasure." His words were seduction all wrapped in silk.

Dana watched as he pulled his shirt over his head. With the top of him bare, he exuded strength, power and muscular endurance. He had a beautiful chest and his dark coloring made him look even more beautiful to her. He tossed the shirt aside, then sat down in a wing chair to remove his shoes and socks. After that was done, he stood and went back to his pants, tugging the belt from the loops.

He smiled over at her. "When I told you that I wouldn't push until you were ready, I knew that meant my patience would be tested. I've been wanting you forever and tonight I plan to show you just how much."

Dana continued to watch as he slid down his pants and underwear. She blinked when she saw the size of him. She had felt his hardened erection plenty of times against her but now seeing it in the flesh was putting a whole new spin on things. Jared was loaded. He had been very fortunate when certain body parts had been distributed.

"Umm, interesting," she whispered softly, meeting his gaze and smiling.

He chuckled. "Interesting? Is that all you can say?"

"I'll wait to make sure it can work before making any more comments."

He laughed, loving every moment of sharing this camaraderie with her, while at the same time fire bolts of desire raced through him. "Trust me. It will work. In fact I plan for it to go into overtime."

The room got quiet as the reality of what they were about to do set in. For the longest time, their gazes connected and their minds were of one accord. Naked, Jared slowly walked over to the bed and took Dana's hands in his. He brought them to his lips and kissed her palms.

"You do things to me that no other woman ever has, Dana. You make me feel things. Make me want things. I don't want you to think what we're about to do is just another roll between the sheets for me. It's something I consider exceptional and extraordinary."

The love Dana felt for Jared increased tenfold. She loved him with all her heart. Tonight she wanted to physically connect with the man she loved. Deciding he had talked enough, she tugged on his hands and they tumbled down into the bed.

Jared's body ended up on top of hers and he glanced down at her, feeling the heat of flesh touching flesh, and framed her face with his palms. He studied her features as if implanting them in his memory.

And then he kissed her. Hungrily. Devouringly. And he couldn't stop. He wanted her with a vengeance, a deep-rooted passion that he couldn't understand. He heard the gentle moan of passion that escaped her lips, and felt the warmth of her fingers caress his naked skin as his tongue continued to ravage the sweetness of her mouth. Finally, the need to breathe and to shield her from pregnancy made him pull away. "I have to protect you," he said with hot desire running rampant in his voice.

He slowly stood, crossed back over the room for his pants. He fished through his pocket, pulling out her underwear instead of his wallet. He glanced over at her and smiled. "Nice color."

She gave him a short laugh brushed with embarrassment. "Glad you like it."

Tossing them aside he then checked his other pocket for his wallet, pulled it out and retrieved a condom packet. Several. He knew she was watching as he put it on, and was overwhelmed by the sensations that rammed through him as he prepared to bury himself in her softness.

After he finished the task he glanced up and met her gaze. "What do you think?"

He saw the heated desire in her eyes, saw the slight shivering of her body. "I think," she said softly, "that more than anything, I want you inside of me, Jared."

Jared inhaled sharply as he felt a tightening coil in his lower region. He should have known she would say or do something to endear her to him that much more. He wanted to fight it but couldn't. And he knew what he was feeling had nothing to do with the length of time it had been since he'd had a woman. It had everything to do with this particular woman.

He slowly walked over to the bed, slid in and pulled her into his arms. Emotions he'd never felt before took their toll and he kissed her while giving in to his overheated senses. He then moved from her lips to her breasts, determined to top what he'd done to them the other day. The lips and tongue torturing her now were those of a man who wanted to make his woman as wet as she could get. Torture was too mild a word to use for what he was doing. He took his time reacquainting himself with the taste of her skin, the feel of her flesh, liking the way her nipples hardened in his mouth as he feasted on them greedily.

When her scent became intoxicating and way too potent, his hand moved in slow precision and reached downward to touch the most intimate part of her, finding her not just wet but completely drenched. He vividly remembered a scene from one of his dreams that he longed to act out. He shifted his body and moved away from her breasts, began tracing a path down her chest to her navel with his mouth, glorying in the sensual taste of her naked skin.

He continued to trail kisses all over her. Rolling her on her stomach, placed kisses all over her spine, the center of her back and all over her shoulders. He then gently rolled her back over and met her gaze. By the look in her eyes he knew she was trying to contemplate his next move. He leaned back and without saying a word, his hand traveled between her legs, parting them just seconds before he lowered his mouth to her with hungry intensity.

Of their own accord, her hips lifted to him and to make sure they stayed there, he grabbed hold of them, held them as he greedily devoured her in this very intimate way. He heard her moan with every insistent stroke of his tongue. He tasted her heat, her fire and her passion. Passion he was both creating and satisfying.

"Jared!"

He quickly pulled back and covered her body with his, interlocking their limbs. He took her mouth at the same time he entered her, sliding inside of her in one smooth thrust as she welcomed him into her body. The same heat consuming her was eating him alive. He began moving as sensations, too overpowering to be real, clamored through him, making his strokes harder, stronger and deeper, robbing him of any logical thought but one. *Don't hold back. Share everything with her and deal with the consequences later.*

And when her body exploded into what seemed like a billion pieces beneath him and carried her to a spiraling climax, he broke their kiss and buried his face in her neck. Kissed her there. Marked her. He continued to take her over the edge with steady thrusts of possession.

That same explosion, the finality of every physical sensation he could think of, overtook him. He hollered out her name as his body shook with the magnitude of an earthquake, the force of a hurricane and the electrifying power of a thunderstorm. What he had found in her arms, inside her body was intense pleasure, too magnificent to measure and too rapturous to describe.

And he knew as the earth slowly ceased spinning and his body relaxed, utterly consumed and feeling like a lifeless weight floating on shafts of air, that this was an experience he'd never shared with any woman before. He was bombarded with the need to hold her and make love to her all through the night.

At that very moment, Jared had to concede that when the time came, walking away from her would be the hardest thing he'd ever had to do.

Shortly after midnight, Jared stood barefoot on the balcony and leaned against the railing. The incessant pounding of the waves beating against the shore matched the raggedness of his breathing and the distinctive hammering of his heart.

Emotions that he had never dealt with before were coming at him from all directions, different angles, crowding in on him. He released a long deep breath as he tried to fight them. But it was useless. Dana had touched him tonight in a way no other woman had, and it hadn't been all physical.

It seemed that after making love to her that first time, an undeniable urge to do so again and again had taken over, and so they had all through the night. He had shared more than just his body with her. He had also shared his soul. It seemed as if she had somehow eased inside his heart and was still snuggled there.

After making love to her the last time he had lain awake while she drifted off to sleep beside him. Sighs of satisfaction had continued to flow through his body long afterward. When he'd glanced over at her, he had been touched by how peaceful she looked. Struggling with feelings that were foreign to him, he had slid out of bed and slipped into his pants. Before he had left the room he had glanced back, lingering in the doorway. The moonlight shining in through the window focused on Dana curled in his bed, her naked body barely covered while she slept. Her bare breasts, firm and full, had tempted him to taste them again.

Bringing his thoughts back to the present, Jared pulled in a broken breath, knowing that no matter how many women he'd slept with before Dana and no matter how many he would sleep with after, he would only find total, complete and satisfying release in her arms. Only hers.

Jared turned slowly, sensing Dana's presence immediately. A lump thickened in his throat when he saw she was wearing his shirt, a shirt that barely covered her.

Their eyes met. Held. And then she said softly, "I woke up and decided that it was lonely in bed without you."

Jared didn't want to tell her the reason he'd left was that he had needed distance from her; he'd been driven to have a few moments alone to get his head back on straight. Making love to her had literally blown him away. Instead he told her part of the truth. "I wanted to hear the sound of the ocean and see the moon and all the stars."

He drew in a deep breath of air, not able to think beyond the need she aroused in him, and then added slowly. "But do you know what I want now more than anything?"

Dana shook her head. "No. What?"

"To make love to you again." A part of him wished he could have mustered enough strength to have said that for the remainder of the night they needed to sleep in separate beds; they were getting into something neither had counted on, something he definitely didn't want. But as she slowly began taking steps, crossing the balcony to him, the only thing he could do was open his arms.

The moment she came close, he gathered her to him, needing to hold her. He felt the willpower he had tried to regain slip away. She pressed against him, needing to be held. She wrapped her arms around his neck and they stood that way for a long moment, body to body, soul to soul. Slow warmth spread from her to him and it seemed that her every curve was molded against his firm muscled length.

And then he swooped her up into his arms and with hurried steps carried her back into the bedroom and placed her on the bed. He leaned down and caught her lips in a kiss that was deep, sensual and demanded full surrender. The sounds of pleasure emitting from her made him want her that much more and his stomach clenched with profound need.

He released her to pull the shirt from over her head, and then proceeded to remove his pants. After taking the time to put on protection, he joined her in bed. She whispered his name and the only thing Jared could think about was demonstrating with his body just what she did to him and how much he wanted her.

The knowledge that she wanted him as much as he wanted her sent his desire skyrocketing in all directions. He intended to spend the rest of the night sharing intense passion with the one woman whose name was more than a whisper on his lips. It was a name that was finding a way to his very soul.

Jared's last thought as he captured her mouth with his was that having her seep into his heart was something he could not let happen. No matter what.

Nine

"Thanks for being here, Dana."

Dana gave Jared an assuring smile when he reached out and took her hand in his and tightened his fingers around it as they sat side by side in the hospital's waiting room. His features were solemn and she knew he was worried about the outcome of his mother's surgery. "You don't have to thank me, Jared. I wanted to be here."

She glanced at the clock on the wall. The doctors had indicated it wouldn't be a long procedure and that someone would be out to talk to the family when it was over. Jared's youngest brother, Reggie, had accompanied Mr. Westmoreland downstairs to the coffee shop, and every so often Jared's cell phone would ring when one of his other brothers called for an update on their mother's condition. His aunt and uncle were here and so were several of his cousins and their wives. One thing she had learned about the Westmorelands was that they were a close-knit family who bonded in a crisis. She admired that about them.

Dana glanced up at Jared. "Can I get you anything?"

He gave her a reassuring smile. "No, thanks, I'm fine." He then leaned closer and whispered softly, privately, "What I really want is something I can't have right now, but there's always later."

Dana felt heat flare into her cheeks and hoped no one noticed the blush that came into her features. After returning from Jekyll Island they had begun spending more and more time together. They had dined at his place and gone out to eat a couple of times this week, had taken in several movies and had also joined his cousins last night at Chase's Place to celebrate Thorn's birthday.

And each time they made love it was better than the last. On the nights that he stayed over, she enjoyed waking up in his arms. There were never any regrets, only complete fulfillment. She could not resist Jared any more than she could stop breathing. The intimacy they shared was tangible, special and so profound, that more than once it brought tears to her eyes.

Tonight she was having dinner again at his place and was looking forward to it. She hoped they had reason to celebrate, and remained positive about his mother's condition.

For the next few minutes she tried engaging Jared in small talk since she knew that he, like everyone else, was watching the clock. His father had returned and was now nervously pacing the room.

Everyone looked up when the doctor walked into the waiting room with an unreadable expression on his face. Mr. Westmoreland, with Jared and Reggie on his heels, quickly walked over to meet the doctor.

"How is she?" James Westmoreland asked in a somewhat shaky voice.

Dr. Miller smiled and he reached out and touched the older man's shoulder. "She's doing fine and test results confirm the lump was nothing but fatty tissue. Sarah is fine and once the anesthesia wears off, she'll be able to leave. Of course I want to see her for a follow-up visit next week."

James sighed deeply and Dana could see relief and happiness in everyone's eyes. "Thanks, Dr. Miller."

"You're welcome." Dr. Miller glanced over at Jared and Reggie. "Which one of you is engaged to be married?"

Jared lifted a brow. "I am. Why?"

The doctor chuckled. "Because that's all your mother talked about from the time they wheeled her into the operating room to right before the anesthetic kicked in. She's really happy about it and is anxious to start planning a wedding. Congratulations." He then turned and walked out of the waiting room.

Jared turned his head and met Dana's gaze. Her fingers tightened on the straps on her purse. It was an unconscious gesture that only he noticed. She had agreed to play out this charade for an additional two weeks, but he understood how everything was placing a toll on her. It was placing a hell of a toll on him as well.

He studied her face, knowing that even after their

"engagement" ended, memories would remain that wouldn't leave him alone, that were bound to creep into his thoughts at any place and at any time.

He sighed deeply as he crossed the room to where Dana was standing, needing the contact, the closeness. "Mom's fine," he said.

Her smile was soft. "I heard and I'm glad," she said so quietly that he barely heard her.

Elated with the news that his mother was okay, and because he was dying to taste Dana's lips, Jared bent his head and brushed his lips across hers.

"If you two keep this up, your Mom's prediction is bound to be true," James said, grinning, coming to stand beside his oldest son.

Another deep sigh escaped Jared's lips. He had an idea but knew he was expected to ask, so he did. "And what prediction is that?"

Mr. Westmoreland looked at Dana then back at his son and chuckled. "That there will be another Westmoreland wedding before the end of summer."

Dana had fallen in love with Jared's home the first time she had walked through the double doors a week ago. The two-story structure, located in one of North Atlanta's most exclusive and affluent communities, was huge and spacious.

When Jared had given her a tour she'd seen that each and every room was breathtaking and expensively decorated, and that included the state-of-the-art theater room she had heard so much about, and a beautifully designed swimming pool. He had five bedrooms, six bathrooms, a huge country kitchen, a living room and dining room as well as a breakfast room, a library and game room. He even had a four-car garage and she had been surprised to discover that he owned a motorcycle. He had explained that because of Thorn, all the male Westmorelands owned a Thorn-Byrd, the brand of bikes that his cousin built.

The house, Dana thought, was very much like the man who owned it, fascinating, interesting and compelling. With all the vaulted ceilings, rich thick carpeting, costly paintings that lined the walls and the expensive antique furnishings, it signified wealth but wasn't overdone. There was nothing ostentatious about the house or the man. It was obvious that Jared liked nice things, but she definitely wouldn't consider his likes eccentric or outlandish.

"Make yourself comfortable," Jared said as he glanced over at her. It was early evening. They had spent the majority of the day at his parents' home after his mother had gotten released from the hospital. He had made all the necessary calls to his brothers, assuring them that things were fine and their mother was okay.

"Do you need my help?" Dana asked as she sat at the breakfast bar and watched how efficiently he moved around in the kitchen.

"No. We're having something light and simple."

Dana chuckled. "Umm, let me guess, hot dogs and lemonade?"

Jared smiled. "No, it's something a lot more filling than that. In fact it's one of the few Westmoreland family secret recipes that Chase will share—a chicken-and-rice casserole. I prepared it this morning before leaving for the hospital, so all I have to do is warm it up. I'm also making a salad to go along with it and thought a glass of wine would be nice, as well."

She watched as he pulled a casserole dish from the refrigerator and proceeded to place it in the microwave. He then pulled out all the items he needed for the salad.

"And you're sure there's nothing I can do to help?" The last time she had shared a dinner with him here, he'd had everything catered.

He glanced up at her and smiled. "I'm positive. You've done enough already. I meant what I said about me appreciating you taking off work to be at the hospital today. It meant a lot to me and I know it meant a lot to my family, especially Mom. I'm so thankful that the test results were good. In a way I had prepared myself for the worse."

Dana heard the catch in his voice and immediately got out of her seat and came around to stand in front of him. She reached out and placed a hand on his arm. "But like you said, Jared, the results were good and that's what's important. She's okay."

Jared nodded and thought that Dana's touch felt hot on his arm. A seductive silence hung over the room as he held her gaze. Desire swirled around in his belly and he hung tenuously on to his control. He wanted her. Always wanted her. Constantly wanted her. And was always amazed at the depth of that wanting.

He recalled vividly and in living color every aspect of making love to her last night. They had returned to her place from the movies, and as soon as the door closed shut behind them, desire, the likes of which he'd never encountered before, had taken hold of him, racked his mind, rammed through his body. He had hauled her to him, picked her up into his arms and had taken her into the bedroom where he had stripped her of her clothes, and then quickly removed his own, barely taking time to protect them both before covering her body with his and making love to her.

The same way he wanted to make love to her now.

He made a move to reach out for her the exact moment the alarm on the microwave sounded. Inhaling deeply, a faint smile formed on his lips. "I guess it's time to eat."

She smiled in return. "Yes, I guess it is."

"Will you go swimming with me?" Jared asked later when they had finished dinner, cleared the table and loaded the dishes in the dishwasher. The last time she'd been over, the lining of the pool was being redone.

She slanted him a teasing grin. "What makes you think I can swim?"

He regarded her with an interest that had her toes curling and the most intimate part of her aching. "I just figured you could, and if you can't then I'll teach you."

Her eyes squinted with amusement. "You're an expert swimmer?"

"I don't do so bad."

Dana thought that if he could swim with the same degree of expertise that he made love then he was definitely an ace. "I can swim," she said, deciding to come clean. "My parents made sure I knew how before my fourth birthday. Living on the East Coast and so close to the ocean meant that I had to learn."

She tipped her head back and looked at him. "But there is one slight problem."

"What?"

"I didn't bring a bathing suit."

"That's no problem. I'm sure there's an extra one around here that should fit you."

He watched her face and saw the exact moment her eyes darkened with disappointment. "Don't bother."

He quickly realized what had bothered her. Reaching out he gently squeezed her shoulders and said, "It's a bathing suit that Delaney left behind, Dana. She used to keep several of them here in case she ever wanted to visit and go swimming." He pulled her to him, needing to hold her. "I've never gone swimming with a woman in this house before," he whispered. He never felt the need to explain his personal life to any woman, but for some reason he wanted to explain things to her.

Dana pulled back, ticked at herself for caring. Besides, he didn't owe her an explanation about anything. It wasn't as if they were really engaged. "Sorry, I don't have a right to come across like that, Jared. What you do is none of my business."

He studied her face for a long time then said, "There's no need to apologize." His breath was warm against her face when he leaned toward her and placed a gentle kiss on her lips. He deepened it then pulled back slowly, not ready to languish her lips yet as he placed tiny kisses around it. "I can say the hell with a bathing suit and let's go skinny-dipping."

Breathless, she smiled against his lips. "Yes, you can say that but then that poses another problem."

He watched as she moistened her lips with a stroke of her tongue, and was tempted to lean down and take that tongue into his mouth and feast on it some more. "What other problem?" he asked, barely able to get the words out.

"I've never swum in the nude."

The thought of her swimming naked ran fluidly through his mind, forming images that made him want to strip her bare, then and there. "You know what they say, Miss Rollins. There's a first time for everything." He leaned down and whispered in her ear, "Come on, let's go for a swim."

When they began walking, Jared slung an arm around her shoulders as he led her to the area where the pool was located. Dana tried not to let the seductive sensations that Jared generated within her, take possession of her mind.

The potent smell of chlorine teased Dana's nostrils as they entered a passageway. He reached out and flipped a switch, bringing light into a huge area filled with lush greenery. To say the pool was impressive would be an understatement. Secured in the privacy of brick walls and a vaulted ceiling made of solid glass, this private place was definitely a swimmer's haven. Dana smiled when they stopped walking and she looked up and saw how the moonlight and the stars reflected through, slanting light against the pool's blue-tinted waters.

"So, do you want a bathing suit or do you prefer going without?" Jared asked as he placed his hands on her hips.

She grinned. "I think I'd feel more comfortable with a bathing suit."

He watched her thoughtfully, wondering if this was the same woman who had played a very enticing game of hide-and-seek with him that weekend. It had been one passionate pursuit and now it seemed that she was trying to go all shy on him. However he was sure a few sizzling kisses would rid her of any degree of bashfulness.

"I may as well warn you that I plan to take the suit off of you the first chance I get," he whispered, leaning down and capturing her earlobe in his mouth and sucking gently.

A breathless sigh escaped Dana's lips and she closed her eyes. It was a good thing he was still holding her by the waist or she would have melted and slid right into the pool. "I kind of figured you'd be trying something like that."

He took her hand in his and drew her away from the pool to an area surrounded by a bevy of palm trees. "At least I gave you fair warning."

He led her to a room off from the pool area that appeared to be a large dressing room. "You can change in here," Jared said, giving her an easy smile. "Towels are in that closet and there's a bathing suit that should fit you in that drawer over there."

She looked up at him. "What about you?"

He gave her that same grin that had endeared him to

her the first time she'd seen it. "I don't have a problem swimming in the nude, Dana."

And with that he turned and left her alone in the room.

Dana nervously fumbled with the buttons on her blouse as she removed it while glancing around the huge room. She saw that all the walls and the ceiling were mirrored and she felt slightly funny as she watched herself undress. She studied the daybed that sat on one side of the room and didn't want to imagine Jared and some woman in it as they watched themselves make love. He had said no woman had ever gone swimming with him in this house but who was to say that no woman had ever made out with him in this room?

Letting out a long breath, she tugged her skirt down over her hips, not wanting the picture of Jared and any other woman to form in her mind. As she'd told him, what he did was his business. But still, the part of her that loved him so much that it hurt, felt pain at the thought of him with someone else.

She tried turning her thoughts and attention elsewhere. Dinner had been delicious and the wine he'd selected had been perfect.

She could tell a huge load had been lifted off his shoulders now that he knew his mother was okay. He seemed more relaxed. Being around him made her feel things, want things and each and every time he had smiled at her, touched her—innocently or otherwise—she found herself hard pressed to keep her emotions under control.

Whenever she looked into his eyes his keen sense of intelligence startled her. He was his parents' first-born, but had not been the heir apparent. Anything and everything Jared possessed was the result of hard work. He deserved all he had achieved and was a man like no other she'd ever known. There was a fierceness about him, yet at the same time an innate gentleness that she found sweet and endearing.

Jared Westmoreland was the man she would love until the day she died.

Dana sighed, as she tied her hair back, trying to remain clearheaded. She couldn't and wouldn't have regrets, no matter what. And she wouldn't dwell on the impossibilities of a future with Jared.

Moments later she glanced at herself in the mirror. Jared had said nothing about the bathing suit being a bikini. It appeared to be brand-new and was a perfect fit, although it showed more skin than she was used to exposing. Jared had seen her naked several times since their weekend together, but for some reason she felt shy around him tonight.

Maybe it was because every time she held his gaze for any period of time she saw desire in his eyes that was so thick it could be cut with a knife. And what he'd said earlier about her not keeping the bathing suit on for long sent passionate chills down her body. He'd said it and she had no reason to doubt it. Grabbing a towel she wrapped it securely around her waist and took a deep breath before walking out of the room.

The first thing she noticed was that Jared had dimmed the lights. The second thing was that he was already in the water, standing in the shallow end, leaning back against the pool's wall. All the way across the room she could feel the strength of him. Knowing he was completely naked only filled her with heated passion and desire. He was built and had the kind of muscles women drooled about. Each and every time she came into contact with his body, she burned.

"Get rid of the towel, Dana."

His words as well as the look in his eyes pulled her to him. She slowly walked to the edge of the pool and met his heated gaze. "And if I don't?"

A smile touched the corners of his lips. "Then I'll be tempted to get out of the pool and remove it for you, and while I'm removing the towel I'll also remove everything else."

Dana tilted her head, picturing both things in her mind. "Mmm, that sounds like quite a seductive threat, Counselor."

She watched as he moved swiftly and agilely through the water and ended up at the side of the pool, within less than a few feet from where she stood. "No threat, Dana. It's a promise."

She took a step back when he eased his naked body out of the pool. She noticed he had on a condom, making it blatantly clear what he had in mind. Dripping wet he stood in front of her. He leaned over and kissed her tenderly while at the same time used his fingertip to loosen the knot of the towel. She felt it fall to the floor, but his mouth kept her too occupied to care. At the moment she was content to let him carry out any threats he'd made.

"You look nice," he said huskily, releasing her lips

and letting his gaze roam over her body. "You're definitely wearing this bathing suit—but not for long."

With a flick of his wrist he released her top and then bending, he caressed her bare shoulders with the tip of his tongue. That was followed by slow nibbling kisses that he placed on her neck before moving to her breasts, taking the hard tips of her nipples into his mouth one at a time.

When she began to shudder he slowly lowered himself down in front of her and began easing the bikini bottom down her legs.

"Your body leaves me breathless, Dana," he whispered as his lips trailed kisses all over her stomach. "And your scent drives me crazy."

His mouth moved downward and he reached out and gently grabbed hold of her hips. Glancing up at her and seeing how she watched everything he was doing while taking measured breaths and gripping his shoulders for balance, he said, "I love kissing you all over."

He felt a shiver flow through her body and whispered huskily, "But I especially love kissing you here."

He heard her moan when his mouth closed over her most intimate part, finding her hot and wet. His tongue flicked out and began stroking her slowly and tasting her completely. When she arched against his mouth, he became greedy, insistent and possessive.

"Jared!"

She screamed his name. He felt her buckle against his mouth as every sensitive nerve in her body exploded. He wanted it all and he didn't let up until her last shudder ended and she became soft and limp.

Standing, he swept her into his arms and carried her over to a huge padded bench and held her. Placing her in his lap he tightened his hold on her and drew her closer, needing the contact and not wanting to question the why of it.

"You're too much, Jared," Dana whispered on a half sigh, barely opening her eyes.

His smile was intriguing. "Is that a bad thing or a good thing?"

"Umm, I imagine it's a good thing," she said softly.

His chuckle was soft and the sound of it sent more sensual chills up Dana's body. "You imagine? You're not certain?"

She hooked her arms around his neck. "Give me a few moments to recoup and I'll let you know for sure."

"You don't have a few moments to spare, sweetheart. I want you too much," he said throatily. And then he was kissing her again, his lips hungry, his tongue hot, intense. Her body immediately responded and began to heat up all over again.

He slowly pulled back. "Come on, let's swim for a while."

He stood with her in his arms and walked over to the pool. "The water is temperature controlled, so it's warm."

They eased their bodies into the pool. After treading water for a few moments, they swam to the other side of the pool then back again. Going to the edge of the pool he gathered her close. Before she could gasp her next breath, he kissed her, touched her all over and completely shattered her sanity.

Mindlessly, she moaned his name when his finger slipped inside of her, stroking her to heated bliss. "Wrap your legs around my waist."

Meeting his gaze she placed her arms around his neck, and when he positioned her body just where he wanted it he slowly eased inside of her, finding she was still moist and hot.

And when he had gone as deep as he could go, Jared's head came down and moments before he covered her lips he whispered the words, "This is as perfect as anything can possibly get."

And then he began moving inside of her, making love to her, taking, giving and sharing. Water lapped against their skin, absorbing the heat of their naked flesh, stroking their passion to a fevered pitch.

It seemed as if it had been months, years since they had shared passion this way and all the longings Dana could possibly endure broke through, encasing her in a storm of emotions and pleasures that ripped through to her very soul. And when he increased the rhythm, she pressed closer to him, urged him to take more as passion swirled around her, driving her through turbulence that could only have one end. Each stroke he made pushed her closer and closer to release. She dug her fingers into his shoulders as liquid warmth gathered, anticipation hovered and pleasure crested.

Jared let out a deep guttural groan when he felt a shudder race through Dana's body and she ground her hips against him, pushing him deeper inside of her, to the hilt. And then he lost it, that final, fragile hold on his sanity. His next powerful thrust connected them in a way that made sensations shoot through both of them simultaneously. Blood pounded in his ears and her name trembled from his lips at the same time that his body shook in a release so strong that he was whirled into a massive impact that stole his next breath.

He felt Dana tremble in his arms, her response shameless, total and complete. The effects tore through him, ripped him in two and demanded that he give up everything, all that he had, whatever he possessed, to the fury of passion that consumed them both.

And as he crushed her to him, he surrendered to the multitude of feelings that drew them together. *She was his.*

Ten

"I want my wife back, Jared. She refuses to see me or talk to me so what do you suggest that I do?"

Jared sighed deeply wondering how Sylvester expected him to answer a question like that when he had his own personal issues to deal with. It had been almost two weeks since his mother's surgery and tonight was the night of Thorn and Tara's anniversary party—and the final act of the play in which he and Dana had been participants. They were supposed to officially end things tonight by breaking their engagement.

"Jared? Are you listening to me?"

Jared turned his attention back to his client who'd been pacing his office for the past half hour. Evidently, Sylvester thought that as his attorney Jared had all the answers, which was a completely false assumption. He was in the business of ending marriages and not trying to find ways to save them.

"Have you tried begging?" Jared decided to ask. The last time he had spoken with Jackie Brewster's attorney, he'd been informed that she was adamant about giving her husband the divorce he'd asked for. She refused to remain married to a man who had wrongly accused her of being unfaithful.

Sylvester frowned. "I'm serious, Jared."

"So am I. According to your wife's attorney, she wants us to proceed. She says there's no chance of reconciliation."

Sylvester, with a defeated expression on his face, dropped down in a nearby chair. "I can't lose her. I love her, Jared, and I will do whatever I have to do to save my marriage. I was wrong. I knew what a good woman she was, yet I was quick to think the worst. It was so hard to accept that someone could actually love me and give me their complete devotion."

Behind his desk, Jared leaned back in his chair. It was odd to watch Sylvester this torn up over a woman. In the past, he'd been quick to end things and move on, usually because he had some other woman waiting in the wings. But that wasn't the case this time. It was obvious Sylvester was in love with his wife.

Love.

With that one word, Dana quickly came into his thoughts. He blinked, refusing to go there. What he felt for her was desire, gut-wrenching desire, lust of the strongest kind. He'd been in relationships before and was an ace at getting out of them whenever things got sticky. And he would be the first to admit that things between him and Dana were definitely getting sticky. It was time to split—with no regrets.

"Isn't there something you can do, Jared? I'm desperate."

Sylvester's words recaptured his attention. He stared up at the ceiling in deep thought for a moment. "Maybe there is," he said, making a quick decision. "I'll do my best to arrange for you and Jackie to have a private meeting, without me or her attorney present. I can't make any promises, but I'll try. Once the two of you are alone, it's going to be up to you to convince her that you're worthy of forgiveness."

He saw the hopeful gleam that appeared in Sylvester's eyes and the optimism that lined the man's features. It was evident he was struggling to hold on to his composure. If there had been any doubt in Jared's mind of just how deeply Sylvester felt about his wife, it vanished at that very moment.

"Are you okay, Dana?" Cybil asked, studying her best friend's face.

Dana looked up from the papers on her desk and forced a smile. "Yes, I'm fine." She quickly glanced away, knowing she couldn't hide her emotions from Cybil.

"If you're fine then why have you been crying?"

Dana began studying the papers on her desk again. "Who says I've been crying?"

"I do," Cybil said quietly, crossing the room to stand in front of Dana's desk. When seconds ticked by and Dana didn't say anything, Cybil spoke again, her voice low and imploring. "I didn't want you to get hurt."

Dana slowly stood from her desk and walked over to the window. She stared out until she was certain that her voice wouldn't tremble with each word she was about to say. "I didn't get hurt. I enjoyed each and every moment I spent with Jared."

"And you fell head over heels in love with him," Cybil said, stating the obvious.

Dana met Cybil's concerned gaze. "Yes, I fell in love with him. I didn't mean for it to happen, but it did. I love Jared with all my heart and I don't have any regrets about it."

Cybil crossed the room to stand in front of Dana. "All right. Now what?"

Dana looked away, to glance back out the window. "Now we've come to the end of our road. Tonight we end things and tomorrow I go back to being an unengaged woman."

Pain settled deep in Dana's heart. How could she go back to the solitary life she'd known after being with Jared for the past six weeks? Not only with Jared, but with all the Westmorelands. For a little while, they had filled a need in her she hadn't realized existed—a need to belong to a family. It was going to be hard going back to being alone again.

"Ben and I are going to the Amelia Islands in the morning to attend the tennis tournament. Come with us."

Dana gave Cybil a reassuring smile. "I'll be fine. I will survive." She chuckled. "It won't be my first broken engagement," she said teasingly.

"But it will be the one that really mattered—pretense or not."

Dana nodded. "Yes, it will be the one that mattered."

"And will you be ready for the questions on Monday? The speculations? The gossip?"

On a long sigh Dana ran her hand through her hair. No, she wouldn't be ready for any of that but she would deal with it. She gave a wry smile. "I'm ready for whatever comes my way, Cybil."

But she knew the moment she'd said the words that they were a lie.

"Why do I get the feeling that you're not in a good mood tonight?"

Jared gave his cousin Storm a crooked smile and lifted the glass of punch to his lips, took a sip and then asked. "I don't know. Why do you?"

A chuckle escaped Storm's lips. "I've often heard if you want a straight answer, then don't ask an attorney a question."

"Yes, I've heard that one, too," Jared said, giving his cousin a wink and taking another sip of his punch. He glanced around, seeing all the people who had shown up to celebrate Thorn and Tara's first wedding anniversary. Even after a year, the thought of Thorn being married was still hard to get used to. Jared never thought there was a woman alive who was brave enough to put up with the surly Thorn Westmoreland. Evidently he'd been wrong. Tara seemed to be handling his prickly cousin very well and it didn't take much to see how in love they were.

Storm's marriage six months ago had been another surprise, and Jared couldn't help but dwell on all the changes that had taken place in Storm's life since then.

The man who had once been Atlanta's most sought-after bachelor, who had been known as *The Perfect Storm* to multitudes of women, the man who swore he would never, ever marry was now a happily married man with a wife and twins on the way.

"What happened?" Jared asked. He suddenly needed answers and he'd force them out of Storm if necessary.

Storm raised a dark brow. "What do you mean what happened?"

"With you and this marriage thing. You swore you would never fall in love but you did and I want to know what happened."

A huge smile stretched Storm's lips. "Since you're engaged to be married yourself, I don't understand the need for this cross-examination. But just in case for some reason the verdict's still out, or you're attempting to find logic in all of this, the answer is simple. Love happened. I met a woman who I couldn't live without. At first I thought it was strictly physical since there was such a strong attraction between us, but then I discovered there was more to it than just being intimate. I enjoyed being with her, going places with her, seeing her smile and sharing my thoughts with her. And she was different from any woman I'd ever known."

Storm chuckled before continuing. "It took me a while to rationalize the depth of my feelings but when I did, I knew just what I wanted and who I wanted. And I also knew what I could lose if I didn't accept the truth and act on those feelings. I needed Jayla in my life, as part of my life, just as much as I needed to breathe."

Jared's troubled gaze met Storm's. "You were vulnerable."

Storm shook his head. "That's a subjective viewpoint, Jared, but also a wrong one. I was in love. I was so deeply entrenched in the throes of it that there was no way I could walk away. Jayla has added meaning to my life in ways I didn't think possible. But then from what I can tell, Dana has done the same for you. It shows every time the two of you are together. I've never seen you this attentive to any woman. For the past ten minutes you've been standing here getting agitated as you wait for her to return from touring the house with Tara. You love her, man. I thought I had it bad, but you have it worse. Hell, you're in worse shape than Thorn was and he hadn't known he was in love with Tara until it was almost too late."

Jared took another sip of his drink. He wondered what his cousin would say if he were to tell him he was wrong, that he wasn't in love with Dana, and that the entire engagement had been nothing but a sham.

Whatever he was about to say died on his lips the moment Dana walked through the patio doors with Tara. Tara and Thorn had had the house built and had moved into it a few months ago. It was a beautiful structure located in the outskirts of town on land that had been in the Westmoreland family for generations.

"Well, there's your lady, Jared. And if you're as smart as I know you are, whatever doubt that's beginning to form in your mind will soon vanish. Dana is a treasure worth having and if I were you I'd go a step further than just putting a ring on her finger. I'd make her officially mine as soon as I could."

"And what about the risk?"

Storm's eyes came swiftly to his. "What risk?"

"Divorce."

Storm shook his head. "You've been handling way too many divorce cases, Jared. When you're in love, you don't think of failure, you only think of success and prosperity. Life is full of risks. Each time I leave the station and head out to fight a fire there's a risk. You don't dwell on the what-ifs, and you have to believe that some risks are definitely worth taking. You have to believe in forever. And with that," Storm said, setting down his glass on the table beside him, "I think I'll go find my wife and give her a huge kiss."

Jared lifted his forehead. "Why?"

Storm gave him a smart-ass grin. "No particular reason. Just because."

Jared watched as Storm walked away before switching his attention back to Dana. She met his gaze and smiled. He smiled back then sighed deeply as he thought of how right things seemed at that moment. From the first, Dana had blended well with his family. And when she stood in a group with his female cousins, as she was doing now, she seemed so much a part of the Westmorelands. It seemed perfectly right for her to be here with them and with him.

As he continued to hold her gaze he suddenly knew that everything Storm had said was true. As much as he wanted to deny it and *had* denied it, the truth was now crystal clear. He *was* in love. He wanted and needed Dana in his life.

He wanted forever.

How many times in the last six weeks had he re-minded himself that their engagement was nothing but pretense? That no matter how much he enjoyed being with her, the time would come for it to end, and for him to go back to playing the field with flashy women who weren't looking for commitment? All the while knowing that his life would become empty without Dana in it.

How many times had he longed to keep things the way they were, but convinced himself that he didn't want or need a woman in his life? That he had seen the ugly side of marriage too much to take the risks for himself? But Storm was right. Some risks were worth taking.

The thought of Dana with someone else, sharing what they had shared was unacceptable. When they had entered into this pretense, he'd had no intention of letting his guard down around her. But he had. And she had eased her way into his heart as easily as any-thing he'd ever seen. He'd tried to put up resistance, had told himself countless times what he'd felt for her was nothing but lust. However, he knew just as sure as he was standing here that what he felt for her was love of the richest kind and if he was completely honest, he could even admit he had probably fallen in love with her the moment she'd stormed into his office. From that day on, he had wanted her with a passion unlike anything he'd ever felt before.

He wondered what Dana wanted. Was there a chance that she had feelings for him? Could she love him? There was only one way to find out. If she loved him, too, it would definitely make things a lot easier, and if she didn't, then he would just have to take the same advice he'd given Sylvester earlier that day. He would beg if he had to, because he had no intention of letting Dana go. Whether it was using reason or resorting to seduction, he would do what he had to do to win Dana's heart forever.

Dana didn't have to ask Jared if he wanted to come in when he took her home that night. She wanted him to and hoped that he would. Tonight was their last night together and she wanted one more lasting memory. Besides, she needed to give him back his ring.

When she had returned from touring Tara and Thorn's house she had noticed something different about Jared. It wasn't anything that she could put her finger on, but she sensed something was up. He'd always been attentive when they were together, but tonight it seemed that he was doubly so. And for someone who was supposed to announce to his family that they had broken their engagement tomorrow, he seemed too much the adoring, doting fiancé tonight for such a thing to be believable. There had been the hand holding and the loving kisses that all painted a picture of a couple who were very much in love.

And then there were the times she had caught him looking at her, sometimes in the oddest way. Once, when their gazes had locked, without warning and right in the middle of Dare's conversation, Jared had cupped her face in his hand and kissed her in front of his family, slowly and firmly, before whispering the words, "Let's leave," seductively in her ear.

So here they were, back at her place and as he closed the door behind them she wondered what he had in mind. But whatever it was, she was determined not to lose her composure. She would get through this night as they said their goodbyes.

"It was a nice party, wasn't it?" she asked, trying to generate conversation.

Jared leaned against the door, saying nothing as he watched her with intense dark eyes. "Yes, it was nice."

"And that motorcycle that Thorn presented to Tara was beautiful, simply awesome. To think he made it with his own hands. I can't imagine all the hours it took for him to do it. That was such a special gift to her."

"Yes, it was."

"It's obvious they are so happy together," she added, knowing she had started to ramble. "It's plain to see how much in love they are."

Jared smiled. "Yes, it is. In fact all my cousins who've gotten married appear to be happily in love."

She met his gaze. "What about Chase? Do you think he'll follow his brothers into matrimony eventually?"

Jared eased away from the door to stand in front of her. "Yes, I think he will, once he finds the right woman."

Dana nodded. She wondered if Jared would ever change his mind about love and marriage or if he would always let what he saw in his profession dictate how his future would be.

Knowing there was something she couldn't put off doing any longer, she let out a long, shaky breath as she lifted her hand and eased the engagement ring from her finger. She handed it to him. "It's time to give this back."

He shook his head as his gaze continued to hold hers. He took the ring from her and placed it back on her finger. "No, I want you to keep it."

She blinked. "I can't do that," she said incredulously, shocked he would suggest such a thing.

"Why not? You wanted to keep Cord's ring."

"But only because I was stuck with all those wedding expenses. Pretending to be engaged to you hasn't cost me anything," she said softly, not wanting to admit that it *had* cost her something. Her heart.

He didn't say anything for a few moments and then he gently took her into his arms and gathered her close. He pulled back briefly, met her gaze and in Dana's mind he was looking at her the same way he had done earlier that night.

She held his gaze and every emotion Dana could think of took hold of her. Every time she thought about the fact that this would be the last time they shared together, that chances were when he walked out the door he wouldn't be coming back, despair took hold of her. But she refused to let their last night together end in gloom and doom. It hadn't started out that way and she wouldn't let it end that way.

Jared leaned down and their mouths joined. Immediately, Dana could tell there was something different about this kiss. It still packed a lot of passion that sent toe-curling sensations through her, but there was a degree of tenderness that touched her deeply, almost brought tears to her eyes. It was as if he was methodically placing his stamp on her.

Moments later when he drew away, she had to hold on to his hand to keep her balance. She could actually hear her heart pounding.

"Let's play one final game," Jared whispered softly.

"A final game?" she asked, thinking of the two others they had played together. Her heart began pounding even harder just thinking about them. And the purely seductive male look in his eyes wasn't helping matters.

He looked at her for several long, quiet moments, then said, "Yes. Let's play Truth or Dare?"

With a sigh, Dana looked down at her hands, her gaze focused on the ring he had placed back there. She looked up at him. "I haven't played that in years, since high school at a sleepover."

"Then you know how it's played?"

"Yes." But something told her that Jared would have his own version of the game. What would his dare be like? And did she really want to bare her heart and soul by telling him the truth about anything he asked?

Jared kept his gaze leveled on her. "Okay then let's get started. You go first," he murmured softly.

Dana heaved a deep breath. "Truth or dare?" she challenged.

A smile spread from Jared's lips to his entire face. "Truth."

"Okay." She paused for a moment, wondering what she could ask him and decided to go easy. "What did you enjoy the most about Thorn and Tara's party tonight?"

"Being there with you."

Dana's breath caught and goose bumps formed on her arms with his response. She hadn't expected him to say that. Before she could recover he said, "Truth or dare?"

She decided she would stick with the truth. "Truth."

"What did *you* enjoy the most about the party tonight?" he asked.

Dana sighed. She had hoped he wouldn't ask her that. She had enjoyed a lot about the party tonight, but she knew what she'd enjoyed the most. She met his gaze and told him the truth. "The moment you kissed me in front of everyone."

She saw the darkening of Jared's eyes. She heard the deepening of his breathing. Both sparked desires within her. He reached out and touched her chin, and then his finger moved slowly down the center of her neck to where her pulse was pounding. "Truth or dare," she challenged again, barely able to get the words out.

Although it was impossible, it seemed his eyes darkened more. "Dare," he said huskily.

Dana swallowed past the lump, especially with Jared's hand still there on her neck, drawing lazy circles with his fingers, stimulating both her mind and her body. She could only think of one dare at the moment. "I dare you to kiss me like I'm the only woman you could ever want." A part of Dana knew how badly that must have sounded, but it was her dare and she wondered what he would do about it.

Jared felt his groin tighten in response to Dana's dare. He doubted that she knew how beautiful and sexy she looked, waiting to see what he would do. Fulfilling her dare wasn't a problem since in his mind she was the only woman he could ever want anyway. But she didn't know it and maybe it was about time she did.

He reached out and gently pulled her to him. There was no waiting, and his mouth took hers with all the urgency and need that he felt. He heard her whimper the moment his tongue entered her mouth, and as he began mating his mouth with hers, he felt the shiver that ran down her body. He had kissed her a number of times, but now he was kissing her as the woman he had singled out to spend the rest of his life with, and he was determined to let it show in his kiss. All evening he had longed to kiss her this way. That kiss in front of his family was merely meant to tide him over until now. Until this. His heart was filled with love and his body was wired with sensuous need. Together, both were causing him to overload.

When she grabbed the back of his head, locking their mouths, his hand eased under her blouse, unhooked the front catch to her bra to touch her breasts. Her felt the tips hardened beneath his fingers, felt her body's response to it in her kiss. She moaned in his mouth and the sound sent fire through every nerve in his body. Then when breathing became a necessity, he slowly pulled back, reluctantly breaking off the kiss.

Dana swallowed a frustrated groan. She hadn't wanted him to stop kissing her. Thanks to him she knew how it felt to come apart in a man's arms. She'd discovered all the pleasure a person could experience in making love.

"Truth or dare?"

A heated flutter floated around in her chest, a tingling sensation took root in her stomach. She nervously bit her bottom lip, looked up at him and met his gaze and said, "Dare."

He smiled, seemingly pleased. Then said, "Give me your underwear."

Dana blinked, wondered if she'd heard him right, although she knew that she had. The room felt charged when she lifted her skirt. The heat in his gaze intensified and her breathing pattern became irregular.

Holding his gaze, she slowly eased her bikini panties down her legs. When they were completely off, she balled them up in her hand and handed them to him.

He took them. "Thanks."

Now it was her turn. "Truth or Dare?"

His deep penetrating gaze met hers. "Dare."

A wicked gleam appeared in her eyes when she said, "Give me yours."

Jared chuckled quietly as his hands went to his belt and he pulled it out of the loop. Next he eased down his zipper. Dana watched as he removed his jeans, then the pair of black briefs he was wearing. She inhaled deeply when he stood before her naked from the waist down. Completely naked and totally aroused.

He held her gaze. "Truth or Dare."

She gave him an intimate smile. "Dare."

"I dare you to take off the rest of your clothes."

Dana's heart began beating faster as she began unbuttoning her blouse to take if off. She then removed her bra that was half off anyway. Next was the skirt that she eased down her legs along with her half slip. Her body shivered at the intense desire she saw in Jared's gaze as he looked at her. His eyes seemed fixated with the area below her navel.

"Truth or Dare?" she asked softly, feeling totally exposed, yet at the same time, utterly sexy while standing nude before him.

"Dare," he said throatily, as if that one word had been torn from deep inside his throat.

She nodded, wondering if they would ever get back to truths when it was much more fun being daring. Just looking at him standing in her living room more naked than dressed, made her feel warm, wet and wanton. "Take off the rest of yours, as well."

All he had to do was pull his shirt over his head and he was done. "Truth or Dare?" he challenged in a husky voice as his gaze moved down the length of her. She felt her body burn everywhere his eyes touched. She also felt her blood simmer slowly through each of her veins.

"Truth," she responded, letting out a slow breath.

"Now that we're naked, what do you want us to do?" he asked. The magnitude of desire in his eyes had her body burning.

She held his gaze. They were back to the truth again. Everything feminine within her yearned for him, actually ached. The area between her legs was throbbing unmercifully. And she could think of only one way to end the torment. "I want you to make love to me. Here. Now. And don't hold back on anything."

Her words were both a truth and a dare, Jared thought, as he filled with need and desire, and an over-powering love slammed into him. Something within him snapped and he wanted to give her exactly what she'd asked for.

He reached out, pulled her to him and kissed her, drowning in the sweet moistness of her mouth. He wanted to touch her, taste her, mark her as his. And although he knew such a thing wasn't possible, he wanted to seduce her into loving him as much as he loved her.

He tugged her down on the carpeted floor and let out a low growl of need when he left her mouth to devour the rest of her. His tongue was hot and the skin it tasted increased the fever and the hunger inside him. And Dana wasn't helping matters. Her hands were touching him everywhere, letting him know that she was driven by the same fierce urgency. When she took him into her hand, running her fingers down his hot, slick shaft, he sucked in his breath. She was burning for him the same way he was on fire for her and he knew of only one way to put out the flames.

"No more," he said, pushing aside her hands, his arousal beyond the point of control. He quickly covered her body and entered her, sheathing himself deep. Breathing raggedly, he began thrusting inside of her, holding her gaze as he moved in and out, mating with her like a man who was about to take his last breath and this was the only thing that could sustain him.

Dana followed Jared's frantic rhythm, kept up with his nonstop pace and sucked in a breath at the impact of each and every thrust. Pleasure tore through her relentlessly, urged her to wrap her legs around his hips and pull him deeper inside of her. She wanted this, had asked for it. And he was giving it to her.

"Jared!"

She gave herself to him in torrid abandonment. Shudders, unyielding and unrelenting, rammed through every part of her body, from the top of her head to the tip of her toes. A mass of sensations bombarded the area between her legs where their bodies were joined. And when he picked up the pace, increased the already frantic rhythm, and deepened his steady thrusts, she lifted her body off the floor, needing and wanting everything he had to give.

"Dana!"

Jared's body shook with the force of an orgasm that shot him into ecstasy, filled him with wondrous sensations. A deep guttural growl of satisfaction ripped from deep within his throat and he felt his body explode inside of her. He never knew, never even thought that making love to a woman could be so climactic and earth-shattering, until he'd made love with her. He had never before mated this wildly with a woman, never before wished the rapture would never end.

A short while later, he collapsed on the floor beside her and pulled her into his arms. He wrapped his arms around her as she lay sprawled lifelessly across his chest, the hunger they had for each other satisfied.

"Truth or dare?" she whispered, pressing her lips against the hollow of his throat and gently sucking there.

His breath caught and he felt himself getting hard all over again. "Truth," he said when he was able to breathe normally again.

"What are you thinking?" she asked, somehow finding strength to lean up and stare down at him.

His heart reacted immediately to her question. "I'm thinking that what we just shared is amazing, and that every time we've made love was incredible. I also think that you're beautiful, sexy and a woman any man would want to claim as his. And that I want you in all the ways a man could possibly want a woman. In bed and out of bed. I'm also thinking about the fact that we didn't use protection, but I'm not bothered by it because I don't want things to end between us tonight."

Dana lightly traced her fingers through the hair on his chest. Was he trying to say he wanted her as a lover? That things didn't have to be over after tonight? But how would he explain to his family as to why she had gone from being his fiancée to nothing more than his lover. But then another part of her knew she wanted more from Jared, a lot more than he was willing to give. She refused to sell herself short and it was best to walk away now to save herself heartbreak later.

"Truth or dare, Dana?"

His challenge interrupted her thoughts. She looked at him. "Truth."

He reached out and captured her hand. "What are you thinking?"

She inhaled deeply, then released a slow, shaky breath. "I'm thinking that I can't settle for an affair with you, Jared."

"That's good because I don't want an affair."

At the confused look that appeared on her face, he sat up and pulled her to him and placed a slow, lingering kiss on her lips. When he released her he said, "I want something more than an affair, Dana. I want you to be the woman I come home to every night."

She frowned, not sure she understood what he was saying. "I don't understand."

With a shuddering sigh he said, "Then maybe it's time to put all game playing aside and speak only the truth."

He couldn't help but think about how much he loved her and needed her in his life. "These past six weeks, pretending to be your fiancé, the man you are going to marry, have been the best weeks of my life. And tonight when I realized it was about to end, I had to face a number of truths. One of which was the fact that I have fallen in love with you."

Dana blinked, seeming thunderstruck. "You have?"

His smile showed a perfect set of white teeth. "Yes, and more than anything I want to make our engagement real." He lifted his hand to her face to caress her cheek. "But getting what I want really depends on how you feel about me, Dana."

He saw the moment tears began forming in her eyes. "Oh, Jared, I love you, too, and more than anything I want our engagement to be real."

He chuckled with both joy and relief and pulled her into his lap. "I'm damn glad to hear that. So, Dana Rollins will you marry me? Be my wife, the mother of my children and the love of my life for always?"

He framed her face in his hands and continued. "Will you let that ring you're already wearing be a symbol of my love and promise? And will you believe that I will honor you, protect you and make you happy?"

He watched as more tears came into her eyes at the

same time a soft chuckle escaped from her throat. "Yes, I'll marry you, Jared, and be all of those things."

An overpowering gush of happiness erupted from Jared's throat. "You do know this means you'll have all the Westmorelands as family?"

Tears made her choke back her laughter. "Thank God. I'd become attached to them and didn't want to give them up even though I thought this would be our last night together."

When his arms tightened around her she leaned down and rubbed her cheek against his chest. "You're a pro at making seductive proposals, Jared Westmoreland."

He grinned as his heart raced with unmeasured joy. "Am I?"

"Yes."

"Umm," he said as heat began stroking his body all over again. "I'm also pretty good at other things."

She met his dark penetrating gaze as she stared at him. "Are you?"

"Yes."

She leaned down, her lips mere inches from his. "Show me these other things. I dare you."

In one smooth move he quickly had her on her back. Their gazes locked and he knew he would love her for the rest of his life.

And that was the naked truth.

Epilogue

Two months later

Just as Sarah Westmoreland had predicted, there was another Westmoreland wedding before the end of the summer.

As Jared carried his wife down the church steps, she laid her head against his solid chest as rice rained down on them. Out of the corner of his eyes he saw his parents. He noticed his mother dab tears of joy from her eyes. To say she was happy was an understatement. But then, he knew she was already checking out her remaining five single sons to see who she should set her mark on next. He chuckled. She even had his cousin Chase within her intense scope. No one would be safe from matrimony if Sarah Westmoreland had her way.

When he and Dana were seated inside the limo, he

pulled her into his arms and kissed her with all the love he felt in his heart. His tongue swept inside to caress the walls of her mouth thinking that he would never get tired of the taste of her.

Their next stop was the grand ballroom of the Atlanta Civic Center. It amazed him how his mother and Aunt Evelyn, along with the long-distance assistance of his aunt Abby in Montana, were able to put together such an elegant wedding once he and Dana had set a date.

Jared released Dana's mouth and looked down into her smiling face. "How much ruckus do you think we'll cause if I tell the driver that we want to skip the wedding reception and go straight to the airport to catch our plane for St. Maarten?"

A smile touched the corners of Dana's mouth. "Oh, I think more than we're prepared to deal with. Your mother and aunts might never forgive us."

Jared grinned. "You're right. I guess the least we can do is show up."

"I agree."

He reached out and pulled her into his lap. It wasn't an easy thing to do considering her wedding dress. It was beautiful and she had looked gorgeous in it when she had walked down the aisle to him. Her best friend's husband, Ben, had given her away and Cybil had been her matron of honor. Delaney, Shelly, Tara, Madison, Casey and some of Dana's girlfriends from college had been her bridesmaids. Jayla had had to sit this one out since she was about to deliver at any moment. Dare had been Jared's best man and his brothers and the rest of his cousins stood in as his groomsmen.

Sylvester Brewster had asked to sing a song at the

wedding as a way to show his thanks for all Jared had done in getting him and his wife back together. After Jared had set up the meeting between them, the two had agreed to marriage counseling to make their marriage work. They were in love and wanted to put this episode behind them and move on.

Dana lifted her hand to admire her rings. She then looked at Jared's hand to see his matching gold band. She glanced up at him. She loved him totally and completely. An idea suddenly popped into her head. "Later tonight, when we're all alone I think we should play another game."

Jared lifted his forehead. "I thought Truth or Dare would be our final one."

She shook her head, grinning. "Why stop when you're having fun? And I have the perfect game for us."

She had peaked his curiosity. "And what game is that?"

"Spin the Bottle."

Jared smiled as he thought of all the possibilities and decided he could definitely put an interesting twist on that game. "Okay, I'm up for it."

Dana chuckled. "I thought that you would be."

And then with a shuddering sigh she pulled his face down to hers, her lips parting as she let him take possession of her mouth in a kiss that was full of all the passion she had come to expect from him. And as she returned his kiss with provocative urgency and overpowering passion, she knew that the best day of her life had been when she had agreed to become Jared's counterfeit fiancée.

* * * * *

THE CHASE IS ON

Prologue

"Never trust a Graham."

Sixteen-year old Chase Westmoreland slid onto the stool at the counter in his grandfather's restaurant. The old man turned and spoke while placing a huge glass of milk and a plate filled with cookies in front of him.

"Why? What's wrong, Gramps?" Chase asked as he immediately attacked the stack of cookies.

"What's wrong? I'll tell you what's wrong. Carlton Graham stole some of our secret recipes and passed them on to Donald Schuster."

Chase stopped eating as his eyes grew large. He knew how his grandfather felt about the Westmoreland family recipes. They had been in the family for generations. "But Mr. Graham is your friend."

Scott Westmoreland frowned at his grandson. "Not anymore he isn't. Our friendship ended along with our partnership two weeks ago. I never thought I'd live to see the day he would betray me this way."

Chase downed a huge gulp of milk and then asked, "Are you sure he did it?"

Scott Westmoreland nodded, his features tired and full of pain and disappointment. "Yes, I'm sure. I'd heard that Schuster had added a couple of new dishes to his menu that taste just like mine, so I went to investigate for myself."

Chase nodded. "And?"

"They're mine all right. Schuster won't say where he got the recipes, but I knew they are mine."

Chase sadly shook his head. He'd always liked Mr. Graham and his chocolate chip cookies were the best. His grandfather's were all right, but Mr. Graham's had a special ingredient that made them mouth-wateringly delicious. "Did you ask Mr. Graham about it?"

"Of course I did and he denies everything, but I know he's lying. He's the only person who knows exactly what ingredients I use. He must feel guilty. That's probably the reason he's not wasting any time moving his family out of town."

Chase's eyes widened. "The Grahams are moving away?"

"Yes and good riddance. It wouldn't bother me any if I never saw another Graham again. Like I said, they can't be trusted. Always remember that."

One

The present

He needed an attitude adjustment.

That thought flashed through Chase Westmoreland's mind as he turned the corner to pull into his
restaurant's parking lot. Six months of abstinence, he
concluded, had to be the reason he'd been in such a
bad mood lately.

It had nothing to do with the fact that in the last
three years, all of his four brothers and his baby sister
had gotten married. Even his cousin Jared, the die-hard
bachelor and divorce lawyer, had recently fallen victim.
Chase was sick and tired of varied family members
looking at him with a knowing smile on their lips. If
they were waiting for him to be next, then they had a
long wait ahead of them.

And it didn't help matters that his brothers were cocky enough to say he would change his mind when the right woman came along. His comeback to them had been quick and confident. The "right woman" didn't exist.

"What the hell!" He brought his car to a sudden stop in the middle of the parking lot outside his restaurant, which was buzzing with activity. He had forgotten that someone had purchased the building a few doors from Chase's Place. From the way things looked, they were moving in.

He had received notice a few weeks ago that he would have a new neighbor.

He wasn't surprised. Atlanta was a city of international renown that had managed to hold on to its southern charm. And the downtown section where his restaurant was located with its charming neighborhoods, tree-shaded streets and friendly communities, made it a prime area for doing business. If he remembered correctly, someone would be opening a confectionery.

When he'd first heard about it, the news had brought out his cravings for chocolate, but now seeing the mass of confusion surrounding him all thoughts of sweets suddenly turned sour.

Moving trucks were everywhere and taking up parking spaces his customers would need. It was barely six in the morning and he had a huge breakfast crowd. The last thing he needed was someone messing with the availability of parking. It was a good thing he had a reserved spot in front of his restaurant, or there wouldn't be any space left even for him.

He sat in his car, forcing himself to breath calmly as a truck blocked him in. This was Monday, not a good day for his patience to be tested. He was just about to hit his horn when a woman walking out of the building caught his attention. For a moment he forgot his anger. Hell, he even forgot to breathe.

As she talked to the driver of the truck blocking his path, he looked her up and down. She was a prime specimen of a woman. She was dressed in a short baker's smock, and he hoped she had on a pair of shorts since a good gust of wind would show him and anyone else what may or may not be underneath. A smile drifted over his lips. Even with the smock he could tell she had one helluva figure. And when his gaze lit on her face…

His skin suddenly felt overheated as he looked into a medium brown face too beautiful for words. She had a pair of honey-brown eyes and full, moist lips covered in what looked like juicy red strawberry lip gloss. He wanted to get out of his car, walk over to her and kiss the coloring right off her lips. Then there was her hair, a mass of dark-brown curls that tumbled over her shoulders. For the first time in quite a while Chase found himself physically affected by a beautiful woman.

That thought made him take a deep breath and he forced himself to pull back. He was a thirty-four-year-old hot-blooded male and there was nothing wrong with responding to visual stimuli. But he couldn't let a great pair of legs and a gorgeous face scatter his wits. All he had to do was remember his last year at Duke University and Iris Nelson. Thinking of Iris made warning bells go off...the sound of reason.

Sighing deeply, he let his gaze drift over her once more before backing up his car and moving around the truck. He sighed, glad he was breathing again. As soon as he got inside his restaurant he would drink a strong cup of black coffee.

Chase only wished he hadn't noticed the absence of a wedding ring on the woman's finger, making him happier than it ought to.

Jessica Claiborne smiled as she looked around her shop. After moving in she was already set for the shop's grand opening tomorrow morning. She had spent the day doing last-minute checks on inventory and confirming arrangement for deliveries. She had hired two high-school students to pass out flyers about the shop around the community. Since she intended for all of her products to be baked fresh daily, she had made a call to the children's hospital and offered to donate any treats she didn't sell tomorrow. Also, she had signed contracts with a couple of the hotels around town to supply their restaurants and coffeeshops with baked goods.

She glanced out the window. It was a beautiful day in early October. The movers had gotten everything set up on Monday and the artist she'd hired had come that morning to paint her shop's name on the display window. Delicious Cravings was the name she had decided on, and she would be forever thankful to her grandmother for making her dream come true.

Sadness settled in Jessica's heart whenever she

thought about the grandmother she had simply adored and the inheritance she'd been left when her grandmother had died last year on Jessica's twenty-fifth birthday. The money had made it possible to walk away from her stressful job as a corporate attorney in Sacramento and pursue her dream of owning and operating her own confectionery.

She sniffed the air, enjoying the smell of chocolate cooking. Already today she had made a batch of assorted pastries including éclairs and tarts. But what she had enjoyed more than anything was whipping up chocolate nut clusters and an assortment of cookies for her neighbors as an apology for inconveniencing them during her move.

Mrs. Morrison who owned the seamstress shop next door had accepted her apology but declined her treats since she was allergic to chocolate but had said she would love to try her shortcake. The Criswell brothers, who owned the karate school, had accepted her gift and apology graciously, welcomed her to the strip and said they looked forward to patronizing her shop. The only person left was the owner of Chase's Place. Jessica hoped the restaurateur was just as understanding as Mrs. Morrison and the Criswell brothers had been and that he had a sweet tooth.

Grabbing the box she had filled with sweet treats, she walked out the door and locked it behind her. She had hired a part-time helper, an elderly woman who would come in during the busy lunchtime hours.

It was early afternoon but she could tell the restaurant was packed and hoped the business would eventually trickle over to her once people realized she was open. Before she got within ten feet of the restaurant she could smell the mouth-watering food and realized she hadn't eaten anything since breakfast.

She walked into Chase's Place, immediately liking what she saw. It was a very upscale restaurant that somehow maintained a homey atmosphere. Lanterns adorned each table and the tablecloths matched curtains that hung in the windows. There was a huge counter with bar stools and soft jazzy music coming from a speaker located somewhere in the back.

"Welcome to Chase's Place, where you're guaranteed to get the finest in soul food. Are you dining in or carrying out?"

Jessica smiled at the young woman who greeted her. "I'm the owner of the new confectionery a few doors down and wanted to bring the owner a gift for any inconvenience he might have encountered while I was moving in."

The woman nodded. "That would be Chase and he's in his office. If you follow me I'll show you the way."

"Thanks."

Jessica followed the woman down a hall that led to the back of the restaurant. Everything looked tidy, even the storage room they passed. The hostess knocked when they reached the office door. "Who is it?" a deep, husky voice called out.

"It's Donna. Someone is here to see you."

"Hell, I'm surprised anyone can get through with all that chaos that's been going on in the parking lot. I have a good mind to go over there and give my inconsiderate new neighbor a piece of my mind for all the problems she's caused me the last couple of days. I couldn't get my own deliveries through for—"

Chase stopped talking when his door swung open and the woman he had checked out Monday morning walked into his office past a speechless Donna. "I guess I've saved you a trip. I would think, considering the circumstances, you would have been just as understanding as my other neighbors and…"

Whatever the woman was saying Chase had stopped listening mere seconds after she walked into his office. Heat flared through all parts of his body and his full concentration centered on the shorts and tank top she was wearing.

Up close her legs were more of a turn-on than they had been on Monday morning. He blinked. The closer she got, the better she looked, especially those moist strawberry lips. She was angry…sexy as hell.

In addition to the honey-brown eyes and curly dark hair that tumbled around her face, she possessed perfect cheekbones and a cute perky nose. He couldn't help noticing that the mouth that was moving was beautifully shaped and ready to be kissed.

"And I hope you choke on these!"

He was jolted from his lust-filled thoughts when a box was suddenly shoved against his chest. It took only a split second for him to realize his visitor was leaving. When the door slammed shut, he looked at Donna, ignored the silly smirk on her face and asked, "What the hell did she say?"

He watched Donna's try to hide a laugh. "I think,

boss, that you've been thoroughly told off. I can't believe you weren't listening."

No, he hadn't been listening. He looked down at the box.

"That was supposed to be a peace offering," Donna explained. "She came to apologize for the inconvenience over the past couple of days. I think that was downright neighborly of her. I guess she hoped you'd be more understanding of the chaos she caused while moving in."

Chase nodded, suddenly filled with regret that he hadn't been more understanding. But he'd been in a foul mood for the past week and had wrongly directed his anger at her. She was a woman after all, and a woman, or actually the lack of one, was the root of his problem.

Granted he wasn't the ladies' man his twin brother Storm had been, but usually he could pull out his little phone book and contact any number of women, who, like him, were more interested in getting down than getting married. But for some reason doing so didn't suit him. The last woman he dated had read more into the relationship and he'd had one hell of a time convincing her that bedding her didn't mean he'd be wedding her. He wasn't into serious relationships of any kind and had told her that in the beginning. Evidently somewhere along the way she'd forgotten.

He dragged a weary hand down his face. Some women saw the single Westmoreland men as challenges. His brother Storm's philosophy—before his wife Jayla had entered his life—had been that he enjoyed women too much to settle down with just one.

Chase believed in learning from his mistakes, and his biggest one had been a woman by the name of Iris Nelson.

While in college at Duke, he had seemed headed for a pro basketball career when an injury had ended his dreams. He'd found himself facing an endless future when Iris, the girl he had fallen in love with, decided that with no chance at the pros he was no longer a good prospect.

Over the years he'd become wary of opportunistic women who only entered relationships to find out what was in it for them, and when the going got tough, they got going. Making women secondary in his life was the best way to eliminate the chance of a repeat heartbreak.

"So what are you going to do?" Donna asked, interrupting his thoughts.

He didn't have a clue. One thing was certain, he owed his new neighbor an apology. "Tell Kevin to prepare a today's special to go and be generous with the servings."

Chuckling, Donna nodded. "You think you'll find her soft spot with food?"

He looked down at the box he held in his hand and inhaled the aroma of chocolate. "Wasn't that her game plan?"

Donna gave him a long look before slowly shaking her head and closing the door behind her as she left.

Chase placed the box on his desk. The top was marked Delicious Cravings. He thought of how she'd looked Monday morning when he had first seen her and just moments ago standing in the middle of his office. The name was definitely appropriate.

He opened the box and immediately fell in love—with the sweets. Yes, he definitely owed the woman an apology and before the evening ended he would make sure she got one.

That man had a bad attitude!

Jessica took a deep breath, refusing to get any more upset than she already was. How dare he say she was inconsiderate? She was one of the most considerate people she knew. It was one of the reasons she had walked away from her high-paying job as a corporate attorney.

She had gotten fed up with having to fight for things she didn't believe in, pushing policies that ruined people's lives, being forced to put corporate profits before the consumers' best interests.

And her consideration for her family's wishes was the only thing pushing her to seek out members of the Westmoreland family to right a wrong made against her family years ago. The nerve of them thinking her grandfather had been a dishonest man! He had been one of the most honest men she knew and if it was left up to her, she would give the Westmorelands a good piece of her mind and tell them just what she thought of their accusations. But before taking her final breath her grandmother had made her promise to come to Atlanta to clear the Graham name without starting World War III, and she intended to do that. After doing research on the area, she decided Atlanta would be a good place to live and not just visit. And so she had made the decision to relocate to the area.

She sighed as her thoughts drifted back to the owner of Chase's Place. He had reminded her of dark chocolate of the richest kind and she knew one of the reasons she had gone off on him the way she had was that she couldn't afford to get caught up in his sheer beauty. Even with his horrible attitude she had to admit that he was handsome as sin. Taller and well-built, his features took her breath away. He had reminded her that she was a woman, something she often tried to forget.

The last thing she needed was to get attracted to a man. She refused to get so carried away that she forgot how deceitful they were. She had learned her lesson even if her mother never had. Jeff Claiborne may have been the man who had fathered her, but he was also the man who had kept her mother dangling on a string for over fifteen years with promises of marriage. When Jessica had been born he had given her his name, but her mother's last name had remained Graham.

It had taken her grandfather's paid investigator to deliver the news that there was no way Jeff Claiborne could ever marry Janice Graham. He was already married to another woman and had a family living in Philadelphia. The news had been a terrible blow to her mother—one that she had never recovered from. She took her own life rather that live with the heartache and pain.

At the age of fifteen Jessica had watched as her mother's coffin was lowered into the ground and had vowed never to give her heart to any man. She wouldn't be fooled by a man as deceitful as her father had been, one man who could take undying love and abuse it in the worst possible way.

Her grandfather, angry and hurt over what Jeff Claiborne had done, had made sure the man didn't get away unscathed. He had paid a visit to Jeff Claiborne's wife and had presented her with documented proof of her husband's duplicity. Jennifer Claiborne, a good woman, hadn't wasted any time filing for a divorce and leaving her husband of eighteen years. And Jennifer had gone one step further by welcoming Jessica into her family, making sure she got to know her sister and brother, and making sure Jeff Claiborne contributed to her support. She knew Jennifer had been instrumental in helping to set up the college fund that had been available when she had graduated from high school.

Savannah and Rico were as close to her as any brother and sister could be. And Jennifer was like a second mother to her. She'd known she could always go visit her extended family in Philadelphia.

Jessica heard a knock at the door and frowned. Dusk was settling in but she could plainly see through her display window that her unexpected visitor was the man from the restaurant.

She had a good mind to ignore him. For the last couple of weeks since moving to Atlanta she had begun thinking she had finally found peace, but now he was convincing her otherwise.

She heard his knock again and decided that she wouldn't hide. Like everything else in life she would deal with her problems, and in this case, her problem was him. He had sought her out and she supposed she needed to make nice because she'd be seeing him a lot.

This building was not only the place she would work but thanks to space above the shop, it was also her new home.

Deciding she had let him linger long enough, she made her way to the door and unlocked it. She took a deep breath before opening it. "What do you want?"

He had been standing with his back to her, looking up at the sky. The day had been beautiful but it seemed that tonight it would rain. He turned around and as soon as their gazes locked she felt the temperature go up about one hundred degrees.

He still reminded her of rich dark chocolate rum balls but now something else had been added to the mixture, she thought, as her gaze moved from the baseball cap on his head to the features in his face. A slight indention in the bridge of his nose indicated it may have been broken at one time but she didn't even consider that a flaw. Nothing, and she meant nothing, distracted from this man's good looks.

Jeeze. That wasn't a good sign.

And to make matters worse, his smile was so potent that she was forced to grip the doorknob to support her suddenly wobbly knees. Forcing her eyes away from that smile, she met his gaze once more and it angered her that he had this kind of effect on her. "I repeat, what do you want?" she all but snapped.

His grin widened. He was either oblivious to her less-than-friendly mood or else he chose to ignore it. "I came to apologize and to deliver a peace offering," he said, widening that killer smile even more and holding up a bag that smelled of delicious food.

"I was out of line earlier," he said. "And I do understand how it is moving in. The only excuse I can give for my behavior is that this has been one hell of a week. But my problems are not your fault."

His apology surprised her, but it didn't captivate her as he had evidently assumed it would. Long ago she had learned to be cautious of smooth-talking men.

"Will you accept my apology?"

She jutted her chin. "Why should I?"

"Because it will prove that you're a much nicer person than I am and someone with a forgiving spirit."

Jessica leaned against the doorjamb, thinking that she was definitely a much nicer person than he, but she wasn't all that sure about having a forgiving spirit. She inhaled deeply, deciding she didn't want to accept his apology. She didn't like the chemistry she felt flowing between them and she also decided she didn't like him. She knew it all sounded irrational, but at the moment she didn't care. "There are a lot of things I can overlook, but rudeness isn't one of them."

Chase lifted a brow and frowned. "So you aren't going to accept my apology?"

She glared at him. "At the moment, no."

His frown deepened as he peered down at her. "Why?"

"Because I don't feel like it. Now if you'll excuse me I need to—"

He held up a hand, cutting her off. "Because you don't feel like it?"

"That's what I said."

Chase felt frustration take over his body. He had dealt with many unreasonable people, but this woman gave new meaning to the word. Yes, he had been rude. But he had apologized, hadn't he?

"Look," he said slowly, while trying to overlook the irritation plastered on her face. "I know things got off to a bad start between us, and for that I apologize. And you're right. I was rude, but now you're the one who is being unreasonable."

Jessica sighed deeply. The dark-brown eyes focused on hers were intense, sharp, and to-die-for, but still…

"But still nothing, Jessica Lynn," she could hear her grandmother saying in the recesses of her mind. *"You can't judge every man by your father. You can't continue to put up this brick wall against any man who gets too close."*

Sighing again, she smoothed a hand down her face. Her grandmother was right but the need to protect herself had always been elemental. For some reason she had an inkling that the man standing before her was someone she should avoid at all costs.

"Please accept my peace offering as I did yours, okay?" Chase asked, interrupting her thoughts. "By the way, everything was delicious, especially the chocolate chip cookies. They're my favorite and I haven't tasted chocolate chip cookies that delicious in years. They were melt-in-your-mouth delicious." He slanted her a smile. "And I didn't choke on any of them."

"Too bad," she said dryly. Their gazes held for a moment, and she knew she was a puzzle he was trying to figure out. No doubt other women didn't cause him any trouble. He probably flashed his smile and got whatever he wanted. Just like her father.

She wrapped her arms around herself knowing he didn't intend to leave until she accepted his apology. "Okay, I accept your apology. Goodbye."

He grabbed the door before she could slam it shut in his face. He held up the bag and smiled. "And the peace offering?"

She snorted a breath. "And the peace offering," she said reaching for the bag.

Chase chuckled. "Now we're getting somewhere." Instead of giving her the bag he held his hand out to her. "We haven't been properly introduced. I'm Chase Westmoreland. And you are?" he asked taking her hand.

Jessica knew if she had a lighter skin tone he would have seen all the blood drain from her face. "Westmoreland?"

He grinned. "Yes, does the name ring a bell? There's a bunch of us living in Atlanta."

Deciding she wasn't ready to tell him just how familiar it was, she shook her head. "No, I recently moved here from California."

He nodded and after a few moments he said smiling, "You never told me your name."

She blinked, recalling that she hadn't. "I'm Jessica Claiborne."

His smile widened. "Welcome to Atlanta, Jessica. Do you have family here?"

"No," she answered truthfully, "I have no family living here." Her head was still spinning at the realization that he was a Westmoreland.

There was a bit of silence between them when Chase remembered the bag he was holding. "Oops, I almost forgot. Here you go," he said handing the bag to Jessica. "It's today's special. I hope you enjoy it."

"Thanks."

He hesitated for a moment then said, "I guess I'd better get back. The dinner crowd is arriving. Will you be living upstairs?"

"Yes," she said, gripping the bag in both hands. She needed to get away from him to think.

"Well, every once in a while if it's a late night, I sleep over my place, too. If you ever need anything, just let me know."

Don't hold your breath, Jessica thought, closing the door on temptation.

Two

Jessica leaned back in the chair and licked her lips. That had to have been the most delicious meal she'd eaten in a very long time. The smothered pork chops had been tender, just the way she liked and the mashed potatoes had made her groan out loud. No wonder Chase's Place was packed. The dessert, a slice of carrot cake, had been melt-in-your-mouth delicious. And she knew baked goods. Her grandmother had been the best baker she'd ever met.

She'd always enjoyed baking because of all the times she had spent with her grandparents in the kitchen growing up. She had even considered going to culinary school instead of law school. But her grandfather had talked her out of it, saying there were enough cooks in the Graham family.

As she cleaned up, Jessica glanced around her apartment. It was just the right size for her, with a large living room, a bath, a small kitchen and a bedroom. She loved the hardwood floors and the huge window in the living room.

She smiled at the thought that she actually owned this place, the entire building. Downstairs in the shop, there was a huge cooking area and a small office in the back. It had been just what she'd been looking for. According to the real estate agent, all the buildings were newly renovated and business in the area was always good. She moved over to the window and glanced out again at all the people gathered at Chase's Place.

Her breath suddenly caught when she noticed Chase walk out of his restaurant with another man. It was plain to see the two were related since there were distinct similarities in their features. But Chase was the one holding her attention. The sun had gone down, but the faint light illuminated him. He looked good in his jeans and black pullover shirt, and even from where she was standing she could see his perfectly chiseled features.

She sighed deeply, and as if he had heard, he glanced toward her window and their eyes met. She felt it, the moment their eyes connected, a jolt in the lower part of her body, a current of electricity that spiked up her spine. Both feelings suddenly rejuvenated that part of her that had been dormant since her first year of college. The one and only time she'd ever had sex had been an awful experience she hadn't ever wanted to repeat.

But now, looking at Chase perpetuated more than mild curiosity; for a single moment she wondered if making love with him would be different. She blinked, and stepped away from the window. How could she have forgotten just who Chase was? He was a West-moreland, for heaven's sake! She refused to become a lust-crazed lunatic over someone from a family of liars who had accused her grandfather of being a thief. It didn't matter to her that Chase was the epitome of everything male. He was a Westmoreland and that meant he was definitely off-limits.

"Who is she?"

A smile caught the corner of Chase's mouth as his attention was drawn from the window where Jessica had been standing back to his brother Storm. "Need I remind you that you're married?" Chase replied.

Storm chuckled as he shook his head. "No. Jayla is the love of my life and all the woman I'd ever need, and the girls are the icing on the cake," he said of his three-month-old twin daughters. "But it seems to me that she has gotten your attention."

The smile faded from Chase's lips. Jessica Claiborne had definitely caught his attention and from the moment they met. "Her name is Jessica Claiborne. We didn't hit it off at first."

Storm's lips tilted in amused humor. "And now?"

Chase leaned against the building. "I think she still doesn't like me."

Storm lifted his brows. "First impressions can be changed if you work hard at it," he said as he watched his brother's gaze shift back to the window where the woman had been standing earlier. He glanced at his watch. "I have to go. I just wanted to make sure you knew about the christening on Sunday."

"Yes, Mom mentioned it. I think the restaurant is perfect for the after-christening dinner."

Storm smiled. "Are you sure? I wouldn't want you to go to any trouble."

"No trouble for my nieces. Consider it done. Tell Jayla that I'll call her sometime tomorrow to discuss the menu."

"Ok, I'll do that."

Chase watched his twin brother get into his car and pull away. He hesitated for a moment not ready to go back inside and glanced at the confectionery again, wondering whether Jessica had enjoyed the meal he'd had prepared for her. There was only one way to find out.

Shoving his hands into his pockets he walked past Mrs. Morrison's seamstress shop until he stood directly in front of Delicious Cravings. Ignoring the Closed sign on the door, he knocked a couple of times then rang the doorbell. Moments later a soft voice asked. "Who is it?"

"Chase."

She slowly opened the door and glared at him. "What do you want now?"

The bitterness that was still in her voice surprised him. He would have thought that if his apology hadn't done the trick, certainly a meal from Chase's Place had smoothed her over. Evidently not. He heaved a sigh.

She had folded her arms over her chest and he wished she hadn't done that. Although he was a leg man first, he was a breast man second and the position of her arms clearly empathized what a nice, firm, full pair she had. At that moment he actually envied her tank top.

He cleared his throat and said, "I saw you standing at the window."

Her gaze sharpened. "So?"

He smoothed a hand across his forehead. Maybe where she came from, people were unfriendly and unpleasant, but here in the South people were warm and gracious. "Is it too much to hope that you enjoyed dinner?" he asked.

She actually seemed surprised by his question. "Of course I enjoyed dinner. Why would you think that I hadn't?"

"Your attitude."

Jessica clamped down her jaw down from jutting out. Okay, so once again he hadn't seen her at her best, but there was a reason for it. He was a Westmoreland and she was a Graham.

Sighing, she dropped her hands to her side. "Look, don't take it personally, but I don't like you."

Chase leaned in the doorway and crossed his legs at the ankles. "Why?"

She waved her hand impatiently. "I'd think it would be obvious."

He lifted a brow. "You think we're opposites?"

She drew in an angry breath and met his gaze. "I don't know you that well, but I'd say we're as different as day and night."

Chase straightened and shot her a grin. "Then that explains it."

She narrowed an eye. "Explains what?"

"Why we're attracted to each other. Opposites attract."

Jessica snorted a breath. "I am not attracted to you!"

Chase's grin widened. "Yes, you are, and I'm attracted to you as well," he said, standing with his legs braced apart, his gaze intense, and shoulders squared.

"Believe whatever you want."

"Would you like to prove otherwise?"

She raised a questioning brow. "How?"

Chase shrugged. "Never mind, this isn't a good time to—"

"Wait! If there's a way I can prove that I'm not attracted to you then let's bring it on," she snapped.

Chase met her gaze. "Fine with me if you're sure that's what you want to do."

Jessica's shoulders were rigid with anger. "And just what is it we need to do to prove it?"

"Kiss."

At first Jessica was stunned. But then she figured it would be just like a man to want to prove anything by locking lips. Well, he would find out that she didn't enjoy kissing any more than she had making love. This was destined to be the shortest kiss on record.

She met his gaze and smiled. "Like I said, let's bring it on."

The way Chase returned her smile had her thinking that maybe, just maybe, she'd made a mistake. And when he walked past her into her shop, she had a sinking feeling in the pit of her stomach that that was definitely so.

* * *

Damn, Chase thought as he gazed at Jessica's mouth. He was going to enjoy every minute, every second that he devoured it. He bet it was as sinfully sweet and delicious as all those treats she whipped up. Sweeter.

As he continued to stare at her, pure, unadulterated lust rushed through his veins, pricked every pore of his skin and slashed waves of heat through his body. He could even go so far to say that he felt the cells in his groin reproducing.

Need propelled him from where he was standing across the room to her. He gently clasped the back of her head and pulled her closer, her lips mere inches from his. "I intend to kiss you witless," he whispered huskily.

She jutted her chin and narrowed her gaze. "You can try."

He smiled, liking her spunk. Chase hoped like hell that she put all that haughtiness into their kiss. "Open your mouth for me, sweetheart," he whispered in a deep, throaty voice.

Releasing a frustrated sigh, Jessica opened her mouth to tell him a thing or two, but with lightning speed he seized the opportunity and planted his mouth firmly on hers, silencing whatever she was about to say.

He groaned deep within his throat. His tongue thick and hot captured hers and savored it like spicy gingerbread. She had never been kissed this way before; never in her wildest imagination had she envisioned something like this happening to her.

Chase devoured her mouth like a dessert he had to

have, doing passionate, provocative and illicit things to it. The man was skilled, trained, experienced and knew just what to do to make those purring sounds suddenly erupt from deep within her throat.

She couldn't believe it. With his kiss, sensual urges—intense and strong—that she didn't recognize attacked her entire being, demanding that her body react and respond to him. She was grateful for the strong arms holding her close; otherwise she would have melted to the floor by now. She felt intense fire licking its way through her veins, her insides were simmering in heat. She was mesmerized to the point of no return.

But that's not all she felt.

His hardness, his strength, one hell of an erection was cradled between her thighs. She felt delirious, and when an involuntary shudder raced through her, she suddenly realized something. She was kissing him back. She never kissed men back. The thought overwhelmed her, overloaded her senses and sent intense heat rippling through her body.

If this didn't beat all. They had just met that day. He was a Westmoreland. She didn't like him. She didn't like kissing. She needed to breathe.

As if he'd read her last thought, he slowly released her mouth. As she stared up at him she couldn't believe they had shared something so powerful, provoking and intimate. A part of her wondered what one should say after such a stimulating encounter. But at the moment she couldn't say anything. The only thing she could think about was the way his mouth felt and how much she'd enjoyed kissing him.

"Let me go on record to say I only ended the kiss

so we could breathe," he whispered, reaching up and sliding his fingers through her hair. "We might be opposites, but like I said earlier, Jessica, we do attract."

The huskiness of his words sent shivers all through her and her skin was beginning to feel hot all over again. She could actually feel her blood sizzling. He took a step back and a warm smile tilted the corners of his lips.

"Best wishes on opening day tomorrow," he said softly.

She watched as he turned and walked out of the shop, closing the door behind him.

"I'm looking forward to working for you, Ms. Claiborne."

It had been a busy grand-opening day. The huge crowd had come and gone and they were now able to relax and take a breather. Jessica smiled at the woman, old enough to be her grandmother, and replied, "I'm looking forward to working with you, too, Mrs. Stewart. I'm just so grateful that you could help me out. I'd feel a lot better if you called me Jessica."

Delicious Cravings had officially opened at eight o'clock that morning. Jessica had been quite busy and was grateful when Ellen Stewart had walked in the shop at eleven to help with the lunch-hour traffic. But no matter how busy she'd gotten, she couldn't forget the kiss she had shared with Chase last night. It had been amazing.

Switching her thoughts elsewhere, she watched Mrs. Stewart as she dusted off the counter, thinking the woman was a huge asset to the shop with her knowledge of retail sales as well as her genuine friendliness. It seemed she knew everyone who had come in. She was a definite plus for business. But then so was Chase Westmoreland.

Most of the people who had dropped by to make a purchase had mentioned that Chase claimed her treats were to die for. She hated admitting it, but she owed him a degree of gratitude as well, although the last thing she wanted was to owe a Westmoreland anything.

"I think it was very nice of Chase to send you customers. He's such a sweetheart."

Jessica stopped placing brownies in the display case and turned a curious gaze to Ms. Stewart. "You know Chase?"

The woman chuckled. "Of course I do. I know all the Westmorelands. Although most of the people living in Atlanta are transplants, there are still a few of us natives hanging around. I knew those Westmoreland boys and their cousins when they were in elementary school. In fact, I taught most of them."

Jessica nodded, remembering Mrs. Stewart had mentioned she had retired as a teacher over fifteen years ago. "They got into mischief like boys would do but I didn't know a more respectful group," Mrs. Stewart added. "Did you know that his brother Dare is the sheriff of College Park?"

Jessica lifted a brow. "No, I didn't know that."

"Well, he is and a good one at that. And then there's Thorn, who builds motorcycles and races them. Stone writes blockbuster books. There are also a bunch of Westmoreland cousins, like Jared, the well-known attorney. Oh, and I can't forget Storm, Chase's twin brother, although they aren't identical."

Jessica raised a brow, finding all Mrs. Stewart was telling her intriguing. "So I guess that means you know their parents as well."

Mrs. Stewart smiled warmly. "Yes. The Westmorelands are wonderful people. I knew the grandparents, too."

Jessica leaned against the counter. "Really? I understand that Chase's grandfather used to own a restaurant years ago."

Mrs. Stewart chuckled as she wiped off the counter. "Yes, and just like Chase's Place, it served the most delicious home-cooked meals around. Truckers made up the bulk of Scott Westmoreland's busy clientele, but people would come from miles around to eat his food made from secret family recipes handed down through generations. I understand Chase uses some of those same recipes and guards them like a hawk, especially after what happened when his granddad discovered that someone gave away the secret recipes to his chili, beef stew and broccoli casserole."

Jessica swallowed deeply. "How did that happen?" she asked innocently.

"I'm not sure but Scott claimed his partner, a man by the name of Carlton Graham, gave—"

"That is not true. He would not have done such a thing!"

At Jessica's strong defense of Carlton Graham, Mrs. Stewart eyed her curiously before saying, "I recall Carlton and Helen moved to California to be near their daughter and granddaughter." She lifted a curious brow. "Is there any chance Carlton Graham is a relative of yours?"

Jessica nodded, knowing there was no way she could lie to the woman. "Yes, he was my grandfather."

Mrs. Stewart's eyes widened. "Does Chase know that?"

Jessica shook his head. "No, and I don't intend to tell him until I can prove my grandfather's innocence."

"And how do you plan to do that?"

Jessica shrugged. "I'm going to start digging around in my spare time. Someone stole those recipes and deliberately made it look like my grandfather had done it. I promised my grandmother before she died that I would clear the Graham name of any wrongdoing."

Mrs. Stewart nodded. "You might want to ask Donald Schuster since it was his restaurant that ended up with the recipes."

Jessica lifted a brow. "Is he still around?"

"Yes. He's done well over the years. There's probably over a hundred Schuster's Restaurants nationwide, a few in every state, even out in California. And people claim they have the best chili around—chili some say was derived from a Westmoreland recipe."

Jessica nodded. She had heard of the chain of restaurants and had even eaten at one. "What can you tell me about Chase?"

Ms. Stewart sighed deeply. "He's a decent man who unfortunately had his heart broken years ago by a woman he met while at college. It's my understanding they met at Duke University where Chase had gotten a basketball scholarship. Everyone said that she clung to him like glue while he had a promising future in the pros. But when an injury ended any chance of that happening she dropped him like a hot potato. He's never dated another woman seriously."

The two were silent for a few moments then Ms. Stewart spoke again. "I'd like to give you a little advice if I can."

Jessica nodded. "Sure."

"Don't wait too long to tell Chase the truth about your connection to Carlton Graham. It will be better if he hears it from you than from someone else, and if you start asking questions that's bound to happen."

She leaned closer and paused a moment as if searching for words to explain. "Although all of this happened over eighteen years ago, Scott Westmoreland was deeply hurt by what he saw as an outright betrayal. In fact, he had a heart attack not long after that."

Jessica's eyes widened. She hadn't known that. "He did?"

"Yes, although I can't blame it all on stress involving the recipes. Scott was a heavy smoker and I'm sure that played a huge part in it, too, especially since he eventually died of lung cancer."

The older woman sighed deeply. "I'm not saying your granddaddy did or didn't do what the Westmorelands claim. All I'm saying is that they believe that he did it. Chase, the one closest to his grandfather, took the old man's pain and suffering personally and for years he'd tried to make Schuster admit they were preparing foods using Westmoreland recipes. Schuster refused to do so, and since there wasn't any proof, Chase eventually let the matter drop. But I doubt very seriously that he's forgotten about it."

A short while later, with only ten minutes left to closing time, Jessica was alone in her shop. She knew she had earned some pretty good profits for the first day. She sighed as she made her way over to the display case to pack up what was left of today's inventory. She had made prior arrangements with the children's hospital to donate any treats left from that day and knew someone was on their way to get them.

She couldn't help remembering what Mrs. Stewart had told her about Chase and the girl he'd fallen in love with at college. And although she hadn't wanted to feel sympathy for him, she had. The worst thing for someone to do is kick you when you're already down, and his ex-girlfriend had done just that. She hoped that over the years he had realized that he was better off without her. She wished at some point her mother had realized that she was better off without Jeff Claiborne.

She heard the tinkling of the bell on the front door, and turned, thinking it was the courier from the hospital.

Her breath caught in her throat when she saw it was Chase.

Three

"Hello, Jessica."

All day Chase had had her on his mind, and a part of him needed to see her, to see if what they had shared the day before had been reality or make-believe. And seeing her now let him know it had been real. She was as beautiful as he had remembered, everything about her was as much of a turn-on as he'd recalled.

When she continued to look at him without saying anything, he said, "I thought you probably didn't have time to eat lunch so I brought you dinner."

He watched her nervously nibble on her bottom lip and his guts clenched. "Thanks, but you didn't have to do that. I had planned to go to one of those hamburger places down the street."

He frowned. "The food at Chase's Place is tastier and better for you." He crossed the room and handed her a doggie bag. "You may want to get started on this while it's still warm."

Jessica took the bag from him and placed it on the counter. Chase was the last person she wanted to deal with right now. Seeing him here, in her shop, sent flashes of the kiss they'd shared through her mind. A part of her wanted to be angry at him for making her feel the way she did, but it was hard for her to continue to be mad at a man who went out of his way to be nice to her. And he was being nice....

She heard the tinkling of the bell on the door and turned around as a woman walked in. "Hello, I'm Gloria Miller," the woman said. "I'm here to pick up your donation for the children's hospital." She glanced over at Chase and smiled. "Hi, Chase."

"How are you, Gloria?"

"I can't complain."

Jessica couldn't help wondering if Chase knew practically everyone or everyone knew him. "I hope the children enjoy these," she said, handing the woman the sealed box.

The woman grinned warmly. "I'm sure they will. Thanks for this delicious contribution." Moments later she was gone.

"That was thoughtful of you," Chase said as he glanced out the window and watched Gloria pull off.

Jessica shrugged. "No big deal. I operated on the cautious side today and baked more than I needed. I don't want to sell anything that isn't fresh tomorrow so I thought I'd donate what was left to the children's hospital."

"How will you handle the overstock inventory tomorrow?"

"I hope to bake only enough. I don't mind having a few items left but not as much as I had today. And speaking of today, I want to thank you."

Chase grinned. "You already have."

Jessica shook her head. "I'm not talking about dinner," she said. "I'm talking about all the referrals. A number of people who came in mentioned you had sent them and I appreciate the business."

He leaned against the counter. "I'm sure I wasn't the only one. The Criswell brothers dropped by for lunch and they were telling everyone about your fudge and how delicious it tasted. So they're responsible for increasing your business, too."

Jessica nodded. "I'll thank them as well when I see them." She walked over to the door after checking her watch. "It's closing time."

Chase checked his watch. "So it is."

When Chase didn't make any attempt to leave, Jessica put up the closed sign and locked the door. She also pulled down the shade to the display window, and the moment she did the interior of the shop got somewhat dark and way too intimate. "Will you get the lights, Chase?"

"In a moment."

She watched as he crossed the room, stopping directly in front of her. "Do you know what I thought about a lot today, Jessica?"

She didn't respond right away and she refused to meet his gaze. "No, what did you think about?"

He reached out and touched her chin, forcing her eyes to meet his. "The kiss we shared last night."

A part of her wanted to shout for him to get over it, but how could she expect him to when she hadn't? She had thought about it a lot that day as well. "We barely know each other, Chase. We just met yesterday. Things are moving too fast."

"You're right," he said gently, evenly. "So this is what I'd like to propose."

She lifted a brow. "What?"

"That we take the time to get to know each other."

"Why?" she asked, trying to understand. "Why should we do that?" The last thing she wanted was to become seriously romantically involved with anyone. She had a lot on her plate starting up her business. And all of her spare time was devoted to starting her investigation. The first person she intended to talk to was Donald Schuster. He was the one person who she hoped could help prove her grandfather's innocence.

"I think the answer is obvious," Chase said, interrupting her thoughts. "You don't like me. That bothers me because I don't understand why. Whenever I get within ten feet of you, I can feel your guard going up. I'm also bothered by the fact that I'm very attracted to you and I don't like being this drawn to a woman I don't really know. Hell, I didn't get much work done today for thinking about you."

"Then I suggest that you try shifting your attention elsewhere."

"I doubt if that will work. I want you."

Jessica went numb. She'd never met a man who expressed his interest in her so blatantly.

"I hope my directness didn't shock you."

She met his gaze. Yes, it had shocked her. Her heart was flip-flopping in her chest, not to mention the heat that had settled in the pit of her stomach. In California, men enjoyed playing games and you rarely knew what they were thinking, where you stood or what their intent was. "You're an attractive man, Chase, and I'm sure you date," she decided to say.

He smiled. "Not much and especially not a lot in the past six months." When she opened her mouth to continue, he pressed two fingers across her lips. "I'm not asking you to marry me, Jessica. I just want us to get to know each other. You're new in town and I'd like to show you around, introduce you to people, and spend time with you."

"You're a man. You'll eventually want more than that."

"Will I?"

"Yes." Panic gripped her. Never before had a man made her lose all sense of logic. Chase Westmoreland was powerful, dangerous and all male, and those three things had her worried.

Chase knew to tell her that she was wrong, that he wouldn't eventually want more, would be an outright lie. He glanced over at the bag sitting on her counter. "Go ahead and enjoy your food." Then, without missing a beat, he asked, "How about a movie tomorrow night?"

She blinked then stared into his eyes. He was smoothly changing the subject and they both knew it. "A movie tomorrow night?"

"Yes, a movie," he whispered, and the deep sensuous tone of his voice vibrated her nerve endings. "I'll pick you up around seven."

Her senses told her the last thing she needed to do was to begin dating a Westmoreland, but he might have some of the answers she needed. She couldn't overlook that fact. "A movie sounds nice. I'll be ready at seven." She then reached for the doorknob. "Now you can leave."

She pushed a wayward curl back from her face, inhaled and waited. His gaze was locked on hers, arousing her, making her nipples harden against her blouse. She wondered if he was aware of her body's response to him. His scent made her want to nuzzle her face into his neck and

She closed her eyes, refusing to go there. When she slowly opened her eyes, he was there, his lips mere inches from hers. She inhaled sharply. The stir of sensual need suddenly overwhelmed her.

"You feel it like I do, Jessica," he whispered. "Don't ask me why it's happening because I don't know, but it's as if this place, this time, these moments between us were meant to be and we don't have any control over anything."

Jessica tipped her head back, refusing to look at things that way. But when he raised his fingertips to her lips, she instinctively parted them. He was right. It was as if neither of them had control over the moment. She didn't want to get romantically involved with him but a need to kiss him again was sending sensual charges all through her body. And from the way he was looking at her, she could tell he felt them.

She struggled to push down this passionate side

she hadn't been aware she had. She was an ace at confrontation as an attorney, but Jessica was a novice when it came to the kind of deep-in-the-gut sensations that had her lips quivering.

"Please let me kiss you, Jessica."

With the sound of his voice, deep, husky and sexy, he didn't have to ask twice and she tilted her lips up to him. The moment their mouths connected, she swallowed a groan and let his tongue do all kinds of naughty things, pushing her pulse into overdrive and causing tingles to erupt inside her stomach. This kiss was based on more than mutual attraction and gratification. There were elements taking over that scared her to death. He was a fantastic kisser and knew he would be a great lover…but she didn't intend to sleep with him. Ever.

If only she really meant it.

She pulled back. He needed to leave. Now. "Goodbye, Chase."

He smiled. "Goodbye. I'll see you tomorrow night at seven."

And then he was gone.

The following evening Jessica breathed deeply as she crossed the room to open the door. It was exactly seven o'clock and, not surprisingly, Chase was punctual. She glanced down at herself. She had dressed casually in a pair of jeans and pullover sweater.

Jessica felt her pulse shudder when she unlocked the door to find Chase standing there. As expected, he was looking tall, dark and gorgeous. She wondered if he had any idea how he had disrupted her sleep the past two nights. "Chase."

"Jessica."

"Would you like anything to drink before we leave?" She felt another shudder pass through her when she noticed how his gaze was lingering on her mouth. A part of her wished more than anything she was immune to his robust masculinity but unfortunately she wasn't.

"No. Do you have any chocolate chip cookies left from today?"

Jessica couldn't help but smile. He sounded just like a little kid being set loose in the toy section of a department store. "Yes, I do and I remembered that they are your favorite. I've boxed them up already. You can have them when we get back."

"Oh, really…" he said as a smile spread over his face.

Jessica grinned. "Yes, really. Now are we ready to leave?"

"Let's go."

"Are you hungry?"

Jessica glanced up at Chase as they walked out of the theater. She couldn't help but chuckle. "Are you kidding? I'm the one who ate most of the popcorn, at least two hot dogs, not to mention a super-size drink and a box of gummy worms."

A corner of Chase's mouth tilted in a smile as he took her hand in his. "It's okay. I'm not a big fan of junk food."

"Umm, I can imagine. Who comes up with the menu for Chase's Place?"

"Usually I do, but Kevin gives his input."

"Kevin?"

"He's my cook but every once in a while if he's out, I do the cooking. Kevin and I are the only ones who know the Westmoreland family recipes and he's bound by a legal contract never to divulge our secrets. I had to take such measures after what happened to my grandfather years ago. He got burned putting too much trust in his partner."

Jessica swallowed the thick lump in her throat. She already knew the story, at least her grandmother's version. Now she wanted to hear Chase's. "What happened?"

"Years ago, a man by the name of Carlton Graham did most of the cooking while my grandfather handled the administrative duties. The two worked together for years and then had a dispute over something and parted ways. A few weeks later Granddad found out that Carlton had sold the secrets of a few of the Westmorelands' prize-winning recipes to a rival restaurant. Needless to say my grandfather never got over the betrayal. Those stolen recipes had been in the Westmoreland family for generations."

Jessica had to bite down on her lips to stop from coming to her grandfather's defense as she'd done with Mrs. Stewart. "And how did your grandfather know who stole the recipes?" she asked, trying not to give Chase a reason to question her interest.

By now they had reached Chase's car and he opened the door for her. "Because nobody else knew the ingredients. Also, my grandfather kept his recipe book under lock and key and no one else besides Carlton had access to it."

So of course he blamed my grandfather, she thought as she slid into the leather seat of Chase's sports car. "What about other people who worked at your grandfather's restaurant?"

Chase shrugged. "As far as I can remember—I was only fifteen or sixteen at the time—the only other people who worked there were two waitresses, Miss Paula and Miss Darcy, and neither knew the recipes. Their job was to wait tables and take care of the customers."

Jessica nodded, thinking she had asked enough questions. The last thing she needed was for him to become suspicious.

She wished she could level with him and tell him that she was Carton Graham's granddaughter, but to do so would be a mistake until she could prove her grandfather's innocence.

Chase closed the door and walked around the car to get inside. He turned to her before starting the ignition. "You never said if you were hungry."

She shook her head and met his gaze. "No, I'm not hungry but if you are then we can stop and get you something."

He smiled. "I have an even better idea. How about if we go back to your place so I can dig into those cookies? And it would be wonderful if you have some milk. There's nothing like a big, cold glass of milk with chocolate chip cookies."

Just for a second Jessica wondered if taking Chase back to her place and inviting him inside was a good thing. But they had said they wanted to get to know each other better and she had found out some information from him tonight. On Monday she would ask Mrs. Stewart about the waitresses who used to work for Chase's grandfather to see if they were still around. Maybe she could talk to them as well.

"Yes, I have milk and after such a wonderful evening the least I can do is take you back to my place and let you indulge your taste buds a little."

A corner of Chase's mouth tilted into a smile as he started the car. "Umm, indulge my taste buds? Now that's certainly one way of looking at it."

Four

"I don't think you really know how delicious these cookies are, Jessica."

Jessica leaned back in her chair and smiled, pleased with Chase's compliment. "I bet you say that to all the girls."

After taking a huge swallow of milk Chase licked his lips and smiled. "No, honestly, I don't. In fact most of the women I've dated couldn't cook worth a damn, which is probably the reason I was such an asset to them. If nothing else, I was able to feed them."

She grinned and wished she wasn't so affected by that smile of his. He had been at her place for over an hour, and during that time she had sipped her coffee while listening to him tell her about his family. She could actually feel the love he had for his siblings although he tried convincing her that his four brothers were nothing but pains.

However, he had spoken fondly about his baby sister Delaney, who would be flying into town tomorrow from the Middle East with her husband and son. A christening was planned on Sunday for his brother Storm's twin baby girls. And a christening dinner party would be held after the church service at Chase's Place.

"You've let me do a lot of talking, now it's your turn," Chase said, interrupting her thoughts.

She lifted a brow. "It's my turn?"

"Yes, tell me about yourself, Jessica."

For just a second she pressed her lips, together wondering what she could say that wouldn't lead him to make a connection to her and Carlton Graham. And if he remembered her grandfather then there was a strong possibility he would remember her grandmother as well.

She leaned forward, knowing she would have to be careful about what she said. She didn't want to deceive him but, for now, the less he knew the better. "I was born in Sacramento, California, but went to law school at UCLA and—"

"Law school? You're an attorney?"

She heard deep surprise in his voice and smiled. "I was and I guess legally I still am since I'm still licensed there. I worked for a huge corporation and was hired right out of law school. But over the years I saw just how much integrity the company lacked and often had to defend a lot of their practices that I knew were wrong."

She took a sip of her coffee, remembering those times. "I probably would have still been there if it hadn't been for my grandmother. She died and left me an inheritance that I used to open Delicious Cravings."

Chase bit into another cookie. "What about your parents?"

"My mom was a single parent," she said quietly. "For fifteen years she believed my father would marry her, only to find out that he'd strung her along. He couldn't marry her because he was already married with a family living in Philadelphia."

She watched Chase go still. Saw the anger that came into his eyes and studied the frown that bunched his forehead. "How in the hell was he able to pull that off?" he asked.

Jessica sighed. "He was a salesman and traveled a lot. His home base was in Pennsylvania but he dropped in and paid us a visit whenever he was in town. He was able to pull off his duplicity for fifteen years because my mother never questioned his comings and goings."

She took another sip of her coffee then added, "I hated him the most when he would show up unexpectedly. My mother was a different person around him. She became weak, vulnerable and dependent. If he said *jump* she would purr, *How high?*"

Chase nodded. Although he had known Jessica only for a few days he knew she did not take after her mother. He couldn't picture any man dominating her that way. More than likely she had seen her mother live that kind of life and refused to live it herself. "How did your mom find out the truth?"

A part of Jessica wondered why she was telling him any of this, but she knew the reason. She had discovered earlier that she felt comfortable with him. "She didn't find out. My granddad did. It had always bothered him that my father never married my mother and I guess he thought fifteen years was long enough. He also got suspicious of my father's drop-in visits and hired a private investigator who ferreted out the truth."

Chase wiped his mouth, then tossed his balled-up napkin into the garbage can that sat across the room. "How did your mother handle it when she found out the truth?" he asked, turning his attention back to her.

A shudder went through Jessica when she remembered that time. "She didn't handle it. In fact she was so devastated, so humiliated, that she overdosed on sleeping pills."

"I'm so sorry," Chase whispered and reached across the table, taking her hand in his. "That must have been awful for you."

Jessica's heart began beating wildly when Chase's hand enclosed hers. She studied his hands for a moment. They were large, strong and comforting. "It was," she said quietly. "I was fifteen and all alone except for my grandparents. I went to live with them after that. They were super and helped me through a very difficult time. Jennifer was also there for me."

"Jennifer?"

"Yes, Jennifer Claiborne, my father's legal wife. She divorced him after she found out what he'd done. Being the warm, loving and caring person that she is, she opened her arms and heart to me. She sent for me every summer so I could get to know my brother and sister and she became my second mom. She also demanded in the divorce decree that my father establish a college fund for me like he had for my sister and brother."

Chase smiled. "She sounds like one hell of a tough lady."

"She is and I know I can call on her if I ever need anything. She's always been supportive, and considering the circumstances, I think that's admirable. A lot of women would not have done all the things she did to help me put my life together after Mom died."

"What about your father?" he asked, leaning forward. Jessica's nostrils couldn't help but absorb his aftershave, which mingled with his masculine scent and was making her pulse rate escalate.

"After the divorce my father sort of dropped out of everyone's life. Last I heard he was living somewhere in New York."

"The bastard," Chase said, anger and disgust evident in his voice. "What made you decide to move to Atlanta?"

Jessica paused at his question. She couldn't tell him the real reason she had chosen Atlanta. "Mainly the cost of living. Compared to other progressive areas in the country, Atlanta gave me more for my buck and when the real estate agent located this building and said it included an apartment on top, I knew it was perfect."

She slowly pulled her hands out of his and leaned back in her chair. "I think you've eaten enough sweets for one night, Mr. Westmoreland." She glanced at her watch. "Besides that, I can sleep in late on Saturdays, but you can't."

Chase grinned. "True, but you'll need breakfast, too,

so how about joining me tomorrow? Kevin can throw down with grits and eggs."

She cocked her head and studied him. "Is that an invitation?"

"Yes, that's exactly what it is. Then if you aren't too busy you can go to a game with me around noon."

She lifted a brow? "A game?"

"Yes, I coach a basketball team of teens at the community center in College Park, and there's a game tomorrow. Chase's Crusaders against Willie's Warriors."

Jessica shook her head grinning. "Hey, I thought this was football season."

"To some people it is, but to parents who want their sons to become the Michael Jordan of tomorrow, every season is basketball season. So will you go with me?"

Jessica smiled. Although she knew she should turn him down, she said, "Basketball in October, how can I resist? By the way, who's Willie?"

Chase chuckled. "He's the coach for the other team and owns a video franchise a few blocks away. He played professionally for the Pistons a few years ago. We went to high school together and have remained good friends."

Jessica nodded. Of all the things they had talked about tonight, he hadn't mentioned anything about his dream to play for the pros. She watched him as he stood.

"Will you walk me to the door?"

"Of course."

He strolled across the room to check out her cooking pots as well as the molds that were sitting on the candy-making table. "One day you're going have to let me watch you make a batch of chocolate candy."

"Umm, maybe one day I will." She tried concentrating on what he was saying and not on what he was wearing, but there was something scrumptious about a man with wide shoulders and muscled arms in a black pullover sweater. Add a pair of denim jeans on a well-built body with firm thighs and what you got was one hell of a sexy man.

They walked together as she led him out of the kitchen to the door. Jessica tried to downplay the flutter in her stomach but couldn't, since she knew there was a good chance…a really good chance…that he would kiss her good-night. She hated admitting it but she was looking forward to his kiss.

"Breakfast in the morning?" he asked when they reached her door.

She shrugged. "Maybe. But the game is a definite."

"All right, I'll pick you up at eleven."

He leaned forward, his lips just inches from hers. "We're going to have to do something special next Wednesday," he said softly with his gaze totally transfixed on her mouth.

"Why?"

"We'll have known each other a week then." A corner of his mouth curved into a smile. "I can tell you're beginning to like me. For a while there I was worried."

They were standing so close that Jessica could feel the warmth of his breath across her face and the manly scent of him had settled firmly in her nostrils. "You want me to like you?" she asked, voluntarily scooting closer to him as he placed his hands at her waist.

"Yeah, I want you to like me. I'm a likable guy, but I can have my bad days just like anyone else."

"I'll try and remember that."

"Please do."

And then he lowered his mouth to hers. She had a pair of incredible lips and he would never get tired of kissing her. And her taste was so damn good. He wouldn't get much sleep tonight. He already knew that. So he figured he needed to remember every moment of this, every lick, every nibble, to get him through the night.

He liked the sound of her moaning. He liked the way her tongue was mating with his, and he liked the way she was sliding her hands up his shoulders. But more than anything, he loved her hot taste. He knew if he didn't stop now and pull back he would be tempted to sweep her into his arms and take her upstairs.

Moments later he broke off the kiss and whispered. "You are one hell of a woman." Jessica watched as he opened the door and walked out.

Closing and locking the door behind him, she inhaled deeply. Chase Westmoreland was as delicious as the chocolate treats she loved, but she couldn't allow herself to give in to the craving.

"You were missed at breakfast."

Jessica smiled as she stepped back to let Chase inside. As he walked into the middle of the shop with a cup of coffee in his hand, the morning sun that flowed through the display window highlighted his features and she immediately felt a sense of longing and desire.

"I decided to use my time doing something else besides eating," she said. "Win or lose I believe Chase's Crusaders deserve a treat so I spent the morning baking cookies."

Evidently surprised, he cocked his head and stared at her. "You did?"

She grinned. "Yes, I did. I figured it was the least I could do to contribute to such a worthy cause. I think it's wonderful that you're taking the time to spend with them."

Chase shrugged. "It's no big deal. They are a wonderful group of kids. Besides, I love basketball. It was my dream to play in the pros but an injury stopped me. So I finished college and came back here."

She nodded. "That's when you decided to open your restaurant?"

He smiled and leaned against the counter. "No, that idea didn't come until three years later. Like you, I got a job in corporate America, working as a financial adviser. It didn't take me long to get fed up with office politics and make a career change."

He laughed. "Believe it or not, the idea for opening a restaurant came from my brothers. I'm the one who spent the most time with my grandfather when he was in business. I worked at his restaurant after school and on weekends. So I was the one who he passed all the family recipe secrets to. And since I loved to cook, my brothers—who were all single at the time—usually ended up at my place for dinner, so they suggested I go into business for myself."

He took a sip of his coffee, then added, "I had some money saved, my brothers chipped in and we found the building I'm in now. At first it was a family affair where everyone pitched in and worked, even my parents. But when I started seeing a profit I figured that I could afford to hire paid help."

"And now Chase's Place is a popular hot spot known for its mouth-wateringly delicious soul food," Jessica said, remembering something Mrs. Stewart had told her earlier in the week.

His smile widened. "Yes, and I'm very proud of that."

"You should be. Have you given any thought to franchising?"

"Yes, especially lately. But I have to be certain that the warm, friendly, family atmosphere I've worked so hard to achieve won't get lost."

He glanced at his watch. "Are you ready?"

She smiled. "Yes, I just need help getting the box of cookies out to your car."

She moved across the room to go into the kitchen, and he placed his cup on the counter and intercepted her. She glanced up at him and immediately felt a flutter in her stomach. Warning flags went up—as they had last night—signaling her that they were moving too fast; it was too soon and that she shouldn't get involved with him. He was a Westmoreland—the enemy. But whenever he looked at her the way he was doing now, the last thing she wanted to dwell on was bad blood between their families.

"Let's make plans for next week," he whispered, as one corner of his mouth tilted into a smile.

"What kind of plans?" she found herself asking.

"Dinner at my place Wednesday night around eight."

She lifted a brow. "But I thought you closed early on Wednesday. At six."

His mouth curved even more. "I do. A lot of people around here go to prayer meetings at their church which usually include dinner. But I just happen to know the owner of Chase's Place and he's given me permission to bring a special guest after hours."

She chuckled. "Oh, he did, did he?"

"Yes, he did."

Again, warning flags were flapping around in her head, but at that moment she chose to ignore them and said, "I'd love to have dinner with you Wednesday night."

"Thank you."

And then he leaned down and kissed her.

"We were totally surprised when Chase mentioned he had invited someone to today's game," Tara Westmoreland, the wife of Chase's brother Thorn, said smiling. "And we think it's wonderful."

Jessica was confused. "Why would you think that?" she asked. When she and Chase had arrived at the community center he had taken her to a group of four women. Three he had introduced as his sisters-in-laws—Shelly, Madison and Tara; the other was his cousin Jared's wife, Dana.

It was Shelly, Dare's wife, who answered. "Because Chase is a very private person and he's never brought a date to any of the games before."

Jessica shrugged as she leaned back on one of the bleachers. The game would be starting in less than ten minutes. "I'm not really his date. We met this week when I opened a confectionery a few doors down from his restaurant. I moved here from California, and since I don't know anyone in town he was kind enough to invite me along today."

Madison, who was married to Stone, grinned as she patted Jessica's hand. "Trust me, he never would have brought you over to us if you weren't his date. Chase guards his privacy like a hawk." The other three women agreed and nodded knowingly.

Jessica blinked, not sure what to think. She didn't want anyone assuming that she and Chase were involved. They weren't. She glanced down at the basketball court and saw Chase talking to his brothers and cousins. Anyone who saw the group of men would know they were related. She had met the Westmoreland men earlier and found them to be nice, likeable people, although she hadn't wanted them to be.

On the car ride over, Chase had surprised her by inviting her to his nieces' christening as well as the dinner party he planned to host afterwards at his restaurant tomorrow. To include her in such an important family affair was a bit too much and she had declined. Besides, she had made plans to meet with Donald Schuster tomorrow. She had called him yesterday and he had agreed to meet with her at his home.

"Chase's looking this way again," Tara said grinning. "Smile for Chase, Jessica, so he'll know you're okay and aren't suffering from our company."

Jessica couldn't help but smile. These Westmoreland women were too much. She really liked them. She met Chase's gaze and smiled. He smiled back before directing his attention back to the group of youngsters on his team.

"Don't look now but here come the guys," Dana said, smiling, seeing her husband and his cousins climbing the bleachers toward them.

"They will be as curious about you as we were," Shelly whispered to Jessica grinning.

Jessica shot the women a nervous look. "Surely they aren't going to ask me anything about my relationship with Chase?"

Tara chuckled. "No, they're depending on us to pump you for information and later they'll corner us and expect us to come clean and divulge everything that we know."

"But don't be surprised if Dare asks you questions," Shelly added, grinning. "It's the cop in him so don't take it personally. Besides, he's the oldest of his brothers and is somewhat protective, although he'll never admit it." She leaned back in the bleachers and shook her head and chuckled. "And now that he sees how taken Chase is with you, he's bound to get downright nosy."

Jessica stared at the women, not sure if they were serious. It didn't take long for her to realize they were. She swallowed, thinking the last thing she needed was Sheriff Dare Westmoreland asking her a lot of questions.

By the time the Westmoreland men had reached them she had tried to contain her nervousness.

"So, where are you from, Jessica?" Dare asked, not missing a beat as he eased into the spot next to Shelly.

Jessica forced a smile. "Sacramento. Have you ever been there?"

"Yes, for a law enforcement convention a few years back. It's a nice area," he responded.

"Yes, it is a nice area," she agreed.

"Why did you leave?"

Jessica knew everyone was waiting for her answer. She wasn't one to get rattled easily, but Dare Westmoreland was doing a good job of shaking her composure. It wasn't that he was outright rude in his questioning, but she hated being placed in a situation where she had to explain herself to anyone. But in this case she would. It was obvious that the Westmorelands were a close-knit group and a part of her envied the care and concern that they had for each other.

"Job stress," she finally said, leaning back on the bleacher and tucking a strand of hair behind her ear. "I was an attorney in a—"

"You're an attorney?" Jared cut her off by asking.

Her gaze moved from Dare to Jared who she knew was the attorney in the Westmoreland family. She smiled when everyone fell silent. "Yes. I went to law school at UCLA and then went to work for a large corporation. Starting off I loved my job but over the years I discovered just how much the company lacked integrity and more than once I found myself defending practices that I knew were wrong."

"So you walked away?"

Her gaze moved from Jared to Tara and felt a sense

of relief at the look of admiration in her the other woman's eyes. "Yes, but not before I had what I considered a workable plan. My grandmother passed and left me an inheritance, so I decided to use it to fulfill my dream of opening my own business. I've always enjoyed baking with chocolate and I decided a change in areas and careers was what I needed."

"Why Atlanta?"

Breath held, Jessica shifted her gaze from Tara back to Dare. There was something in his dark-brown eyes that made her wonder if he suspected that there was a lot more than what she was sharing with them. She forced herself to hold his gaze while saying, "I knew someone who used to live here and remembered her saying how nice it was. Besides, everyone knows this is a city on the move. There's something for everyone."

Dare opened his mouth to ask her another question but before he could get the words out, the buzzer sounded, indicating the start of the game. Everyone's attention shifted from her to the activities on the court below. Jessica let out a silent sigh and started to relax somewhat, but then she noticed Dare was still studying her curiously and knew she would have to stay on her guard around him.

"You have to be proud that your team won," Jessica said hours later as she and Chase walked out to his car. After the game the parents had served refreshments. Her delicious baked treats had been a big hit.

"Yes, I am. I think the guys did a good job. They showed good teamwork and that's what's most important, the team and not individual egos. If we can instill that mindset into them now, they'll be better athletes if and when they make it to the pros."

He glanced at his watch. "My sister Delaney and her family should have arrived by now and everyone will be over at my parents' place. Would you like to go over there with me for a while?"

Jessica inhaled deeply. She had enjoyed herself with the Westmorelands at the game today but the last thing she wanted was to continue to give them the impression that she and Chase were an item. "Thanks for the invite, but I think I'm going to turn in early tonight. This has been one busy week for me. The grand opening was great but tiring, and I want to spend the rest of today and tomorrow relaxing."

"All right." He looped an arm around her shoulders as they continued walking toward his car. Chase, Jessica was discovering, was a very nice person and she didn't want to think about what his reaction would be when he found out she hadn't told him everything about herself. But for now, she couldn't. Until she could come to him with proof of her grandfather's innocence, the less he knew the better.

Five

As Jessica drove through the security gate that led to the Schuster estates, she was glad Donald Schuster had agreed to see her. After telling her that he had remembered her grandfather, no doubt he was curious about what she wanted.

As she approached the huge ranch-style home set on what had to be at least four acres of land, she couldn't help but think how quickly she could prove her grandfather's innocence if Mr. Schuster were to tell her who had given him the Westmoreland secret recipes. Then she could present her findings to the Westmorelands and proceed with her life as she had planned. If nothing else, this week had shown her that people wanted a pastry shop in the area and more than once she had been approached with the idea of supplying pastries for neighboring businesses.

Moments later Jessica found herself knocking on a huge wooden door and blinked when a butler dressed in a starched uniform answered. "May I help you, Miss?"

She smiled. "Yes, I'm Jessica Claiborne and I'm here to see Mr. Schuster."

The butler nodded. "He's expecting you."

The butler led the way, and Jessica followed, glancing around at the extravagant surroundings. Everything she saw said *money,* but there was something about the place that reminded her of a museum more than a home.

She stopped when the butler paused and opened a door that led out onto a glassed, enclosed patio. An older man, who would have been close to her grandfather's age had he lived, was sitting in a wheelchair looking out over a huge lake.

"Mr. Schuster, your guest has arrived," the butler announced.

The man immediately turned the wheelchair around to look at her. A smile touched his aged face. "Come in," he said in a strong voice. He offered her a chair across from him. "You said you wanted to ask me questions about your grandfather and that episode with the Westmoreland secret recipes."

Jessica nodded. "Everyone thinks my grandfather is the one who gave them to you."

The man waved a frail hand in the air. "No one gave me anything. Although some of my entrées may have tasted like Westmorelands' they weren't. I tried to tell Scott Westmoreland that, but he was too bull-headed to listen, and I guess it didn't help matters that he knew I'd been trying to convince your grandfather to become my partner. But there was this friendship thing between him and Westmoreland and nothing would shake that."

Jessica was saved from saying anything when the butler brought in a tray of iced tea. When she found herself alone with Mr. Schuster again, she said, "Evidently something did shake their friendship, since he stopped working with Scott Westmoreland."

"Yes, but he would have eventually gone back. The two got into it all the time but they would always resolve their disagreements and get back together. They made a hell of a team. Your grandfather was a great cook and Scott, bless his stubborn hide, was one hell of an entrepreneur. And I understand his grandson Chase Westmoreland is just like him. He's a fantastic chef and has a good head for business when it comes to running a restaurant."

Jessica smiled, thinking that the older man had paid Chase a nice compliment. "And you're sure there's no way you were using any of the Westmoreland recipes?"

The older man chuckled. "At my age I wouldn't bet my life on anything, but my cook at the time said they were was his own recipes, and I had no reason not to believe him."

Jessica nodded again. "Could you tell me his name?"

"Theodore Henry. But we called him Teddy for short."

"Does he still work for you?"

"Heavens no, he stopped working for me years ago.

But I understand Teddy owns a catering company in town."

Jessica took a huge sip of her tea then set the glass down and smiled. "Thanks, Mr. Schuster, you've been a big help and I appreciate you taking the time to see me. I intend to find Mr. Henry and talk to him."

"Hey, Chase, will you quit looking out that window? Jessica hasn't returned yet. If I didn't know better I'd think you were really smitten with her."

Chase turned and frowned at his brother. "I just met her a few days ago, Thorn."

Thorn shrugged, smiling smugly. "So? All it took was a couple of seconds for Tara to knock me off my feet."

Better than her knocking the hell out of you. Chase shook his head, reminiscing. He could vividly recall the night Tara and Thorn had met. Tara had been so mad at Thorn he was lucky she hadn't whacked him. "No one is knocking me off my feet," he finally said.

"If you say so."

Chase inhaled deeply. Sometimes he wished he'd been born an only child.

"Dare thinks there's something suspicious about her," Thorn added.

Chase raised his eyes heavenward. "Dare's a cop. He thinks there's something suspicious about everyone."

Thorn chuckled. "That's true. I don't think he was too happy that she was so close-mouthed about herself and her family."

Chase leaned against a table, remembering what Jessica had shared with him the other night. It wasn't exactly something he'd want to share with the whole world if it had happened to him. He'd felt touched that she had told him as much as she had. "She's a private person, Thorn. Let it go."

Thorn smiled. "Hey, it doesn't bother me if your woman has secrets."

"She's not my woman."

"Who isn't your woman?" their sister Delaney came up and asked.

"The chocolate chip lady," Thorn said grinning. "She makes the best damn chocolate chip cookies."

Chase narrowed his eyes. "She made them for the guys on the team, but I couldn't help noticing that you, Stone and Dare grabbed a few."

Thorn shrugged. "They looked too tasty to pass up and they reminded me of the cookies Grampa's cook used to bake before they went their separate ways years ago. And as far as your team goes, all that sugar in a teenager's mouth isn't good. Think of all the cavities. We did their parents a favor."

Chase was about to say something when he noticed Jessica's car pulling into the parking lot.

"Looks like your woman is back," Thorn said as a smile tilted a corner of his mouth.

Chase shrugged nonchalantly. "So? What of it?"

Thorn rubbed his chin. "That's what I'm wondering myself," he said as he walked out of the room.

It was close to five o'clock by the time Chase had tidied up his restaurant and taken out the last of the trash. His brothers had hung around to help, but he was glad when they'd finally left. They had ribbed him enough for one weekend.

He locked the door to his restaurant and glanced over at Jessica's place wondering what she was doing. She'd said she would spend the weekend relaxing and he didn't want to bother her, but a part of him had to see her.

What he had told Thorn was true. He and Jessica had known each other for only a few days. But he had to admit that in such a short length of time he had learned more about her than he had about some women he'd dated for a full month. He'd learned about all the unhappiness she'd had in her life and how much she enjoyed baking. He liked talking to her and felt comfortable telling her about the injury that had kept him from going to the pros. But he hadn't mentioned anything to her about Iris and the broken heart she had dealt him during that time.

He smiled when he thought of the hit Jessica had been with the kids on his team and their parents. Everyone had appreciated her thoughtfulness in wanting to reward the team with goodies. There hadn't been a shy bone in her body while interacting with everyone, including his family. He liked the way she smiled when she found something amusing, but he also thought her frown was absolutely adorable. During the short time they had known each other, he had told her more about himself than he had shared with any woman before.

But how could he trust her, or any woman? After the episode with Iris, trust wasn't something that came easily with him, especially when it involved a woman. He was a private person, reluctant to talk about his personal business and he pretty much kept things to himself. He did share a close bond with his brothers and cousins, and once in a while he would talk to them about things that were important to him but never about women. No woman had ever gotten close enough to him again to cause that type of grief. They came into his life and they went out of his life. That's the way he wanted it and that's the way he intended to keep it.

So why was he becoming obsessed with Jessica Claiborne?

He strolled over to his car to leave, and just as he was about to unlock the door he paused. Inhaling deeply he turned and began walking toward Jessica's shop. With every step he took he tried to convince himself that he was just being neighborly by checking in on her. He didn't have to go inside. He would just say hello and leave.

But moments later, when she opened the door, all thoughts of leaving suddenly left his mind. It was obvious that she had recently showered. And that she wasn't wearing a bra under her tank top. He blinked, not wanting to stare. She had great-looking breasts. They looked full, firm and lush pressed against the soft fabric of her top. Damn, he shouldn't be looking at her breasts. He wished he could do more than just look at them. Tasting them wasn't such a bad idea right about now.

He tore his gaze away from her chest and his eyes moved downward. She was wearing shorts that showed off her gorgeous legs and he suddenly felt his attraction for her get sharper, more intense.

He should be avoiding Jessica like the plague. Their

relationship was not what his brothers assumed. But still, he was man enough to admit that there was a flicker of forbidden desire that clenched his guts whenever he saw her, came this close to her. Why was he putting himself through such madness? He sucked in a deep breath and smelled her scent—like cinnamon, spice, everything sensual and everything nice.

"Chase?"

He heard his name and then remembered he was standing there and hadn't said anything. "May I come in?" he finally asked.

Her legs somewhat shaky, Jessica met Chase's stare. Getting rid of him would be easy enough. All she had to do was refuse his request to come in. But for some reason she didn't want to. She tried to tell herself that this intense attraction between them had gone on long enough and it was time to take drastic action. Telling him that she was Carlton Graham's granddaughter would guarantee that he would walk away for sure, but she wasn't ready for that to happen. She couldn't tell him who she was until she could also prove her grandfather's innocence.

She sighed deeply and took a step back. When he was inside with the door closed behind him, she saw the heated look of desire in his eyes. Her first instinct was to run, head up the stairs, but she had a feeling he would only come after her. So she might as well stay put and get something they both wanted. For someone who didn't like kissing, she was becoming obsessed with doing it. Her mouth had practically been branded Chase's Place.

Jessica made a move toward Chase, as if drawn by a magnet. At the same time, Chase moved closer to her. "This is crazy," she said in a breathless whisper as she walked into his arms.

"Yeah, totally insane," he said huskily, pulling her closer to him.

She tilted her face up, and he did what was becoming as natural as breathing; he captured her mouth with his, blazing the heat already sizzling between them, satisfying their need to taste each other.

Kissing him got better each time. He had that special technique of letting his tongue sweep the corners of her lips, first sipping her gently like fine wine before deepening the kiss and sucking her tongue into complete submission, mating wildly with it and driving her insane. Only with Chase could she allow herself to open fully and take part in such an intimate exchange. He had the ability to arouse feelings that she wanted to explore. She wasn't able to do anything but stand there, hold on and shudder in his arms.

Moments later, he pulled back, reached out, palmed her face in his hand and brushed a kiss over her forehead. "I wanted to check on you to make sure you were okay." Then, knowing that was really a lame excuse, he added, "And more than anything, I wanted to taste you again."

Giving in to this uncontrollable desire, he leaned closer and kissed her mouth again, wishing he could kiss her forever. He finally lifted his head and their gazes met. And he knew what they had agreed on earlier was true. This was crazy. But that didn't stop him from kissing her again before he finally left.

* * *

She never was good at counting sheep, Jessica thought a few hours later as she lay in her bed gazing up at the ceiling. Who could think of sheep when thoughts of Chase Westmoreland filled her mind?

The taste of him was still fresh in her mouth, and she didn't want to think about the feel of him. Her breath was coming out in short gasps just thinking about the size of the erection that had been cradled between her thighs as he had continued to kiss her deeper and deeper.

She'd known she could have pulled back to stop him at any time but she hadn't wanted him to stop. So he hadn't, until it became obvious that if they continued she would have found herself on the floor with her shorts off, legs spread, and Chase naked between them. After kissing her into sweet oblivion, he had told her that he hoped she slept well tonight then left.

Jessica wasn't sleeping at all. She snapped her eyes shut. Instead of a flock of sheep flooding her mind, she saw Chase as she had seen him earlier that night, just moments before he'd left. He had been standing in her shop, gazing at her with so much desire in his eyes.

She almost jumped when she heard the phone ring and quickly reached over to pick it up while glancing over at the clock. She smiled and sat upright in bed. How could she have forgotten the call she got around this time every Sunday night?

"Hello."

"Hello, Jess, how did things go?"

Jessica's smile widened upon hearing Jennifer's voice. "The grand opening was wonderful."

"Sorry I missed it."

"Trust me, I understand." And she did. Jennifer Claiborne had been appointed school superintendent in Philadelphia, and since the school year had only started a month ago, she hadn't been able to get away.

"Have you heard anything from Savannah lately?" Jessica asked about her sister who was a year older and worked mostly out of the country as a photographer.

"Yes, she called today and said she had tried contacting you, but you weren't home. And she couldn't reach you on your cell phone. Of course she didn't leave a message. You know how she hates talking into those answering machines. I also talked to Rico today and he said to let you know he'll be in your area next week and plans to stop by."

Jessica grinned. "And I'm going to look forward to his visit," she said. Rico was four years older, a private investigator and she simply adored him.

She and Jennifer talked for over an hour. She told her about the information she had gathered to prove her grandfather's innocence.

"And you're sure Chase Westmoreland doesn't have a clue who you are?" Jennifer asked for the second time.

"Yes, I'm sure. He knows me as Claiborne so there's no way he could make the connection." That was the way she wanted things until she was able to tell him everything.

"Well, I hope you're not making a mistake by not telling him the truth up front."

Jessica shook her head. "He's a Westmoreland. He wouldn't trust me. Like his grandfather didn't trust my grandfather."

"It also seems to me from what you've told me about him that he's a nice guy. Possibly someone you could become interested in."

Too easily, Jessica thought, remembering the intense attraction she and Chase shared. "You know how I feel about having a serious relationship, Jennifer."

"Yes, and like you I have reasons to feel that way, but there's a need within all of us to be loved by someone."

Jessica sighed. Until she had met Chase she would have denied that such a need existed, but now…

"I'd better let you go. I'm sure you have a big week ahead of you."

After hanging up the phone, Jessica shifted to a more comfortable position in bed. She couldn't dismiss another type of need trying to take over her mind and body. It was a need she had never experienced before, but one she always encountered whenever she and Chase kissed. It was the need to take things further and enter into a scorching affair with him, based on need, not love, something she had never done before. She wasn't sure if she could handle it. And if she couldn't stand the heat, she should probably just stay out of the kitchen altogether.

Six

"So you remember the two waitresses who used to work for Chase's grandfather?" Jessica asked Mrs. Stewart while restocking the display case with fudge.

"Paula Meyers and Darcy Evans? I sure do," Mrs. Stewart said smiling. "Paula still lives in College Park but Darcy moved to Macon a few years ago to be closer to her family."

"And what about Theodore Henry? Mr. Schuster's former cook?"

"Yes, I knew him, too. He was a single man, nice-looking, soft-spoken, pretty much kept to himself. He rarely went to church, but he didn't bother anybody. He did what he had to do at Schuster's and minded his own business."

Jessica nodded. She intended to speak to Mr. Henry

and Paula Meyers by the end of the week. Getting together with Darcy Evans might take longer since she would have to drive to Macon to do so.

She preferred speaking to everyone in person. From her days as an attorney she learned that face-to-face communication was much more effective than discussing anything over the telephone.

Hours later, after Mrs. Stewart left for the day, Jessica found herself alone in her shop as she tried to decide what would be tomorrow's craving of the day. But the only craving she could think about was the one she had for Chase. She couldn't erase from her mind the enjoyment she got kissing him. It didn't take much for her to remember the gentle yet thorough sweep of his tongue inside her mouth, assailing her senses with every stroke, and how he would feast on her lips. He had the ability to dismantle each and every wall she erected around herself.

And that wasn't good.

She glanced at the clock. She had an hour left before closing time. When Donna, the waitress from Chase's restaurant, had dropped in earlier to buy some brownies, she had casually mentioned that Chase had to leave town unexpectedly for Knoxville, something about a screwup in one of his deliveries, and that he wouldn't be back until Wednesday.

Jessica had accepted Donna's statement with a small shrug, which she hoped indicated her indifference. But the truth of the matter was she wasn't indifferent. How could she be when the thought that she wouldn't be seeing Chase again until Wednesday made her miss him already?

They were supposed to have dinner at his restaurant—after hours—to celebrate a week of knowing each other. He wasn't interested in anything other than enjoying a good wholesome time with a woman, based on friendship and nothing else. Okay, so they did throw a lot of kissing into the mix, she thought. But still their relationship was based on friendship, although that might crumble when he found out her true identity.

She sighed when she heard the phone ring and reached to pick it up. "Delicious Cravings."

"Yes, I'm returning a call to Jessica Graham. This is Paula Meyers."

Jessica smiled. "Yes, Ms. Meyers. Thanks for returning my call."

"Are you sure there won't be anything else, Chase?"

Chase glanced up from looking at the invoice. He was eager to leave Knoxville and head home but it seemed that Sam Nesbitt's daughter was on the prowl again. Storm had dated Cyndi once and now, with Storm happily married, it was obvious that she had shifted her attention to his single brother. "I'm positive. Looks like everything is in order."

"I would definitely agree," she said, giving him a thorough once-over while licking her lips.

Seeing her lick her lips did absolutely nothing for him. If it had been Jessica's lips, there'd be no way he would have been able to downplay the thrill and excitement that would have rushed through him.

"I'm about to close shop, Chase. I know a place where we can go and…get it on."

Chase lifted a brow. Storm had warned him that

Cyndi Nesbitt didn't mince words or waste time. She spoke her mind and told you exactly what she wanted, and most of the time she could get pretty damn graphic. As he gazed at her, he knew she could probably deliver on her offer of recreational sex. But the fact of the matter was he wasn't interested. The only woman he wanted was back in Atlanta.

Placing a polite smile on his face, he said, "Thanks for the offer but I have a few more stops to make before returning to Atlanta sometime tomorrow. Tell your father that I'm sorry I missed him."

A disappointed pout curved her lips. "Yeah, I'll be sure to tell him."

Later that evening Chase was back at his hotel. After taking a shower he lay on the bed and found his mind filled with thoughts of Jessica. Inexplicable warmth flowed through his bloodstream. He had never met anyone quite like her. He shifted his body and rubbed the back of his neck. Okay, he knew he shouldn't be thinking about her so much, but the blind truth was that he couldn't help himself. It was nothing more than a sexual attraction fueled by six months of him doing without, but still, there was something about Jessica that drew him, made it impossible for him to want any other woman but her.

He leaned forward and picked up the business card he had placed on the nightstand earlier, the card Jessica had given him on Saturday for Delicious Cravings. Sighing deeply, he picked up the phone and began dialing. When it began to ring he glanced at his watch. It was close to eight o'clock and he hoped he wouldn't be disturbing her.

"Hello?"

At the sound of her sweet voice he released a long, deep breath. The warmth flowing through his bloodstream increased as he settled back against a huge fluffy pillow. "Hi, Jessica. It's Chase."

Jessica curled her body as she lay on the bed and a heated sensation flowed through her stomach. She took a deep breath. The sound of Chase's voice was doing things to her. "Chase, how are you?"

"A whole lot better now that I'm talking to you."

A thrill shot through Jessica at his words. He definitely knew how to break through a girl's defenses. "I had to leave this morning on an unexpected trip to Knoxville," he was saying, reclaiming her attention. "I've been having problems with my suppliers and I thought a face-to-face meeting was warranted."

Jessica nodded. "I've heard that Knoxville is a beautiful city."

"It is. I gather that you've never been here."

She smiled. "No, I haven't."

"Then I'll have to invite you to come with me the next time I make a trip this way."

Chase murmured the words low, in a deep, husky tone. His breath seemed to transcend the phone lines and warmly caress her ear, heating the flesh along her spine. His invitation wasn't helping matters. "I'd like that." She ignored the warning bells sounding in her ears. She and Chase were moving a little too fast, but she didn't see them slowing down any.

"So, how was your day?" he asked.

She didn't want to think of her meeting that

afternoon with Paula Meyers. The older, sweet and seemingly gentle woman hadn't been able to tell her anything about who might have passed the Westmoreland secret recipes on to the cook at Schuster's restaurant. Jessica would be taking a drive to Macon to talk to Darcy Evans the next afternoon. When she had called, the woman hadn't seem too excited to talk with her.

"Today was wonderful," she said. "Business was good. In fact I got another contract to supply pastries for a nearby hotel."

"Sounds like you're doing well. But then, I knew that you would."

When Jessica tried uncurling her body, heat ran down her spine again. "Thanks." A few moments into the conversation she asked, "So when will you be coming home?"

"Sometime Wednesday. You haven't forgotten about our dinner plans, have you?"

She took a deep breath, not wanting to tell him that she hadn't thought of much else. Even the disappointing dead end with Paula Meyers hadn't dampened her thoughts of sharing a meal with Chase on Wednesday night. "No, I haven't forgotten. I'm looking forward to it," she said truthfully.

"So am I." After a few moments he said, "I'm sure you've had a busy day and need your rest so I'll let you go. Good night, Jessica."

She hated that their phone conversation was coming to an end. "Good night, Chase, and thanks for calling."

After hanging up, Jessica traced the lines of her lips with her fingertips, remembering the time it had been

Chase's tongue and not her finger caressing her lips. The memory sent an arousing shiver through her. As she stretched out in bed she could hear the steady tap of rain beating down on her roof.

Cuddling her pillow she shifted her body into a comfortable position knowing that the moment she closed her eyes, thoughts of Chase would consume her, even while she slept.

Darcy Evans was hiding something.

Jessica could feel it. The woman, who appeared to be in her mid-thirties, said she had only agreed to talk with Jessica because of the respect she'd had for Jessica's grandfather. Eighteen years ago she had been a seventeen-year-old unwed mother in need of a job and Carlton Graham had talked Scott Westmoreland into hiring her as a waitress. She hadn't worked there long when Scott and Carlton parted ways.

"So you have no idea how the Westmoreland recipes could have gotten into the hands of the cook at Schuster's restaurant?"

Jessica watched the expression on the woman's face. As she stood leaning her hips against the closed door, she replied, "How would I know something like that? I was just a waitress."

Yes, how indeed? Jessica wondered as she continued looking at the woman. "And you were a waitress there for a couple of months?"

"For four months actually."

"And during that time you never worked in the kitchen?"

The woman's eyes flared. "And just what are you accusing me of?"

Jessica sighed. "I'm not accusing you of anything, Ms. Evans. I'm just trying to find answers to an unsolved puzzle."

The woman lifted her chin. "Why bother? Scott Westmoreland and Carlton Graham are dead. What does it matter what happened with those recipes?"

Jessica picked up her purse and stood. "Because although they've passed away, their descendants deserve to know the truth, and until they do, my grandfather's honesty will be questioned. That's unfair to him. I want to prove he wasn't guilty of any wrongdoing."

Jessica watched the woman tense up and look around the small apartment as if not wanting to meet Jessica's eyes. "Your grandfather was a good man."

Jessica smiled. "Yes, I think so, too, but he died knowing there was a blemish on his character and that always bothered him. And I'm asking that if you remember anything that you think might help clear his name, will you please let me know."

"I won't remember anything," Darcy Evans said, much too quickly, Jessica thought as she was ushered out the door.

Chase turned and glanced around the room. His office had been transformed into a place he almost didn't recognize. While in the kitchen preparing the dinner he would share tonight with Jessica, he had given Donna instructions on how he had wanted things set up, and it appeared his ever-efficient waitress had gone overboard. The way she had changed a section

of his office into an intimate dining area for two definitely met with his satisfaction, but what was up with
the lit fireplace and all the flowers and candles? There
was no way he could dine in here with Jessica and not
think of seduction. He would want to kiss her, take her
upstairs to the small apartment he used on occasion,
and undress her. Then he would run his hands all over
her breasts, stomach and thighs, not to mention touch
that area between her legs that had definitely become
his own delicious craving. He felt a tightening in his
loins. He wanted to do more than touch her there. He
wanted to taste her, devour her and watch her eyes
fill with the pleasure he was dying to give her as she
opened her legs wider and his tongue continued to—

"Everything meets with your satisfaction, boss?"

Jerked out of his racy thoughts, Chase turned and
met Donna's excited features. He sighed. "You kind of
went overboard, don't you think?"

Donna chuckled. "Well, considering how things
went the first time Jessica Claiborne walked into your
office, I figured you needed all the help you could get,
and I have a feeling that she likes to be wined and
dined like the rest of us."

Chase nodded as he studied the woman he had
hired six months ago. Donna had become someone
he could depend on. Although he didn't know a lot
about her personal life since she kept that pretty private, he did know that she was twenty-three and was
attending school at night to earn a degree in business
management.

A few hours later when he was alone Chase's primitive instincts kicked into gear. His staff had cleaned

everything up and left for the day. He hadn't seen Jessica since Sunday and although he had spoken to her on Monday night from Knoxville, he had talked himself out of calling her again on Tuesday. He had convinced himself that his desire for her was natural and he would just have to ignore the low burning need that always simmered in his gut whenever he was around her. Tonight the two of them would celebrate a week of knowing each other, although he didn't want to dwell on the fact that he'd never commemorated a week of knowing any other woman.

He sighed, almost impatient to see her again, to kiss her, talk to her, then frowned, wondering what the hell was wrong with him. He didn't have long to ponder that question when he heard a knock at the door.

Ignoring the racing of his heart, Chase opened the door and for a moment just stood there staring at the woman standing in front of him. She was dressed in a skirt and blouse that would have looked simple on any other woman. The outfit did a pretty nice job of emphasizing her full, firm breasts, tiny waist and curvy hips. And, he thought, glancing downward to take a look at her legs, which could easily be seen thanks to the shortness of her skirt, there was definitely temptation there, especially with the high-heeled sandals she wore. Her scent, hot and seductive, also triggered something within him. Like he wasn't heated up enough already.

He didn't say anything for a moment and watched as she nervously swept her bottom lip with her tongue. Pure unadulterated lust hit him with the force of Mount St. Helens erupting.

"I hope I'm not too early, Chase," she said softly, glancing up at him.

His gaze came to rest on her mouth when he said, "No, you're right on time." And I want to taste you bad.

He took a step back, let her in, then closed and locked the door behind her. The air surrounding them seemed to quiver and the need to take her into his arms and kiss her was slithering through every vein in his body.

"I thought I'd contribute dessert," she said, handing a covered container to him. "Chocolate cheesecake."

"Thanks." He slowly felt his control slipping and knew he had to get a grip. Grip, hell! He placed the cake container on a nearby table and reached out and pulled her into his arms. As soon as his lips captured hers he knew kissing her was becoming an addiction. It should be against the law for any woman's mouth to taste this sweet, this delicious, this able to whet his sexual appetite.

He hadn't known how much he needed this until now. He needed to bury his mouth in hers, suck her tongue, feel her breasts pressed against his chest, and hear the way she moaned when he kissed her. And then there was the way her body automatically connected to his groin, fitting his arousal dead center between her thighs—the part of her he craved most.

Damn if he didn't put a stop to this madness, he would be taking her right here, right now. Slowly, reluctantly, he lifted his head and almost drowned in the heated look in her eyes. "I thought it would be best if we dined in my office," he whispered against her moist lips. "That way no one would see the lights on in here and assume I'm open for business." In other words, he didn't want any interruptions.

"All right."

He suddenly felt warm again and he inhaled deeply, trying not to focus on her mouth. Trying to pull himself together, Chase picked up the cake container off the table and placing a hand at the center of her back, he led her down the hall. Neither said a word. When they reached his office door he pushed it open and watched as she walked into the room.

Her gaze immediately went to the table set for two, the lit fireplace and the flowers and candles. She didn't say anything for a moment, turning slowly. The eyes that met his were like a soft caress and did nothing to cool his desire, only heightened it.

A smile tilted the corner of her mouth when she said, "You didn't have to go to all this trouble, Chase."

Yes, I did, he thought, as he slowly strolled toward her, covering the distance separating them. He placed the cake container on his desk and to keep from reaching out and touching her, he tightened his hands into fists at his side.

The way her hair tumbled around her shoulders, made her look sexier than ever, and now, within the close confines of his office, her scent, a delicious fragrance that was the very essence of her, further ignited that primal instinct already playing havoc with every part of his body. Kissing her earlier definitely hadn't helped matters.

"I hope you enjoy dinner. It's a Westmoreland secret recipe for chicken and dumplings."

Jessica swallowed. The last thing she wanted to hear anything about was a Westmoreland secret recipe. "Is it good?"

He chuckled. "I'll let you decide." He walked over and pulled out a chair at the table. "Come and let me serve you."

She nodded and sat down at the table. Jessica watched as he expertly served the food, struggling to remain calm and fighting not to stare at him. She hadn't realized until now just how much she had missed him these past couple of days. Nor had she realized how much she had needed him to kiss her. He had such a dark, handsome, sophisticated look, yet her senses told her that there was a hint of something untamed about him.

"Let's dig in," he said after they'd said grace.

During dinner they talked about a number of things. He even gave her pointers on how to promote her business on the Internet. Afterwards, they savored the cheesecake she had brought.

"Did you enjoy dinner?" he asked softly sometime later, when they stood in front of the fireplace enjoying a glass of wine.

She smiled. "Yes, I enjoyed everything. The chicken and dumplings were to die for."

She glanced around the room at the flowers and candles then turned back and looked at him. "Everything was nice, Chase, but I'm wondering…"

When she hesitated and didn't finish what she was about to say, he asked, "Wondering what?"

She nervously bit her bottom lip. "I'm wondering

if perhaps it's a little too much for two people who've decided to be just friends."

Chase had crouched down in front of the fireplace to add another piece of wood to the flames. He lifted a dark brow and glanced at Jessica. "When did we decide that? We talked about things moving too fast and slowing them down a bit. We also agreed to take the time to know each other better. But I don't recall saying we wouldn't be anything more than friends. In fact I'm counting on just the opposite. I don't want to be only your friend."

He studied her as he stood, watching every nuance of her features as the words he'd spoken sank in. "What are you saying?" she whispered softly, her voice the only sound in the room other than the resonance of the fire crackling in the fireplace.

He sighed, knowing he had to give her the bare truth. No frills, no gimmicks, no lies and definitely no game-playing. He wanted to be her lover and not her friend. Usually he didn't move this fast with any woman, but with Jessica he was driven to do so. "We've already discussed the issue of us being attracted to each other. But there seems to be another problem, a deeper one."

Her brows furrowed in a frown. "What?" She tried to downplay the churning in her stomach as he looked at her. His dark eyes, shadowed by long lashes, were doing things to her.

His features were serious when he said, "I want you, Jessica, and I think you want me as well. We can do whatever we want to skirt around that fact, avoid it or ignore it, but eventually the final result will be the same."

She lifted a brow. "The final result?"

"Yes."

"Which is?"

"We *will* become lovers. If not tonight, then some other night. The chemistry between us is too strong for us not to. I would never force or trick you. But I will try my best to seduce you."

Seduce you…Chase's words flowed through her mind and as much as she didn't want them to, they stirred a sensual need in her. They did more than that, they ignited something deep and elemental. She turned to study the flames in the fireplace, but they were nothing compared to the ones inching through her bloodstream at that very moment.

For two solid days she had tried keeping her mind focused on finding out how Schuster's cook had gotten hold of the Westmoreland secret recipes, but Chase had always lurked deeply in her thoughts.

She heard him come to stand behind her. She breathed his masculine scent, and knew that what he'd said was true. Considering their families' history, an involvement with him was the last thing she needed. But he was right. Sooner or later they *would* sleep together, even though she hadn't liked sex in the past. She knew that with Chase things would be different. He'd already changed her mind about kissing.

"Jessica?"

He whispered her name just moments before he reached out and gently turned her around. Dark-brown eyes studied her intently, searching her face, heating her insides and melting her resistance. For longer than she cared to remember, she had been an independent woman, placing no aspect of her life or livelihood into a man's hands. But then those hands had never belonged to Chase Westmoreland.

The truth of the matter was that she wanted his hands to hold her, snuggle her close to him, touch her all over, give her the pleasure she had dreamed he had given her just last night. Just thinking about it made her pulse fierce, her breathing erratic, her heart beat wildly and generated an intense amount of heat between her legs. She drew in a shaky breath knowing what she was going through was more than mere lust, but at the moment she didn't want to define anything.

She struggled against the need to be sensible versus her desire to be wanton. There was a heartbeat of a pause, and then she reached out and wrapped her arms around Chase's neck and brought her body against the hard solid plane of his. She felt how aroused he was through his slacks and the intense sexual need she had been fighting since first meeting him took control.

"Chase," she murmured softly, deciding to throw caution to the wind and take what she wanted for the first time in her life.

"Yes?"

"Seduce me."

Seven

Seduce me...

Jessica's words sent Chase's libido into overdrive. He gazed at her, thinking that not only did he plan to seduce her, he intended to drive her wild. "Will you join me in another glass of wine?" he asked quietly against her ear.

She nodded as a shiver passed through her, uncertain of his plans for her. But whatever they were she would be a willing participant. She met his gaze and held on to it. "Yes."

Emotions were churning inside her as she watched him pour them each another glass of wine. "I propose a toast," he said huskily, gazing at her with those dark penetrating eyes that had her body simmering. "To seduction."

Jessica let her gaze shift from him to stare at the

hand holding his wineglass in midair. This wasn't the first time she had studied his hands and wondered how they would feel on her. Even now, just thinking about it had her senses overheating. She swallowed deeply as she clicked her glass to his then slowly drank her wine. When she had taken a couple of sips he reached out and gently eased the glass from her hand and placed it beside his on the table. He turned to a CD player that sat nearby and after he had turned a knob, soft jazz filled the air.

"Let's dance," he whispered, pulling her into his arms.

Jessica could feel her body tremble from the hardness of his pressed intimately to hers. She gave in to the seductive moment surrounding them and closed her eyes as the soft sound of the music lulled her, sharpened her feminine instincts. She nestled her face against his throat, breathing in his manly, arousing scent. The light stroke of his fingers on her back inched lower, past her waist to caress her backside. His touch was driving her insane, making her want things she'd never had. Molten heat filled her entire body.

More than once her pelvis pressed into him; she was fully aware of his erection, large and thick, and she was surprised by her ability to make him want her that much. He splayed the palm of his hand inside her buttocks, bringing her closer to him, making her breathing shallow and the area between her legs even more damp.

All too quickly, the song ended. She glanced up and met his gaze. She saw the heated look in his eyes, noted the raw primitive expression on his face mere seconds before he leaned down to connect his lips to hers. Hands that she had been studying earlier reached out and cradled her head, delving into her scalp, as he mated his mouth with hers, slowly, easily, thoroughly.

Then he deepened the kiss, sucking her tongue into his mouth, letting her know just how much he wanted everything he could get and driving her mad in the process. He ground his aroused body against hers and she groaned as he continued to kiss her with a passion that had liquid heat flowing between her legs, making her want him there. *Oh, yes, right there.*

She felt his fingers inching up her leg, moving slowly toward her inner thigh and the feel of him touching her made her suck in a quick breath. He pulled back, releasing her mouth and the look he gave her was so incredibly sexy it made a deep quivering need invade her insides.

"I think you have on too many clothes," he whispered as he reached out and began unbuttoning her blouse. "I want you naked." He continued to hold her gaze. "Do you have a problem with that?" he asked softly as he eased the buttons out of the buttonholes.

She reached out and held fast to his arm. Not to stop him but to hurry him along. His slowness was almost killing her. "No, I don't have a problem with it," she whispered, reveling in the warmth of his skin beneath her fingers.

When the last of the buttons had been undone and he saw her flesh-colored lace bra, he inhaled sharply. His hands went first to the front fastener and, with a quick flick of the wrist, her bra came undone and her breasts sprang free.

Jessica heard the deep sound of male appreciation that erupted in his throat and her stomach clenched at the way he was staring at her breasts. There was hunger in his eyes. She held her breath as he eased the bra from her shoulders, letting it join her blouse on the floor.

"I've wanted you from the first day I saw you. It wasn't here in this office. It was before then. That Monday morning I saw you move into your place," he whispered. "The first thing I thought was that you had a gorgeous pair of legs," he said smiling wryly. Then his features turned serious when he added, "Gorgeous legs or not, I didn't want to get involved with you, but I soon discovered I could do nothing to stop it from happening."

He breathed in deeply. "I want you so much," he groaned just moments before leaning down and capturing one of her nipples with his mouth.

Jessica sucked in a deep breath when his mouth connected to her turgid nipple, licking at it, sucking it into his mouth and lavishing it with the warmth of his tongue. He was assaulting her emotions to the third degree, causing a purr to erupt deep within her throat, making her legs give way.

As her knees buckled, he brought her body closer to his, holding her up, not letting her go anywhere while his mouth switched breasts, tormenting the other as he had its twin.

"Chase." Jessica moaned his name on a soft sigh as her hand reached out to hold fast to his head, not wanting him to stop what he was doing to her. He was filling her with passion to a degree she'd never known could exist.

He pulled back. "I want to taste you some more," he whispered throatily, holding her gaze, making the ache within her even more profound.

She inhaled sharply and to her amazement she heard herself say, "Then do it."

The smile he gave her melted her insides and destroyed any resistance that might have suddenly popped into her mind. She watched as he undid her skirt to let it slide down her legs and pool at her feet, leaving her wearing nothing but a pair of flesh lacy thong panties.

"Sexy as hell," she heard him growl in a deep, rough tone before going on his knees and gently easing her panties down. Then he leaned back and looked up at her, letting his gaze roam all over her. His eyes came back to the area between her legs. When she saw him lick his lips she knew what was coming next. She had heard about it, read about it, but had never experienced it herself. In a few moments she would. Chase would make sure of it.

He eased closer to her and leaned over and placed a kiss on her navel, licking the area around it, making it wet then blowing warm air on it, making the heated warmth between her legs intensify. She watched him as a flush of desire surged through her.

He slowly made his way downward, past her navel, and before she could catch her next breath he was kissing her there with the same intensity that he had applied to her mouth. And to make sure she wasn't going anywhere—like she would even consider such a thing—he placed a firm grip on her buttocks, holding her still while igniting her entire body into flames.

She heard the guttural growls he was making as he kissed her and, of their own accord, her hands clutched his head. He sank farther into her warmth, deepening the kiss and tasting her in a way no man had ever done before.

With a groan, she thrust her hips closer—as if his mouth wasn't planted in place firmly already—but what she wanted was for the waves that were insistently pounding at her insides to finally drown her. It was evident that Chase would not be rushed. He intended to feast on her until he got his fill, until his hunger to taste her this way was assuaged.

But her body suddenly exploded and she screamed his name. She tried pushing him away from her, but he gripped her buttocks tighter, firmly locked his mouth to her as his tongue moved inside her wildly, uninhibitedly, stroking her, tasting her thoroughly. He didn't release his grip until the last tremble had left her body, and then he didn't stop what he was doing, but continued to taste her as his hands gently stroked her hips.

Finally, he lifted his head, eased back on his haunches and looked at her. The look in his eyes made her breath catch. He wanted more. A lot more. And as she watched him lean forward and nuzzle his face in the area between her thighs, heaven help her but she wanted more, too. "Make love to me, Chase," she whispered.

He pulled back, looked up at her, eased to his feet and then swept her into his arms.

Chase gazed down at the woman he was holding. Usually he wouldn't do what he had just done until he got to know the woman better, but Jessica was a deca-dent delicacy and he couldn't have resisted sampling her that way even if he had wanted to. And now that he had tasted her, his craving had intensified. She was utterly delicious.

He held her tenderly while walking up the stairs and couldn't help but notice how she cuddled in his arms, rubbed her cheek against his chest, causing his breathing to quicken, his libido to go into overdrive.

When he reached the bedroom he drew in a deep breath, crossed the room to the bed and lowered Jes-sica. He had felt her heat the moment she had walked into Chase's Place tonight, and now he wanted to get all into it again. But first he had to get as naked as she was. Looking at her lying there on his bed without a stitch of clothing was making him lose control of all coherent thought. Tasting her was nice, definitely a mouthwatering experience, but what he wanted to do more than anything was get inside her.

As he stood back to unbutton his shirt, he watched her watching him. The moonlight streaming in through the windows bathed her in a translucent glow, making the coloring of her body as luscious as the chocolate she used to bake with. "Say something," he whispered when the quiet stillness in the room got unbearable and it was obvious what he was doing had her complete attention. He tossed his shirt aside.

He watched as she stretched her naked body while a smile touched the corners of her lips. He liked the fact she wasn't shy or bashful. Nor was she ashamed of showing her body to him. She laughed quietly, sexily. "What do you want me to say?"

Heat flooded his brain when she took her tongue and licked her lips. He swallowed the lump in his throat as his hands went to his belt buckle. "You can say anything."

She paused, as if taking in his words, and when she licked her lips again he sucked in a quick breath. He watched as she eased to the edge of the bed, her face coming in direct contact with his midsection. She reached out and pressed her hand against the large, heavy erection clearly showing through his slacks, using her fingers to explore the firmness of it through the khaki material. "Umm, at the moment, I can think of only one word to say," she said softly and in a voice he found incredibly sexy.

"What's that?" he asked, barely able to get the words out as she continued to explore him, squeeze him, cup him.

She lifted her gaze to meet his and with a deep, throaty sound she said, "Hurry."

He smiled as he took a step back and quickly pulled the belt from his pants before easing both his underwear and slacks down his legs. He stood before her as naked as she was and got heated watching her eyes roam over him. "What are you thinking?" he asked in a strained voice.

"What I thought the first time I saw you. That you remind me of rich dark chocolate," she whispered. "And that I would definitely like to have some of it."

He chuckled and slowly moved toward the bed. "Baby, I intend for you to have all of it."

He joined her on the bed, urging her back to the middle of the mattress. Without wasting any time he pinned her body beneath his weight. "But first," he said, leaning in and bringing his face down to hers, "I need to kiss you again."

Jessica smiled. She knew all about his kisses, was well aware of how delicious and X-rated they were. Ever since meeting Chase she had become aware of the extent of the sexual desire she had stored away, denying its existence. Before she could ponder why, his mouth captured hers, making her forget everything but the way he was working his tongue inside her mouth. Memories of what he had done to her while on his knees in his office, along with what he was doing to her now, sent sensuous shudders all through her, tumbling her emotions and getting her body overheated.

When he finally released her mouth, he whispered quietly, so incredibly sexily in her ear, "Open for me, Jessica."

Instinctively she spread her legs as he continued stroking his tongue back and forth across her lips. She felt him lift his lower body and she unconsciously lifted hers. "Now take me in," he whispered hoarsely.

He leaned up and met her gaze and she knew what he was asking her to do, which was something she'd never done—lead a man into her body. But she would do it. She wanted to do it. Before, when she had made love that one time in college, things had been over before she could blink, leaving her feeling cheated, unsatisfied, disappointed. But Chase was making sure she was a part of what they were doing. He was allowing her to be more than a willing partner. He fully intended her to be an eager participant.

Reaching out she came into contact with the hairy

surface around his navel. Her fingers paused, liking the feel of the rough texture of hair there on his stomach. When her fingertips began caressing him there, she heard his sharp intake of breath.

"Jessica."

Her name was a tortured groan from his lips and she smiled as her fingers moved downward until she got hold of him. He felt hard, firm, big in her hands. She blinked. *Too big.* She wondered if they would fit.

She glanced up and met his gaze. As if knowing her thoughts he smiled and said, "Perfectly."

She breathed in deeply, deciding to take his word for it. Besides, holding him in her hand was making her lose control of all rational thought. The only thing she could think about was that the huge, thick object she was clutching would soon be inside her, mating with her and...

She blinked again. "What about protection?" she suddenly asked.

She could tell from the expression on his face that he had forgotten just as she had. He sucked in a deep breath. "Damn, I'm usually not this careless. Sorry," he said, shifting his body off her to retrieve a condom packet from the nightstand drawer. He ripped it open with his teeth and quickly sheathed himself.

She smiled, although she still wondered how they would fit. "I sort of got carried away with the moment, too." She paused, then quickly added, "I'm on the pill to regulate my periods but I haven't slept with anyone for over eight years—"

"Eight years?" A shocked look took over his features.

She nodded. "Yes, not since my first year at college. It wasn't anything like I thought it would be and was over quickly." A part of Jessica couldn't believe she was discussing this with Chase as if they were having a conversation about the weather.

"And you haven't done it again since then?"

Jessica swallowed before answering. "No, this will be the first time since then."

Returning to her, he bent his head, took her lips, dipped his tongue into her mouth, kissing her with such gentle tenderness Jessica thought she would faint. Then he deepened the kiss, reigniting the flame between them, causing her body to ache for him once again.

"Lead me in, Jessica," he said moments later, breaking off their kiss.

His breathing was choppy and his whispered words made her entire body pulse. Holding him firmly in her hand, she guided him to her as their eyes met and held. The intensity in his gaze sent heat throbbing through her. She actually felt the muscles in her womb contract. It seemed that every part of her was ready to receive him.

When he was at her entrance she felt him take over. The tip of him eased inside, stretching her, and as he lowered his hips and she lifted hers, he went deeper. She sucked in a deep breath when he couldn't go any farther.

Chase raised up slightly and gazed down at her. "You're still... He didn't..." He broke off in amazement. He leaned down, his face mere inches from hers.

Before Jessica could fully understand what Chase

meant by those words, she felt him push his body forward, and the cry of pain that tore from her lips was captured in his kiss. She'd been a virgin all this time. He continued kissing her and she couldn't recall a more precious moment.

Instinctively, she wrapped her legs around Chase's waist as he continued kissing her. Moments later, he pulled back and whispered, "Make love with me, sweetheart."

Her legs tightened around him. Her body was coiled with anticipation of what was next. And when he pushed deeper inside her, locking them legs to legs, limbs to limbs, breasts to chest, she lifted her hips to him.

He began to move. Slow at first, driving her almost insane with the way his body was moving in and out of hers. Then suddenly his strokes quickened and they mated effortlessly, smoothly, fluidly. His hips slammed into her over and over again. As if that wasn't close enough, he took his hand and lifted her and she thought she felt him touch the crest of her womb.

"Chase." She cried out his name, begging for a release that was different from the one she'd had earlier in his office. Different but just as intense. His tongue inside her had been awesome, but his sex inside her, pumping into her fast, solid, hard, was even better. Over and over he continued, nonstop. Every single thrust brought her closer to the edge. She wanted to scream, her throat ached to do so.

And she did.

She screamed his name. Her arms circled his neck and felt all the perspiration that soaked his skin. Sweat trickled down his back, slicked his forehead, and dampened her flesh. But he didn't let up and she cried out again, everything inside her exploding—including him.

She heard his guttural cry just moments before she felt the warmth of his release. He was not holding anything back, determined to make her shatter, break free, blast off to the stars, detonate into ecstasy. And he was there with her, grinding his teeth, pushing deeper inside her as both of them continued to come apart. He relentlessly pounded into her hard and fast, and she felt his second release, just as intense and thick as the first. His head fell back and he screamed her name as explosions continued to erupt between them.

And Jessica knew at that moment that as unbelievable as it might seem, she had fallen in love with Chase Westmoreland.

Chase's body shuddered as he eased off Jessica. They had made love a second time and he'd have liked nothing better than to pin her body under his and go another round. He doubted if he would ever tire of making love to her.

His delicious craving. He'd never known a woman so damn edible.

He glanced over at her. He'd worn her out. She could barely keep her eyes open. After the first time they had made love he had gone into the bathroom. When she had seen him standing at the foot of the bed with the basin of water and wash cloth, she had drawn back and looked at him as though he'd lost his mind, not believing he would even for one minute consider performing such an intimate act on her. She had tried being stubborn about it, but in the end he had kissed her into submission. He had never slept with a virgin before. Even Iris had been experienced.

He inhaled sharply when he thought of the woman who had wounded his pride and broken his heart. When he had been at the top of his game, at the head of the list for the NBA draft, she had been right there, on his arm and in his bed. But after his injury she hadn't wasted time moving on to bigger opportunities and even had the gall to tell him that it wasn't anything personal, but she wanted more from life than to be tied to a cripple. That had been nearly ten years ago. He no longer walked with a limp thanks to the extensive physical therapy he had endured, a very supportive family and the willpower and determination to survive as well as to succeed.

He glanced back over at Jessica and saw she had drifted off to sleep. But still he heard her murmur his name as she shifted in bed and wiggled her bottom to fit into him. His physical reaction to her cradled so snugly against him was immediate. His craving for her absolute. He splayed his palm on her stomach and gently pressed her closer to him, spooning their bodies, and he heard when she murmured his name again.

Chase frowned slightly. The last thing he needed at this point in his life was another woman getting under his skin. Once burned, it was hard not to wear a shield. He had made the decision long ago never to fall in love again. Doing so would only be asking for pain. For that reason he was troubled by his deep attraction to Jessica. Even before they had shared what they had tonight, he had been entranced by her, which wasn't a good thing. When it came to women he wasn't into attachments.

He glanced at the clock on the nightstand. It was a little past midnight. He would need to wake her before four o'clock to make sure she got dressed to return to her apartment. Some of his employees began arriving around five to handle the early-morning breakfast crowd. The last thing he wanted was for anyone to know his and Jessica's business. As far as he was concerned, what they'd shared was too precious for prying eyes at the moment. Everyone would discover sooner or later that they were having an affair, but he wished it to be later and not sooner.

Chase cursed under his breath when he thought about his brothers and cousins. They would try making a mountain out of a molehill but at that moment, Jessica shifted again in bed, bringing her bottom even closer to the fit of his front, and his brothers and cousins were the last thought on his mind.

Jessica slowly opened her eyes and felt a strong, warm arm slung across her waist. A very naked waist. It suddenly occurred to her that she was completely naked and so was the man lying so close beside her in the softly illuminated bedroom.

She peeked at the clock on the bedside table. It was three o'clock in the morning. She felt her pulse quicken at the memory of what she and Chase had shared last night, and all because of Chase's very talented mouth. She closed her eyes as heat flowed through her.

Then something else rushed through her as well.

The stark memory that she had been a virgin. Chase was now the first for her in a lot of ways. The first man to give her a climax and the first man to actually make love to her in the full sense of the word. There had been nothing quick about it and the last thing she felt was cheated.

Jessica felt her face burn with embarrassment when she also remembered what he'd done after they had made love the first time, and the gentle, attentive care he had given her afterward. She had never imagined any man being that caring and concerned with a woman he'd slept with. Just thinking about what he had done to soothe her aches would endear him to her for life. And when they had made love a second time, he had been so gentle and tender it had almost brought tears to her eyes.

A sharp pain stabbed at Jessica's heart when she imagined what Chase's reaction would be when he discovered she was Carlton Graham's granddaughter. She knew Mrs. Stewart and Jennifer were right. She should tell him the truth and continue to go about proving her grandfather's innocence. From just the short time she'd gotten to know Chase, she felt that trust was an important issue to him.

Suddenly, Jessica's breath caught in her throat when she felt his arm shift from her waist as his hand moved slowly downward, toward the juncture of her legs.

"Sore?" he asked, his voice warm and soft, as he brushed his lips across an area beneath her ear.

Jessica opened her mouth to answer but she let out a soft purr instead when his fingers began caressing her feminine core, making scorching heat swirl inside her.

She swallowed deeply and then tried to speak again. "Not too much, thanks to you." She felt the moistness of his tongue as he licked an area against her neck. She immediately gasped for air.

"No thanks needed."

In one smooth move he had rolled her from her side onto her back and she found herself trapped intimately beneath his hard, solid body. The eyes staring down at her were sexy as sin. And immediately she felt the heat simmering within her ignite, flame out of control. Right now, at this very moment, she wanted him to make love to her again. She needed it. Later she would rake herself over the coals for falling in love with him, but for now...

She raised her arms to encircle his neck, bringing his mouth down closer to hers. "Make love to me again," she whispered, meeting the deep intensity in his gaze.

Although she might be the one making the request, she knew that he wanted her just as much as she wanted him. The proof was there in the thick, hard, turgid erection resting so achingly close between her thighs. But she knew that Chase was the kind of man who wouldn't make a move until she'd given him permission to give her pleasure.

And then, slowly, she began to feel him inch his way inside of her. The dark eyes she was gazing up into became even darker. Her body automatically stretched as he went deeper, and flicks of intense heat began consuming her.

"I love being inside you," he growled in her ear, and she wrapped her legs securely around him, locking their bodies as his shaft inched deeper still. When he had gone as deep as he could go, he leaned down and when her lips parted on a low, breathless moan, he claimed her mouth, at the same time as the lower part of his body began moving in deep, penetrating thrusts, over and over again.

And then it happened. Pleasure slammed into her and she was stunned by it. She had reached a climax with him before, but this one almost jerked her body clear off the bed, made her arch desperately against him, and felt as if she was coming apart, fragmenting into a million pieces. Chase lifted his mouth from hers to throw back his head and a deep howl filled the air as he experienced his own pleasure. As if she wasn't close enough, his hands cupped her bottom to bring her closer so he could go deeper, fusing their bodies as one.

Then his lips covered hers and he took her mouth with a promise of more fulfillment as exploding waves drowned them once again, sweeping them off to a place where it seemed their souls had somehow melded.

Before dawn that morning Chase opened the door of his restaurant to walk Jessica home. The air was cool and everything was quiet and still.

He automatically placed his arms around her shoulders and brought her body close to his as they strolled in the darkness past Mrs. Morrison's shop. No words were exchanged between them and Chase wondered if Jessica felt the way he did, that what they'd shared was a dream and one uttered word would bring them awake.

When they reached her door he watched as she unlocked it. She turned back to him and Chase quickly leaned down and pressed a kiss upon her lips. He wondered how one ended what had turned out to be such a very special night. And if she were to invite him in, how would he turn down her invitation when more than anything he wanted to make love to her again—for the rest of the morning and the remainder of the day as well?

The kiss that he had meant to be short and sweet suddenly took on a life of its own, and he found himself kissing her deeply, with abandoned possession and simmering hunger. He knew he should pull away from her, but decided he couldn't imagine having his mouth in any other place at the moment.

Finally, when they heard the loud horn of a semi-truck somewhere in the distance, they moved apart. She met his gaze and he could see the same desire he felt mirrored in her eyes.

"I'd better go inside," she whispered softly. "And thanks again for dinner."

Chase smiled. "Thank you for *everything*."

Jessica's stomach clenched. She both loved him and wanted him. A deadly combination. Without thinking what she was doing she leaned up on tiptoes and brought her lips to his. He took the kiss she offered, added his own little sensual twist.

She slowly pulled back. "Good night, Chase."

A broad grin touched both corners of his lips. "And good morning to you, Jessica." He turned and then walked away.

Eight

The first thing Chase noticed when he walked into Jessica's shop at lunchtime was the slew of customers lined up at the counter that had yet to be waited on. And it appeared she was trying to work the lunchtime crowd all by herself. He wondered aloud where Mrs. Stewart was.

Jessica had glanced up when she heard the sound of his voice. She met his gaze and smiled.

"She called in. She wasn't feeling well and was determined to come in anyway, but I talked her into staying home."

Chase lifted a brow. "And you're trying to handle this crowd all by yourself?"

"Yes."

Before she could blink, he had come behind the counter and snagged an apron off the rack. He then put on a pair of food-handler's gloves. Jessica turned and stared at him. "What are you doing?"

He smiled at her. "Helping out."

"B-but..."

He turned her back around. "You have a customer, Jessica. Don't keep Mrs. Prescott waiting. If I'm not mistaken this is her day of beauty and she can't be late at the salon."

The older woman who was standing on the other side of the counter beamed. "That's right, Chase. And Harry and I will be at your place for Friday's night's special. I'm counting on it being fried chicken, collard greens and potato salad."

Chase chuckled. "And just for you and Mr. Prescott, I'll make sure that it is."

Mrs. Prescott then turned to Jessica. "And don't put up a fuss about him helping out, young lady. I've known those Westmoreland boys since the day they were born. The last thing you have to worry about is one of them robbing you blind."

Jessica couldn't help but smile. That *was* the last thing she was concerned about. But how would she be able to do anything with Chase so close? There wasn't much space behind the counter and she didn't know how she and Chase would share it. She and Ms. Stewart were two relatively petite women, but Chase... well, Chase was well-built, muscular, had a nice set of abs, not to mention a few other qualities she considered outstanding. She'd been an eyewitness to those qualities just last night, and the memory made heat rush into her face.

"Hey, you okay?" Chase leaned over and asked her, almost too close for comfort.

She blinked and tried to control her rapid heartbeat. "Yes, I'm okay." *If you call thinking about last night okay.*

"Why you ask?"

He chuckled. "Because Mrs. Prescott has been trying to give you her money for the past couple of minutes."

"Oh." Jessica turned to the older woman apologetically. "I'm sorry."

The older woman smiled. "That's okay, I understand. I used to be young once."

Jessica swallowed. Had the woman picked up on her attraction to Chase? She was more than ready for the next customer, determined to keep her concentration on her customers and not on Chase. A few moments later she discovered they worked well together. He knew just what her customers wanted and even talked them into buying something extra. For the next hour and a half they had a steady flow of customers, but by two o'clock the store was completely empty.

Jessica glanced over at Chase as he removed his gloves. "Thanks for the help. You're good for business," she said smiling.

"Umm, I hope I'm good for more than just business," he said grinning suggestively as he removed his apron and hung it back on the rack.

Jessica shook her head and chuckled. "Trust me, you are."

His grin widened. "That's good to know."

Jessica sighed. She had meant every word of what

she'd said. Memories of their time together last night had kept her pretty heated much of the day. One thing the busy lunch hour had done was keep her mind occupied and off him…until he had shown up unexpectedly with his offer to help.

Chase glanced down at his watch. "I'd better go before everyone wonders where I took off to." He chuckled then said, "But then I think they'll know if Luanne Coleman has her way."

Jessica raised a brow. "Luanne Coleman?"

"Yes, the woman who was in here wearing the red dress and straw hat."

Jessica nodded, remembering. "Was she the one who held up the line for ten minutes trying to decide whether she wanted a batch of brownies or fudge and didn't make up her mind until you gave her a sample of each?"

Chase laughed. "Yes, that's the one. She and her husband own a flower shop in College Park and she is the town's biggest gossip. It's my guess that after she left here she went right over to the restaurant and spread the word that I was helping you out."

Jessica stared at Chase. "But why would that interest her?"

Chase leaned back against the counter. "The last I heard Mrs. Coleman and the other older ladies in her sewing club are betting on the next Westmoreland to get married."

"The next Westmoreland to get married?"

"Yes. Some are putting their money on me and some on my cousins Ian and Durango." At her confused look Chase chuckled again and decided to explain. "My brothers and cousins and I haven't ever wanted marriage in our future but within the past three years, all of my brothers have gotten married."

"Oh."

"Then a few months ago my cousin Jared surprised all of us by getting engaged. He and Dana got married, so quite naturally everyone turned their eyes on me since I'm the last of my brothers. Although I've told them many times I'd never marry, they don't believe me."

Jessica nodded. "And why not?"

"Because my brothers and Jared always said the same thing—that they would never marry. And although I would be the first to admit that they're all happy, it means nothing to me. The bottom line is that I'll never marry."

Jessica turned away from him, pretending to be absorbed in wiping down the glass case. She didn't want him to see how his words affected her. She may have fallen deeply in love with him, but that was her problem, not his. She had a feeling he was deliberately emphasizing something he'd said last night. She had heard him loud and clear when he'd said he was into casual relationships. A man into casual relationships didn't have marriage on his mind. She was smart enough to know that. Maybe it was time she let him know her position as well. "I never intend to get married either," she said as she wiped off the counter. She didn't look up but felt his probing eyes on her anyway.

"Why not?"

Jessica decided to look at him since he actually sounded confused. "I told you the story behind my father, Chase. What he did affected my ability to trust. Not that I think all men are the scum of the earth like he was, but I pretty much decided I have more to do with my time than worry about whether the man I'm with is trustworthy."

Chase nodded. "Yes, I know what you mean."

Jessica met his stare. "Do you?"

Chase fell silent for a moment then said, "Yes. I do. I got burned in college when the woman I thought loved me dropped me like a hot potato when my injury kept me from playing pro ball."

There was a pause and then he added, "I was quite bitter for a while but soon wised up and decided I was better off without Iris. Still, that hasn't stopped me from being cautious. I'll never trust another woman with my heart again. Trust is important to me. I can't stand deceit of any kind."

She nodded slowly, not wanting to consider the fact that at that moment she was deceiving him. "Umm, so I guess we understand each other."

Chase was quiet. Then he said, "Yes, I guess we do." He looked back at his watch again. "I'd better go." He then looked at her and asked. "What are you doing later?"

"I'm going out."

He raised his brow. "Out?"

"Yes." She decided she didn't owe him any further explanation than that. The last thing she wanted him to know was that she intended to pay a visit to Theodore Henry. The man had refused to return her calls. She had heard from Mrs. Stewart that he would be catering a fund-raising dinner in East Point, a suburb of

Atlanta, tonight. She intended to show up and talk to him whether he wanted to talk to her or not.

"How about taking a two hour drive with me to Chattanooga on Saturday?"

"Chattanooga?"

Chase smiled. "Yes. I'm going there to pick up motorcycle parts as a favor to Thorn. He's busy building a bike for his next race."

Jessica thought about his invitation. She had never been to Chattanooga before and had always heard how beautiful the city was. Although she knew the best thing to do was not get more involved with Chase than she already was, the bottom line was she couldn't help it. She wanted to spend time with him. "I'd love to go to Chattanooga with you Saturday."

His smile widened. "Great. I'll pick you up Saturday morning around eight. Is that a good time for you?"

"Yes, that's a perfect time, and I'll be ready."

For a long moment neither of them said anything, but they stared long and hard at each other. And, as she gazed into his dark eyes, Jessica could feel the heat beginning to rise between them. She wondered what Chase was thinking when he tipped his head back and continued to stare at her. Was he remembering last night in his office and then later in his bedroom? She had enough memories stored for the both of them. Even now, with him standing there, she could vividly remember him kneeling between her thighs and the swirl of his tongue as he greedily devoured her.

She felt her stomach clench and her thighs actually trembled at the memory. As if he'd read her thoughts—was tuned right in to what she was thinking—he took a couple of steps toward her when the bell on the door sounded. A man walked in.

Chase inhaled deeply as he watched as Jessica turned to greet the customer. His entire body felt tight, wound-up, hot. It was as if he'd read her mind and had gotten caught up in her sensuous thoughts, her candid memories of the time they had spent together last night.

Pulling in another deep breath, he watched as a huge smile touched her lips before she raced from behind the counter to be engulfed in the man's arms.

"Rico!"

Chase frowned. Who the hell was Rico? And judging from the gigantic smile on Jessica's lips she definitely knew the guy. Was this the guy she was going out with later? Suddenly, without much glamour or fanfare, an emotion he hadn't experience in a long time attacked his insides. He didn't know who the man was, but he wanted to cross the room and snatch Jessica out of his arms.

He made a move, then caught himself, astounded that he would feel that way. Not since Iris had he felt jealousy for any woman. Fighting for control he leaned back against the counter. Okay, so he usually wasn't the jealous type, but dammit, at the moment he was seeing red.

"Maybe I should leave," he said in a somewhat angry voice.

Two pair of eyes shifted to glance over at him. Evidently the extent of his anger registered. He saw a sparkle in the man's eyes. In Jessica's he saw clear confusion. Hell, he was confused about the way he was acting as well.

"Umm, maybe you *should* leave," the man named Rico said, smiling, although the smile didn't quite reach his eyes.

Chase's frown deepened. He straightened, suddenly filled with a desire go over and smack the man, break the pretty boy's nose.

"Rico, stop," Jessica said, chuckling. She met Chase's hard stare and the smile vanished from her lips. She wondered what had him so upset. Then it dawned on her. She had told him she was going out later today and then Rico showed up. She couldn't help but smile again at the possibility that he was jealous.

She shook her head, knowing that couldn't be possible. Men who were only into casual relationships didn't get jealous. "Chase—" she cleared her throat to say "—I'd like you to meet my brother, Rico Claiborne."

Chase lifted a brow and stared first at her and then at the man. "Your brother?" he asked, clearly astonished. The two looked nothing alike.

"Yes, her brother," the man answered smiling. He slowly crossed the room to Chase. "And you are?" he asked as though he had every right to know. Chase started to tell him off but then he remembered how he and his brothers used to behave with his baby sister Delaney's dates, and decided big brother here was due the same courtesy.

"Chase Westmoreland."

Chase watched a confused expression form on the man's face before Rico turned around to look at Jessica.

Jessica inhaled deeply. She knew that Rico recognized the Westmoreland name and had questions. And she would have to give him answers.

Rico turned back around and offered Chase his hand. "Nice meeting you, Chase Westmoreland."

Chase took the hand the man offered, wondering what the hell was going on. He had picked up on something between brother and sister when he'd given the man his name and that had him confused. "Nice meeting you as well," he finally said. He then cleared his throat and said, "I'm sure you want to visit with your sister so I'll be going."

Rico smiled. "You don't have to leave on my account."

Chase inhaled deeply. Yes, he did have to leave. He had to go somewhere and think about his possessive feelings. "I was about to go anyway. I have a lot of work to do."

Rico nodded.

"Chase owns that huge restaurant two doors down," Jessica was saying. "My shop assistant got sick today and he was kind enough to help me out with the lunch-hour crowd."

Rico Claiborne nodded again, looked over his shoulder at Jessica and then back at Chase and said, "Oh, I see."

Chase frowned. He had a feeling Jessica's brother was seeing too damn much. "Nice meeting you," he said, then crossed the room to the door. Before he opened it he stopped and glanced over at Jessica. "And I'll see you Saturday morning."

She smiled. "All right."

Chase then walked out the door and closed it behind him. For a long moment Jessica didn't say anything but watched as he walked past Mrs. Morrison's shop back toward his place.

"Would you like to tell me what's going on, Jess?"

Jessica turned and met her brother's inquisitive gaze.

"I'm not sure I know, myself, Rico."

Later that night Jessica walked into the ballroom of a community center and glanced around. This was a fund-raiser for a mayoral candidate and like everyone else present, she had purchased a ticket to attend. However, she was only here to get answers from the man whose company would be catering the food.

Rico had been passing through on his way to Florida and had only stayed long enough for them to share a snack and talk. She had explained as much about the situation as she could, leaving out specific details involving her and Chase but she had a feeling he had read between the lines anyway.

Jessica glanced down at her watch. She had arrived during the cocktail hour, so it wouldn't be too difficult to make her way to the kitchen and talk to the cook. All she needed was a few minutes of his time.

Moments later she walked up to one of the waiters who was carrying around a tray of hors d'oeuvres. "I'd like to see Mr. Henry. Is he around?"

The man smiled then nodded in the direction of the kitchen. "He's in there."

"Thanks."

A few moments later she walked into the kitchen and glanced across the room at the man giving orders to a couple of waiters. If this was Theodore Henry then he was a lot younger than she'd thought he would be. This man appeared to be in his middle forties.

She waited until the two young waiters left before approaching him. "Mr. Henry?"

He turned and gave her a pleasant smile. "Yes? How can I help you?" he asked, extending his hand to her.

"I'm Jessica Claiborne. I've tried calling you several times but you never return my calls." Jessica watched as the smile on his face vanished and he coolly withdrew his hand from hers.

"I am an extremely busy man. Besides, I have no idea what you were asking about."

Jessica lifted a brow. "So you knew nothing about Scott Westmoreland's allegations that my grandfather gave you Westmoreland recipes when you were Schuster's cook?"

"Oh, I heard about it but I didn't have time for such claims. I was too busy coming up with those tasty dishes to worry about two old men with nothing better to do than argue over something unimportant."

Jessica exhaled a breath. Although it was killing her,

she was determined to continue questioning the man with polite professionalism. Although she definitely wanted to tell him where he could shove his arrogant attitude. "And just where *did* you get the recipes, Mr. Henry?"

His frown deepened. "Not that I have to answer that, but to clear your mind about any wrongdoing on my part, those recipes have been in my family for years. I told Westmoreland that, but he refused to believe me."

Before giving her a chance to respond or to ask him anything else, he said, "Look, Miss Claiborne, I really don't have time to stand here and discuss something that happened almost eighteen years ago. Evidently it's important to you but it's not to me. Now if you'll excuse me, I have things to do."

"Hey, boss, we're about to leave," Donna said to Chase. "You plan to stay late tonight?"

Chase pushed away from his desk. "Not too late. I just have a little bit of paperwork I need to do."

Donna nodded. "Okay. I'll see you in the morning."

Once alone, Chase leaned back in his chair and glanced around. His office looked normal, nothing like it had the night before. But still that didn't stop the memories from flooding his insides with a heated rush.

He stood for a moment, stretching his legs. As he walked around the room every step he took reminded him of Jessica being here with him last night. He remembered all the times he had kissed her, brushed his lips across her skin, touched her with his fingers, and devoured her greedily with his mouth. He was getting hard just thinking about it.

Damn. He was spending way too much time lusting after Jessica. After all, that's all it was. There was no other explanation for it. That bout of jealousy earlier today had stemmed from possessiveness, nothing more. Hell, he'd had a right to feel possessive after what the two of them had shared. She had been a virgin, for heaven's sakes. He couldn't help but smile. Even she had been surprised by that.

He stretched his shoulders and looked down at his watch. It was close to eleven o'clock. He wondered what Jessica was doing. Was her brother still there? What if he wasn't? He sighed deeply. Damn, but he wanted to see her.

He shook his head. After last night, if he were to show up now, this late, she'd think he was making a booty call. Hmm, although the thought of that sounded nice, he knew, whether he wanted to admit it or not, that he thought of Jessica as more than a convenient body he could use. There was something about her that reached him on all levels, not just the physical one. He wished he had the strength to keep her at arm's length but knew he could not. Even when she wasn't there with him he could feel her presence. Thoughts of her were always embedded deep in his head.

Knowing he had to get out of his office he grabbed his jacket off the rack. Moments later he was locking the door behind him. He tried not to glance over at Jessica's place. But he just couldn't help it.

Fighting temptation with a vengeance, he walked to his car. He was determined not to see Jessica again today. But as he pulled out of the parking lot, intent on going home, he knew that tomorrow was only a few hours away.

Nine

"Hey, Chase, you got somewhere to go tonight?"

Chase glanced up from looking at his cards and met Dare's stare. He and his brothers were over at Storm's place playing a friendly game of cards. At least it always started off friendly. Hopefully tonight they wouldn't have to worry about Storm's loud complaining when he started losing. With newborn twins in the house he figured his brother's boisterous foul mouth would be kept at a minimum.

"What makes you think I have someplace to go?" he asked.

Dare smiled. "Because you seem anxious about something, and you keep looking at your watch."

Thorn chuckled and glanced over at Chase. "And that's a sure sign a woman is involved."

Chase had no intentions of telling them if there was

or if there wasn't. It had been hard going all day without seeing Jessica. Twice he had started over to her place before quickly changing his mind. They would be seeing each other tomorrow when she went with him to Chattanooga and he was satisfied that was soon enough.

Chase threw down his cards. There wasn't a damn satisfying thing about it. He glanced around the table at his brothers, who were staring at him as if he'd lost his mind. "Look, I'm out of here," he said standing on his feet.

Stone lifted a dark brow. "But for once you're winning."

Chase inhaled. No, he wasn't winning. He was losing every minute he was sitting here with them when he could be with Jessica, in her arms, in her bed.

This had turned out to be a good batch of chocolate, Jessica thought as she pulled off her cooking mitt and licked her lips. She had made more than she needed, but she figured the extra would be perfect for moulding into candy for Chase's Crusaders.

Removing the hairnet from her head, she pushed a wayward strand of hair from her face and thought about her disappointing meeting with Theodore Henry last evening. The man was arrogant. And regardless of what he'd said, she believed he had gotten those recipes from somewhere.

Today had been a very busy day and she was glad Mrs. Stewart had felt well enough to return. But the steady stream of customers hadn't stopped her from glancing over at the door every once in a while hoping to see Chase walk in. She knew Fridays were one of the busiest days at his restaurant, but still, she had missed seeing him all day. He'd had dinner delivered to her and the thought of him thinking of her made her smile. She had discovered that Chase Westmoreland—the man she had fallen in love with—was a very thoughtful man.

She glanced around when the doorbell rang. It was close to ten o'clock. Who could that be? Her pulse rate increased at the thought that it might be Chase. Leaving the shop's kitchen, she quickly made her way to the front door. The silhouette of his body through the glass gave him away. She hadn't been expecting him but she could tell by the way her heart was beating and the sizzling heat that was beginning to flow through her that she was glad to see him.

Breathing deeply she slowly unlocked the door.

Chase couldn't help but stare at the woman standing in front of him. She was barefoot and her thick black hair was pulled back into a ponytail, but a lock of hair had escaped and obscured one eye in a way he thought was sexy.

"Chase?"

He stuffed his hands in his pockets to keep them from reaching out and pulling the rubber band from her hair, totally destroying her ponytail and making her hair tumble over her shoulders.

"I was playing cards with my brothers," he said slowly, getting turned on just by looking at her standing there. "I was winning, but I couldn't keep my mind on the game for thinking about you, wondering what you were doing and wishing whatever it was, I could be here with you." He watched Jessica's mouth turn up into a smile and his guts clenched.

"Chocolate," she said softly.

He blinked then lifted a brow. "Excuse me?"

She smiled again. "I was making chocolate. At least I was just finishing up. Would you like to come in?"

Chase smiled. Would he ever. "Are you sure you don't mind?"

She met his gaze. "I'm positive." As he closed the door behind him, Chase leaned against it for support and stared at her. Her reaction to his heated gaze seemed natural, and the darkness of his eyes touched her everywhere, making a low burning need ignite through her. Seconds turned into minutes and neither said anything. If she didn't speak soon, she'd be burned to a crisp. "Would you like some?"

Too late she realized what she'd asked and watched a smile tilt the corners of his lips. It was a smile that was definitely provocative, irrevocably male. She quickly decided to clarify. "Chocolate. I made extra. Would you like to taste some?"

He nodded his head, kept his gaze directed on her. "I'd love to taste your chocolate."

She swallowed as a sharp physical reaction sliced through her and it made her wonder if they were still discussing the same thing. "There's some left on the stove."

Chase followed Jessica to the kitchen and remembered the last time he'd been inside that particular part of the shop. It had been the night he had taken her to the movies and she had invited him in for cookies and milk afterward.

"Where's your brother?" Chase decided to ask, wondering if the two of them were alone. He hadn't seen another car parked out front.

"He's gone. He was passing through and only stayed for a little while."

Chase nodded. "I would never have guessed the two of you were related."

Jessica glanced back over her shoulder at him and smiled. Most people didn't and she understood why. "Our father is African-American but Jennifer, my stepmother, is white. Rico looks like her and my sister Savannah looks like a combination of both of them."

Chase stood just inside the door of the kitchen and glanced around as the aroma of chocolate teased his nostrils. She had definitely been busy. A long table was lined with molds for chocolate lollipops. But what was really holding his attention was Jessica.

He watched as she walked over to an industrial-sized stove. "One thing about chocolate," she was saying, "is that you can never make too much, since it can be stored and reused many times over."

She turned and smiled at him. "The only problem is that tonight I've run out of storage space and I have to get rid of what's left in the pot since I won't be using it. I think it was a really good batch." Chase watched as she stuck her hand into the pot and then tasted the chocolate from her finger.

His gut clenched at the sight of her licking her finger clean, and he felt an immediate hardening of his body as his control began slipping. He met her gaze and doubted that she knew just how aroused he was getting from watching her.

"May I have a taste?" he asked, shrugging out of his leather jacket and walking toward her. He paused long enough to place the jacket on a hook near a small table.

"Sure. Is a spoonful okay or do you want—"

"Your finger."

She lifted an arched brow. "My finger?"

He came to stand in front of her. She smelled good, but he knew without a doubt that she tasted even better. "I want to lick it off your finger. Just like you did."

Jessica swallowed hard. His words made her feel tingly all over, especially in one particular spot. She turned back to the stove and stuck her finger in the huge pot. She shivered slightly as she ran her fingertip along the side and coated it with warm chocolate. She turned and held her hand up to Chase, close to his lips. "Here you go."

Without saying anything, and without his gaze leaving hers, he caught her hand in his to steady it, then stuck out his tongue and licked the chocolate off her finger. His strokes ignited the already simmering flames inside her to a torturous blaze as she watched his tongue gently but boldly caress her finger. She felt a whimper form in her throat and when he sucked her finger into his mouth, devouring it greedily, she nearly came undone. He had to reach out and catch her by the waist to stop her from melting to a heap on the floor.

When he finally released her finger, he smiled at her, licked his lips and said, "You're right. That's a good batch. I've never had chocolate that tasted that good before." Then before she could catch her next breath, he leaned in close to her lips and whispered, "And I want some more."

He kissed her, slanting his mouth greedily over hers. His seductive attack on her mouth put her on hot alert. Immediately her body responded to the feel of her breasts pressed tightly against his chest, the way her middle fit snugly against the hard length of him, and the way his mouth was mating with hers. She could feel the desire between them intensifying. They needed each other badly. He tasted like chocolate, but she figured so did she. And they both intended to indulge to their hearts' content.

Chase finally pulled back. Breathless. Something inside him snapped. The deep sexual need for her that he'd been fighting all day swiftly uncoiled. He wanted her. Desperately. Now.

He lifted up his T-shirt. Tossing it aside, he went to the snap on his jeans. The same fever consuming him was consuming her too and he watched her undo the top two buttons of her smock and pull the cotton material over her head. Within seconds he stood before her without a stitch of clothing on and she wore only a blue bra and matching lacy thong.

Driven by a need that was unlike anything he'd ever experienced before he reached out and pulled the rubber band holding her ponytail in place, letting her hair flow wildly around her shoulders. Then, with a flick of his wrist, he unfastened her bra and slipped it off her. His gaze then went to her thong, and he reached out and traced his finger along the thin scrap of material before bending to gently pull it down her legs.

He smiled and, before Jessica was aware of what he was about to do, he reached his hand into the pot of chocolate, coated his fingers and proceeded to smear the warm, creamy richness all over her chest. She made a purring sound deep in her throat at the feel of his hands coating the dark, sticky sweet substance all over her breasts. Using his fingers and gentle precision he smoothed it all over her skin, rubbing his thumb over the sensitive peaks of her breasts before moving lower.

His hand made a path down her stomach then slid lower, spreading chocolate everywhere he touched. Jessica squeezed her eyes shut as heat suffused her body, causing a burning sensation between her legs. And when he touched her there, covering her in warm chocolate, she leaned forward and pressed her lips against his neck and whispered his name.

She opened her eyes when she felt him sweep her up into his arms and walk across the room to an unused table and placed her on it. Then his mouth was everywhere as he leaned over her and began licking the chocolate from her body. With every stroke, every caress of his tongue she moaned his name, groaned a need, and her hips involuntarily came off the table as he robbed her senses blind in the most primitive way known to mankind.

The quaking of her body alerted him that she was close to coming apart. He quickly gathered her into his arms, sat down in a chair and placed her on his lap, straddling him. Purposefully, he guided himself into her. Instinctively, as if she needed this, wanted him, she pushed her body down on the hard, pulsing erection and threw her head back as her muscles drew him in deeper, clenched him, stealing his breath with every inch of him that her body absorbed.

He pulled her mouth down to his in a kiss that was downright salacious, and he began thrusting his body upward, plunging back and forth, in and out of her, setting a rhythm that was meant to drive her.

"Chase!"

He gritted his teeth, took one final plunge and gripped her hips, locking her body to his, needing the feel of his throbbing flesh exploding within the crevices of her womanly core. The thought of what was happening, the profound degree of intimacy they were sharing, made him nudge her legs wider, wanting to give her everything he had and then some.

He heard her cry out again and then he lost it. When she began convulsing in his arms he was powerless to deny himself another orgasm. A shiver of animalistic need raced up his spine and with a growl of deep satisfaction he plunged into her again. He arched his back and called her name as the most incredible climax took control of his body and mind, sending them swirling with sensations he'd never felt before. Three nights ago he'd thought this innocent whiff of a woman was almost too much for him. Now he wondered how he would survive the passion she stirred each and every time they made love.

What he had just experienced left him weak, sensuously spent and for long moments neither of them spoke. Nor did it seem were they in a hurry to separate their bodies. They needed to remain connected a while longer.

Then he lifted his head and their gazes met and at that moment he knew that what they had shared had been earth-shatteringly special, and that no matter how many times they made love, he would never get enough of her.

And he also realized something else. Jessica Claiborne was getting under his skin, and getting deeper and deeper with every passing second.

Chase awoke to the sound of horns blasting in the distance. It was morning. He glanced over at the woman cuddled beside him, remembering all that had transpired between them the night before. After making love to her in the chair he had swept her into his arms and brought her upstairs to the shower where he washed any lingering traces of chocolate from her body. He had dried her off before sweeping her into his arms to carry her over to the bed where they made love over and over again.

He closed his eyes, thinking there was no other place he'd rather be at the moment than lying beside her. But then the thought of being deeply embedded within the warmth of her body was a damn good idea, too. An even better one. He rubbed a hand over his face. If he kept at this pace he would have to start taking an extra vitamin each day.

He glanced over at the clock. It was nearly seven. His restaurant had opened without him and since his car was parked outside and he was nowhere to be found, Donna and Kevin would be able to guess where he was and what he'd been doing.

He rubbed a hand across his chin. He needed a

shave. But then a slow burn began seeping up his spine making him aware of something else that he needed.

Jessica.

Oh, hell, he had to wake her up sometime. He smiled, knowing just the way he wanted to do it.

Jessica glanced over at Chase when they passed a sign that said they had reached Chattanooga. Situated along the Tennessee River and tucked away among the southern Appalachian Mountains, it was clearly a beautiful city.

She had enjoyed Chase's company during the two-hour drive from Atlanta, although she had slept the first half hour on the road. She was still filled with memories of how he had awakened her that morning. A smile curved her lips.

She sighed as she thought about the conversation they had shared during the past hour or so. He had told her more about his and his brothers' escapades growing up, and she had shared with him memories of her times with Rico and Savannah.

After taking care of the business he had come to Chattanooga for, Chase suggested that they have lunch at a restaurant on the Formal Gardens at the Chattanooga Choo Choo. After a delicious lunch of mouth-watering seafood, they had walked around holding hands, basking in the beauty of the gardens. She hadn't known so many kinds of roses existed.

As they continued walking, enjoying the beauty of so many flowering plants, he pulled her closer to him and whispered. "Last night was special, Jessica. This entire week has been. I want you to know that."

She glanced up at him and smiled. He had told her that twice already. "Spending time with you has been special to me as well, Chase."

They were silent for a moment while they continued walking, headed toward the parking lot and back to his car. He then said, "I'd like to prepare dinner for you tomorrow."

She chuckled, remembering what happened the last time she'd shared dinner with him. "At the restaurant?"

"No, my home."

They had reached his car and stopped walking. She gazed up at him. He was smiling that smile that made her feel warm and tingly on the inside. She had gotten a quick tour of his home when they had gone there that morning for him to change clothes. She thought his home in Buckhead, a very upscale and affluent section of Atlanta, was simply beautiful.

"I've love to have dinner with you tomorrow, Chase. Do you need me to bring anything?"

A sexy smile touched his lips. "Only yourself."

She laughed quietly. "Umm, I think that can be arranged."

He pulled her into his arms and just before he kissed her, he whispered, "I most certainly hope so."

Although Chase had told her to only bring herself, Jessica couldn't resist making a delicious dessert. She smiled as she glanced down at the baking dish filled with banana pudding.

But her smile faltered, the banana pudding suddenly forgotten when Chase opened the door and her gaze connected with his. He stood before her, imposing, undeniably male and irresistibly sexy. The royal blue pullover sweater he wore emphasized very broad shoulders and his jeans fit well-built hips and firm muscular thighs perfectly. She clung tightly to the little composure that she had left while drowning in everything sensual about him.

"I thought I told you that the only thing you had to bring was yourself."

She swallowed. Good grief. His voice sounded just as sexy as the rest of him. "I couldn't resist."

He smiled, moved forward and took the dish from her hand. "And neither can I, Jessica." He leaned down and kissed her, giving any neighbors who might be out and about something to talk about.

He pulled back slightly and whispered close to her lips. "Maybe we ought to finish this inside."

She licked her lips. "Umm, yes, maybe we ought to."

He stepped back, and, as soon as she was inside with the door closed, he placed the baking dish on a hall table and pulled her into his arms, kissing her more ardently than he had a few moments ago. "Kissing you has become addictive," he whispered, as he used his tongue to lick the sides of her mouth and a section of skin beneath her earlobe. "I definitely like the way you taste."

She smiled up at him. "And here I came prepared to be fed, not to become a meal."

He chuckled against her lips before licking them some more. "Oh, don't worry, baby, I'm going to feed you." He pulled in a deep breath and took a step back.

"Come on to the kitchen before I have you pinned up against that door and take you right here and now. I'm just that tempted."

He picked up the banana pudding, then bent his head down to her for another quick kiss. "I hope you have plenty of energy because I intend to put you to work."

She smiled. "Work?"

"Yes, work," he said as he led her into the kitchen. "I intend for you to help me prepare one of the Westmoreland secret family recipes for dinner tonight."

Jessica suddenly went still. "But I thought you said you didn't share the secret recipes with anyone."

He turned around, looked over at her and grinned. "It's okay—I trust you. Now come on. I told you, I planned on putting you to work."

Jessica hesitated. Now was the perfect time to level with him. She should tell him the truth, especially since her investigation had hit a brick wall. There was no one else to talk to for more information. Paula Meyers and Darcy Evans said they had told her all they knew, while Schuster and Theodore Henry claimed they knew nothing. Although there was something about Darcy Evans' and Theodore Henry's version of things that she didn't believe, she had no proof to base her suspicions on. But she wasn't ready to throw in the towel. She was determined to speak to both of them again.

"Jessica?"

She glanced over at Chase. He was looking at her strangely. "Yes?"

"Are you okay?"

She inhaled deeply, wanting to tell him the truth.

But she knew at this moment she couldn't. She couldn't risk what he might do. What if he kicked her out on her butt. She couldn't stand that right now. She would tell him the truth soon. But not today.

She forced a smile. "I'm okay. What do you want me to do?"

Chase placed a typed piece of paper on the counter in front of her. "I've got the recipe memorized but since you're helping I printed it off the computer."

She breathed in as she glanced down at the recipe. "You keep secret recipes stored in your computer?"

He chuckled as he pulled a can of cream out of the refrigerator. "Yes, I intend to pass my business on to one of my nieces or nephews one day."

"What about kids of your own?"

He glanced over at her. The smile he wore wavered just a tad. "I have no intentions of getting married and I don't plan on ever having any. And on the off chance that I do marry—probably a good twenty or thirty years from now—all I'd want from my wife is companionship. Our marriage will be in name only."

Jessica nodded and glanced back down at the piece of paper. Even the thought of a fifty-something Chase marrying a woman in a marriage of convenience bothered her. She loved him, dammit!

"So what do you think?"

His question almost started her. She'd been so wrapped up in her thoughts. "About what? You getting married twenty years from now to a woman you won't love?"

He shook his head and smiled wryly. "No. What do you think about the recipe? Are you up to it?"

He placed the cream on the counter and came to stand directly behind her. He reached out and drew her back against him, her tush snug against his erection. If anyone was up to anything, he most certainly was. She sucked in a quick breath when he slid his hands down past her waist to her hips.

She slowly closed her eyes. At any moment he would start inching up her skirt to slide his hand underneath. From there he would find his way into her panties. If she didn't stop him they would never get dinner done. Besides, she needed a few moments alone to pull herself together. Their conversation about the possibility of him getting married one day had messed with her mind.

She spun around quickly, almost startling him in the process. "Excuse me. I need to wash up before we get started."

Without giving him a chance to say anything, she eased by him, went into the hall bathroom, closed the door and tried to catch her breath.

After finishing off the last piece of baked chicken on her plate, Jessica leaned back in her chair and licked her lips. Every meal that Chase had prepared for her had made her want seconds. But what was so special about the baked chicken and Westmoreland rice was that they had prepared the meal together—working side by side in his kitchen as though they belonged there.

"Don't lick your lips like that," Chase murmured from across the table.

She glanced over at him and raised her eyebrows. "Why not?"

"Because it makes me want to lean over this table and lick them for you."

The air between them started to simmer, and Chase felt the need to take a step back, slow things down, savor their evening together. "Tell me about your grandparents."

She quickly glanced over at him. Panic suddenly fill her. "Why?"

"Because I think considering what you told me about your mother's situation that your grandparents must have had a positive effect on your life."

She smiled. His expression warmed her, and she could tell that he was truly interested. Memories of her grandparents flashed through her mind. "They did. Although my mom and I had our own place, my grandparents were close by." She paused before adding. "They moved to California to be near me and my mom when I was around ten or so. My greatest memories are the ones I shared with them."

Jessica knew that now would be the perfect time to tell Chase that she was Carlton Graham's granddaughter and suddenly decided to do so. "Chase."

He met her gaze and smiled. "Yes?"

She made a small sound in her throat but couldn't get the words out. At least not those words. Instead, she cleared her throat and asked. "How long have you lived here?"

"A little more than a year. Before then I had an apartment in Roswell. I visited a friend in this area and decided I liked it. What about you? Do you plan to live over your shop for a while or are you interested in buying a house someplace?"

Jessica took a sip of her coffee. "I owned a home in Sacramento. It was larger than I needed, but my boss at the corporation where I used to work believed that a big house in a posh neighborhood was a must for the attorneys he employed. And, like an obedient soldier, I did what was expected."

He nodded. "Do you miss being a lawyer?"

She shrugged. "I miss practicing law but not the corporate politics that went along with it. The straw that broke the camel's back was a case I was assigned to work on. One of the divisions of a company I represented made children's toys. We had repeatedly gotten complaints that one particular toy was dangerous and several kids had gotten injured playing with it. But it was a big moneymaker and the company refused to pull it from the shelves. When a child died, we got sued. I had to defend a product that I knew had been responsible for causing that child's death. I couldn't do it and quit."

Chase felt a rush of admiration for her. Instead of getting caught up in the woes of corporate politics and becoming just another company robot, she had taken a stand and had made what had to have been tough decisions regarding her future.

He stood, walked around the table and took her hand in his. "Come on, let's go for a walk."

She lifted a surprised brow. "A walk?"

He smiled. "Yes, the neighborhood has a nature trail. And usually around this time of the evening you can catch a fox or two roaming around. Besides, walking is a good way to work off that huge meal we just ate. And just think we haven't gotten into the banana pudding yet."

She grimaced. "Hey, don't remind me. I don't know where I'll be able to put anything else."

He grinned. "That's what you get for having a hard head. I told you not to bring anything but yourself."

A smile touched her lips. "Well, yeah, but I didn't want you to do all the cooking. Had I known you would put me to work I would have thought twice about doing it."

He leaned over and pressed a kiss to her temple. "You enjoyed sharing the kitchen with me today. Admit it."

Jessica laughed. "Okay, I admit it. Are you happy?"

He raised his hand and cupped her face in it. He smiled down at her and held her gaze. "Yes, I am happy," he said quietly, actually meaning it. His hand tightened around hers. "Come on, let's get out of here and take that walk."

"What do you mean you haven't told him yet?"

Later that night Jessica stared down into the cup of coffee she held in her hand. She had her sister on speaker phone and Savannah hadn't wasted any time giving her the third degree.

"Jessica?"

She raised her eyes to the ceiling. This was worse than Savannah being here in person. Her tone was just that effective. "I hear you," Jessica said, taking a sip of coffee. Moments later she added. "The timing has never been right. Every time I get ready to open my mouth, he says something sweet and I can't bring myself to tell him."

"Sounds like you're making excuses."

Jessica sighed deeply. She was. "It's not easy, Savannah. I told you how I feel about him."

"Yes, but in order to give him a chance to feel that same way about you, you have to be honest with him. Put all your cards on the table."

Jessica gazed down into her cup of coffee again. Of course her sister was right. While having dinner with Chase that evening she had had at least two opportunities to come clean and tell him the truth, but had taken advantage of neither. "If I told him now, without proof of my grandfather's innocence he might think the worst."

"And what if you can't prove your granddad was innocent, Jess? What then?"

Jessica didn't want to think about that possibility. Both Darcy Evans and Theodore Henry were hiding something. She could feel it. She closed her eyes and saw the image of a very handsome Chase Westmoreland smiling at her. Then suddenly another image invaded. It was one of Chase angry at her. The sexy line of his mouth had transformed into a deep frown.

"Jess?"

Jessica opened her eyes again. "Yes?"

"You're special, and no matter what the outcome might be, if he doesn't see how special you are then you're better off without him."

"You think too highly of me, sis," Jessica laughed as she pushed her coffee cup aside. She'd had enough caffeine for one day.

"Hey, I can say the same about you."

For a long moment, neither said anything and then Jessica broke the silence. "You would like him," she said quietly.

"Yes, but as far as I'm concerned, he's already taken. You did say he has brothers didn't you?"

Jessica grinned. "They're taken as well, however he has some very good-looking single cousins."

"Umm, maybe I should come for a visit."

"You know," Jessica said smiling. "Maybe you should."

"Storm says you're pretty serious about some woman."

Chase glanced over at his cousin Quade who had made an unexpected visit to town. Quade worked behind the scenes for the Secret Service and his job protecting the president could take him anywhere. Chase took a sip of his beer before saying. "Storm talks too damn much."

Quade smiled. "Maybe he does." He thought a moment, then said, "So tell me…who is she and how did she manage to get under your skin?"

Chase shrugged one shoulder. Although he rarely saw Quade these days, that didn't diminish their friendship, best buddies since childhood, who rarely kept secrets from each other. "Her name is Jessica Claiborne and she moved here from California. She used to be a corporate attorney but got fed up with corporate politics and decided to try her hand at baking instead. She owns a confectionary two doors down from the restaurant."

Quade lifted a brow. "She gave up law to make candy?"

Chase sat back and smiled. "Yes."

Quade shook his head. "That was some career move. I wondered what her parents thought of that."

Chase spent the next ten minutes or so telling Quade about Jessica's past and her bastard of a father. "That had to have been hard on her," Quade said.

Chase nodded. "I'm sure it was, but, at least she had her grandparents."

Quade sighed. "Yes. It sounds like they were good people."

Chase thought of the woman who was beginning to mean a lot to him. "I'm glad they were there for her."

Quade sat forward. "So how did she manage to capture your attention?"

Chase stood and walked to the window. He remain silent for a moment pondering Quade's question. He turned from the window and shrugged broad shoulders. "Hell, that's a good question, but she's there, Quade, under my skin and the strange thing about it is that I sort of like her there."

Chase saw the surprised smile that touched his cousin's lips. "Next time I'm passing through I'd like to meet her."

"You will," Chase promised.

Ten

"What are you thinking about, Jessica?"

Jessica glanced up and met Chase's gaze. She had been staring down at their clasped hands as they sat at a coffee shop in Lenox Square Mall, thinking how comforting it felt for her fingers to be intertwined in his.

A week and a half had passed since she'd had dinner with him at his home and each and every day she spent with him she was falling deeper and deeper in love. But hanging over her head was the fact that she wasn't being completely honest with him.

Theodore Henry had gotten downright rude and even threatened to file harassment charges if she tried contacting him again. That meant her only hope was Darcy Evans, who hadn't returned any of her calls. She would make it her business to talk to the woman again.

She knew Chase was waiting for an answer, so she forced a smile and said, "Umm, I was just thinking about what a close-knit family you have." And she really meant that. Chase had invited her to a Monday-night football party at Jared and Dana's home to see the Falcons play the Cowboys. They had watched the game on Jared's state-of-the-art home-theater system. She had met Chase's parents and reacquainted herself with some of the family members she had met previously. And she had finally met his sister Delaney and her husband Sheikh Jamal Ari Yasir.

He smiled. "Yes, I have to admit that we are that. I can't imagine it being any other way." He leaned closer to her. "But you and your siblings are close, too, aren't you?"

She nodded. "Yes. Savannah and Rico are great. Jennifer has a sister and a brother but they're standoffish. They think she went a little too far including me in her family. After all, I'm the product of her husband's affair."

"You were also her husband's child. Besides, her husband's wrongdoing wasn't your fault. I think it was admirable of her to accept that and do what she did. But I know that many women's pride would not have let them do it."

Jessica nodded again. "Yes, I know, and that's what makes her so special to me. She made it her business to include me as part of Savannah's and Rico's life and I appreciate her for it. It really helped after Mom died."

"I'm sure it was hard on your grandparents to lose your mother that way."

Jessica sighed deeply. "Yes, she was their only child. For a while my grandfather blamed himself for not finding out about my father sooner. Another part of him questioned whether he had done the right thing at all by hiring that investigator and telling my mother the truth. He never thought she would take her life over it."

Jessica didn't say anything for a while, then added, "For the longest time I was bitter and resented her for what she did, leaving me alone. I had to go through grief counseling to let go finally and realize that the love my mother had for my father was an obsession and a sickness. That's when I promised myself that I would never get that caught up over a man."

Chase tightened his fingers around Jessica's as he once again thought about the relationship they shared. He had to admit that the past couple of weeks had been pretty darn special. They had attended a laser show on Stone Mountain, played tennis together twice and she had watched Chase's Crusaders clinch another win one week only to lose big-time the next. Last Sunday evening, a pack of them led by Thorn had taken their Thorn-Byrd motorcycles on the road to ride all the way to Augusta for dinner. No one in the family had seemed surprised that he'd brought Jessica along, nor had anyone questioned him about the amount of time the two of them were spending together. His family had accepted that they were now an item. He wasn't sure how he felt about that.

"More coffee?"

They both glanced up at the waiter who was making his rounds. "No thanks," Chase replied, releasing Jessica's hand to glance at his watch. "In fact, I'd appreciate our bill now."

When the waiter left, Chase smiled over at Jessica. "Thanks for going shopping with me."

She chuckled. "There aren't many people I know, men specifically, who do early Christmas shopping. You still have two months left."

Chase grinned. "Yes, but like you said, I have a large family. Besides, giving out gift cards makes it easy. The kicker is trying to decide what stores they like best." His grin widened. "The saying 'beggars can't be choosers' doesn't always apply in my family."

After finishing their coffee they walked around the mall again. Although there were two months lefts before Christmas, many of the stores already had their holiday decorations up.

"This place is like a madhouse the day after Thanksgiving. You'll have to come with me that Friday to see what I mean. But the crowd puts me in the Christmas spirit."

Jessica suddenly felt breathless. Thanksgiving was a month away. That he assumed they would still be together had her walking on air. But she quickly came back down to earth when she thought of what was still lurking over her head. She decided to pay Darcy Evans another visit tomorrow. She had to give it one more try before finally telling Chase the truth.

Jessica was grateful Mrs. Stewart had agreed to work a full day so that she could make the trip to Macon to pay Darcy Evans another visit. She hated being a nuisance, but she was determined to give it another try to see if perhaps there was something the woman wasn't telling her.

Darcy wasn't at home but an older woman—Darcy's mother—told her that Darcy owned a hair salon not far away. Thirty minutes later Jessica was parking in front of Darcy's Beauty Box.

Jessica knew the moment she walked into the shop and her gaze connected with Darcy that the woman was surprised to see her. "Ms. Evans, how are you?" she asked, extending her hand. The set-up of the shop was very chic. Jessica was glad there was only one customer sitting under the hair dryer, who wouldn't be able to overhear their conversation.

"Why are you here?" Darcy asked, reluctantly accepting the hand Jessica offered. "I thought we finished our discussion the last time we talked."

A wry smile touched Jessica's lips. "I was hoping that perhaps you might have remembered something else since then."

"No, there's nothing else. I told you everything I know."

"Are you sure?"

Darcy tore her gaze from Jessica's and glanced around the room, looking anywhere other than Jessica's eyes. "Yes, I'm sure."

Jessica still wasn't completely certain and decided to try another angle. She didn't want to push but she needed the truth. "Do you believe my grandfather passed those recipes on to someone who worked at Schuster's, Mrs. Evans?"

Darcy's eyes snapped back to hers. "No, of course not. He was one of the most honest men that I knew. I felt bad when Mr. Westmoreland accused him of doing that."

Jessica lifted a brow. "You were there the day it happened?"

"No. Your grandfather and Mr. Westmoreland had an argument and then your grandfather quit. But he and Mr. Westmoreland were such good friends we all assumed he would be coming back."

Jessica nodded. "Do you remember what the argument was about?"

She watched as the woman tore her gaze away from her again. A few moments passed then she said quietly, "It was about me."

Jessica wasn't sure she'd heard her correctly. "About you?"

The woman nodded. "I was going through a difficult time. My son Jamie who was only eighteen months old at the time was constantly sick, which kept me from work a lot. And when I was there I was so preoccupied worrying about him I was beginning to get my orders messed up."

Darcy inhaled deeply as if remember that time. "Some of the customers started complaining to Mr. Westmoreland. Your grandfather knew how much I needed my job to pay for Jamie's medical bills and asked Mr. Westmoreland to give me another chance. They argued about it. Then I heard your grandfather walked out."

The woman shook her head regretfully. "I felt bad about everything. But Paula Meyers, who had worked with your grandfather and Mr. Westmoreland a lot longer, told me not to worry about it because your grandfather had quit before after having words with Mr. Westmoreland and would be back. When two weeks went by and he didn't return, I got worried and started blaming myself."

Jessica's eyes began softening. All it took was a close look at Darcy Evans to know she was still blaming herself. "I think my grandfather and Mr. Westmoreland would have eventually patched up things, too," she decided to say. "But a couple of things happened right after that. My mother had to be hospitalized for pneumonia and my grandparents flew to California to take care of me."

Jessica smiled, remembering. "While they were there I think they decided that my mom and I needed them closer, especially when they couldn't talk her into moving to Atlanta. They returned home a week or so later and my grandfather found out about Mr. Westmoreland's accusations. His integrity had been questioned by someone he considered a good friend and he was hurt. Nothing he said to Mr. Westmoreland could prove his innocence, and I think that was one of the reasons he felt moving to California was best for everyone."

For a long moment neither she nor Darcy said anything. But Jessica could swear the older woman had an odd look on her face. And if she wasn't mistaken, it was a guilty one. "Are you sure there isn't anything else you can tell me, Ms. Evans?"

For a brief moment Darcy didn't answer, and then she said, "No, there's nothing else."

Jessica still didn't believe her. "It's important to me

that if you do remember anything you contact me. I'm caught in the middle of a bad situation right now."

Darcy lifted a brow. "What kind of a bad situation?"

Jessica knew she had to be completely honest with Darcy and hoped the woman would eventually tell her whatever she was holding back. "I've fallen in love with Scott Westmoreland's grandson Chase."

Darcy nodded. "He's the one that owns that restaurant in downtown Atlanta, right?"

Jessica smiled. "Yes, that's right."

"I always knew he would be the one who would eventually follow in his grandfather's footsteps. He would hang around the restaurant and help out more than any of the others. He always seemed like a nice young man."

Jessica smile widened. "He is. We've been seeing each other for about three weeks now, but he doesn't have any idea that I'm Carlton Graham's granddaughter."

Darcy raised a surprised brow. "He doesn't?"

"No. Because of what happened all those years ago, bad blood was left between the two families. I promised my grandmother before she died that I'd prove my grandfather's innocence to the Westmorelands and end the feud." She inhaled deeply. "I hadn't planned on meeting and falling in love with Chase."

Darcy nodded. "But surely something that happened years ago wouldn't keep the two of you apart."

Jessica smiled wryly. "It might. He was pretty close to his grandfather and I can tell he's still pretty bitter about the entire thing. Besides, honesty means a lot to Chase. I should have told him who I was from the beginning. But I wanted to prove my grandfather's innocence before doing that. Now I can see I made a mistake in waiting."

"What will you do now?"

"Tell him the truth and hope he believes me. Hope he's willing to put the past behind us and move on."

Darcy didn't say anything for a few moments, then asked, "Do you think he will?"

"God, I hope so."

Chase glanced down at his watch thinking Jessica should have returned by now. He had stopped by the shop at closing time to let her know that he had to leave town unexpectedly, and found Mrs. Stewart was still there. The only thing she would tell him was that Jessica had an errand to run and she didn't expect her back before seven o'clock that night.

He couldn't help wondering what sort of errand Jessica had to do that could have kept her away from the shop practically all day. He glanced around when he heard a knock at his office door. "Who is it?"

"Donna."

"Come in."

He watched his most dependable waitress walk nervously into the room. In the months she had worked for him he'd never known Donna to be nervous about anything. But a part of him saw beyond that. For a split second he could see a hint of sadness behind those big brown eyes of hers.

When she didn't say anything he decided to urge her on. "Donna, what can I do for you?"

She looked away, hesitated, then she said, "I came to give you this."

Chase's eyesbrows shot up when she handed him a piece of paper she had in her hand. It took him a quick second to scan it. His eyes widened, and he lifted his gaze, giving her a surprised look. "You're quitting?"

She looked away again and shrugged her shoulders. "Yes. I like working here but I need to start going to school full-time if I ever want to finish. I got a letter yesterday from a college in Tennessee offering me a scholarship to finish my last two years, and I've decided to take it."

Chase smiled. Although he regretted losing Donna, he knew that was an offer that was too good to pass up. Opportunities like that didn't come often. "I'm happy for you, Donna."

At last a smile touched her lips. "Thanks. I'm pretty happy for myself. I keep rereading the letter to make sure I'm not dreaming. They want me to start in January, which means I'll have to pack up and move. With the holidays coming up I didn't want to leave you in a fix, and I wanted to let you know now, although I can probably work another month."

"And I appreciate that. You're going to be hard to replace. And if you ever need anything I'll always be a phone call away."

"Thanks, Chase."

After Donna left, Chase leaned back in his chair. He glanced down at his watch again. He had taken just about all he could stand. He needed to see Jessica. And the thought that he would be leaving town for three days didn't help matters. Hell. He'd been pretty useless all day for thinking about her. To go to her shop and not find her there had been a huge disappointment.

Chase didn't like the way his thoughts were going—he was becoming more and more obsessed with Jessica. For the first time in his life, while holding Storm's twins earlier that day when Jayla had stopped by to meet Storm for lunch, he had actually thought of having kids of his own. For Pete's sake! Just the other day he had told Jessica he didn't plan on ever having kids. Yet when he had looked down at his nieces, he'd actually envisioned Jessica as his children's mother. Panic rose thick in his throat.

He stood, suddenly not feeling at all like himself. He was encountering emotions that were best left alone. Yet for some reason he couldn't leave them alone. Not today. A sharp rush of desire flooded his insides and his main thought as he walked out of his office was that he had to see Jessica.

Chase practically launched himself at Jessica, pulling her into his arms and kissing her the moment she opened the door.

"God, I missed you today," he murmured, easing her back into the shop and closing the door shut with the heel of his shoe. He didn't care that he'd just seen her yesterday and had made love to her last night. That was then and this was now. He leaned down and kissed her.

Jessica tried not to shiver from all the love she felt flowing through every part of her body. She didn't want to think about the possibility that once she told Chase the truth tonight, he would walk away angry and not look back. But she knew what she had to do.

She pulled her mouth from his. "Chase, I have something to tell—"

Before she could finished what she was about to say, he was kissing her again, deeply, with an urgency that obliterated all her thoughts. Knowing this might very well be the last time she shared such intimacy with him, she went for sheer pleasure and attacked his mouth with the same urgency with which he was attacking hers. Moments later they were both groaning out loud.

Chase finally broke contact with her mouth, swept her into his arms and quickly carried her up the stairs. He placed her on her feet next to the bed and immediately began removing her shirt as she reached for the fly of his jeans. Both were crazed with passion, driven by need. Their level of desire had reached a boiling point.

"I want you so bad I ache," Chase whispered when he had completely removed her clothes and she had removed his. He tumbled her back on the bed, went for her breasts and greedily began licking the swollen mounds. She moaned out loud when he sucked a nipple into his mouth. His tongue began licking it, tugging on it; he was driving her crazy by holding the sensitive tip gently between his teeth and not letting go. He then gave the other breast the same torturous treatment.

"Chase!"

"Hold on, baby, I've just gotten started," he murmured, leaving her breasts to travel downward. Jessica sucked in air when his tongue began licking around her navel, circling it, branding it, kissing it.

Then he lifted his head, locked his gaze with hers

and something flickered in his eyes; the heat of it made her breath catch just seconds before he lowered his mouth to her feminine core. Her legs automatically spread for him and it took all the strength that she possessed not to come off the bed under the onslaught of his skillful mouth. But nothing could stop her from shivering uncontrollably when he increased the pressure of his tongue, stroking her with a decadent lick that sent blood throbbing through her veins. She screamed his name but that only spurred him on, making him even more intent on savoring her this way. And when an orgasm hit, splintering her body into a million pieces, she screamed his name again and bucked her hips upward as he continued to ply her with quick and sure strokes of his tongue.

It was only when the last shiver had touched her body that he finally dragged his mouth away. Every inch of her felt sensitive from such a fiery response. He sat back on his haunches and the smile that played at the corners of his lips sent shivers racing through her again. He held her gaze, making her heart pound and she felt an agonizing ache rekindle between her legs.

As if he knew just what she was going through, he reached out and touched her there, began caressing her wet flesh. Then he leaned toward her and, in a voice that was deep, sexy and husky, he said, "Don't relax now, sweetheart. I'm just getting warmed up."

Chase intended to make love to his woman all night.

His woman.

He closed his eyes when a sharpness tore through his heart, almost knocking the breath out of him.

"Chase, are you okay?"

He opened his eyes and gazed down at Jessica. He moved to position his body over her, satisfied that she was primed and ready to take him in. At that moment, he knew. She *was* his woman and he loved her. He loved her. He had never intended for such a thing to happen. But it had and there wasn't a damn thing he could do about it but accept it. And he did, without question.

"Chase?"

His heart pounded against his chest and he leaned down and kissed her lips softly. "Yeah, I'm okay, baby. At this moment I couldn't be better."

She smiled cheekily up at him and said, "Hey, I think that's for me to decide."

Chase grinned as he traced her lips with the tip of his tongue. "Then let me help you make such an important decision."

And then he was back at her lips with that skillful mouth of his, kissing her deeply as his tongue whirled around in her mouth, feasting, tasting, corner to corner, marking every single crevice.

Jessica moaned and closed her eyes when he slipped his hand between their bodies. His fingers touched the soft flesh between her legs, lightly stroking, making small erotic circles, causing sensations to flood her, making her hips buck again.

He finally released her mouth and gazed down at her as she slowly opened her eyes. He was filled with an urgency that he'd never felt before by the recognition of just how much he wanted this woman. Just how much he loved her. And suddenly he became caught up in a raging desire to be inside her.

Now.

He lifted her hips with his hands, anchored his thighs between hers and positioned his aroused member dead center where he needed it to be.

He eased inside her and she automatically adjusted her body to accommodate him, lifting her hips as he went deeper. He arched his hips and pressed forward until he reached the hilt and was buried deep inside her. He fought the urge to move, to stroke her with the rhythm that would send them both over the edge. He wanted to savor being this way, inside her, locked in tight, feeling the moist heat of her clutching him, nearly stealing his breath away.

But he refused to move just yet. He held her gaze, and because he wanted her to know just how he felt at that moment—submerged in the intensity of his love— he whispered, "I love you, Jessica."

He watched her eyes widen, her face fill with disbelief, and then he saw the tears that filled her eyes, the look of happiness on her lips when she said, "I love you, too, Chase."

Damn. He hadn't expected that. And her words were the catalyst that broke his control. His need to make love to her suddenly became as vital as his need to draw his next breath. He began moving inside her in rapid thrusts, stunned by how emotions had taken over his mind, invaded his heart, filled him with a drive to make her truly his.

Never had he known anything as beautiful as what

he was sharing with her now. She was filling an emptiness inside of him that he hadn't known existed. And she was doing it in a way no other woman had. His body continued moving in and out of her as she lifted her hips, wrapped her legs around his waist to hold him tight, melding their bodies together over and over.

"Chase!"

When she cried out his name, he gritted his teeth as the same sensations that began wracking her body invaded his. An explosion erupted and mind-whirling sensations overtook them. He grasped her hips while he continued to ply her with fluid strokes and the full impact of his release. It seemed they were spiraling higher than they had ever gone before, riding wave after wave of sensation so intense he wondered if he could survive. He drove into her again and again as words of love flowed from his lips.

And when his body exploded a second time, and moments later a third, he knew that she was truly his just as he was undeniably hers.

Hours later, Chase tried not to wake Jessica as he eased out of bed. He needed to leave, go home and pack for his trip to Houston. His plane would be leaving in five hours and he would be battling morning traffic to the airport.

After putting on his clothes he walked back over to the bed, leaned down and gently kissed her lips. Moments later he slipped downstairs, deciding to leave her a note. He would also call her when he got to the airport. If this meeting wasn't so important he would change his mind about going. But lately he'd given thought to opening another Chase's Place in Texas and the group of men he was meeting with could make such a venture possible.

He opened the door to her office and glanced around. This was the first time he had been in this particular room and liked how she had things set up. It was small but furnished professionally. He walked over to the stylish oak desk to get a piece of paper and a pen. His hand went still when his gaze fell on a small framed photograph.

He picked it up, blinking, not sure he was seeing straight. It was a photo of Jessica with an older couple who he could only assume were the grandparents she loved. Chase recognized the older couple immediately. They were Carlton and Helen Graham.

Suddenly, he felt as if he'd been punched in the gut. Jessica was Carlton Graham's granddaughter? If that was true, then why hadn't she told him? His hand shook as he placed the picture frame back on the desk. He glanced around and a piece of paper caught his attention. He picked it up. He read the words written on her To Do list for today:

Talk to Donald Schuster again regarding the Westmoreland recipes.

The paper slipped from his hand as he felt a stabbing sensation in his heart. He closed his eyes in denial. There was no way another Graham was betraying a Westmoreland. It couldn't be possible. When he opened his eyes and stared at the paper and the photo once again, he saw that anything was possible. Had Schuster heard that he was thinking about franchising and made some kind of deal with Jessica to get close to him? Damn, she *had* gotten close to him, and he had even trusted her enough to share one of the recipes with her. What was in it for her? A chance to sell her sweets in all the Schuster restaurants around the country? He clenched his teeth. It hurt like hell to know she was an opportunist, just like Iris had been.

He felt angrier than he'd ever felt in his life, anger mingled with deeply entrenched pain. He left the office and raced back up the stairs. For the second time in his life he had given his heart to a woman and look what happened. Never again would he trust blindly.

He felt a tightening around his heart when he walked back into Jessica's bedroom. His body was torn with the love he felt for her and the hurt her betrayal was causing. Exhaling deeply, as if that could expel any emotions he felt for her, he walked over to the bed. "Jessica, wake up."

Fighting sleep, Jessica slowly opened her eyes when she heard the sound of Chase's voice. When he came into focus she saw that he was standing over her with features filled with anger. She pulled herself up in bed. "What's wrong, Chase?"

For a moment he didn't say anything; he just looked at her and the anger was there, clearly, in his eyes. "Chase, please tell me what's wrong."

"Why didn't you tell me you were Carlton Graham's granddaughter? Did you get a kick out of playing me for a fool?"

She sucked in a quick breath, wondering how he had found out, but then knowing it really didn't matter.

He *had* found out and she hadn't been the one to tell him. "No, that's not it at all, Chase. I wanted to tell you but thought I could prove my grandfather's innocence first."

"You can't prove what isn't true."

Jessica was out of bed in a flash. She got into Chase's face, not caring that she was completely naked. "My grandfather didn't take any recipes and I wanted to prove it. But then I fell in love with you and—"

"Hell, you didn't fall in love with me. It was nothing but an act. Do you think I'm stupid, Jessica? I saw that note about you meeting with Schuster today. Are the two of you working together to pry more recipes out of a Westmoreland? What did he offer you? A chance to peddle your sweets in his restaurants?"

Jessica shook her head. "No. How could you think something like that? Schuster has answers. Someone gave him those recipes all those years ago, and since I knew it wasn't my grandfather, I met with him once to see what he could tell me. I'm meeting with him again to get more information out of him if I can."

Chase drew in a deep breath. He wanted to believe her, but all he could think about was her betraying his love. His mouth tightened in a harsh line. "If any of what you're saying is true, why didn't you tell me who you were? We've been seeing each other for almost a month, Jessica, and during that time you've had every opportunity to tell me the truth, but you never mentioned you were related to Carlton."

Jessica swallowed, knowing he had her there. There had been opportunities when she could have shared that fact with him. "Like I told you, Chase, I wanted to prove his innocence first. I was going to tell you when you first got here last night, but I didn't get a chance to. You've got to believe me. Chase. I love you and—"

Chase laughed. It was an unforgiving sound. "Love? Is this how you show your love? By being deceitful? Then I don't want any part of it."

He turned and walked out of the room. Jessica held her breath until she heard the door slam shut behind him. Tears flooded her eyes. She had made a complete mess of things. She hadn't cleared her grandfather's name, and worse—Chase hated her.

Eleven

Chase slipped out of bed. Whenever he traveled he made it a point to stay at the best hotels. But a nice room and a soft bed couldn't prevent his restless nights.

For the past two days he had been so thickly involved with business negotiations that he hadn't allowed anything or anyone to invade his thoughts… other than Jessica. She had managed to wiggle inside his head, although he hadn't wanted her there.

And he couldn't get her out no matter how hard he tried.

Without wanting them to, memories of that night came back to flood his mind. She had actually looked shocked by his accusation. Well, hell, how had she expected him to react? Had she thought he would embrace her with open arms? Overlook the fact that his grandfather and hers had ended up bitter enemies? For heaven's sake, she was a Graham and he was a Westmoreland. He distinctively remembered his grandfather's warning never to trust a Graham. Not only had he trusted one, he had fallen in love with one.

He sighed deeply. And did she actually think he would believe her story about trying to prove her grandfather innocent? That the only reason she had met with Schuster was to find out the truth?

But then he couldn't dismiss the possibility that his reluctance to believe her was the reason she hadn't leveled with him in the beginning. She had known he wouldn't embrace her with open arms. They would have become enemies before having the chance to become friends.

On top of knowing that, there was this thought that had been nagging at him for the past two days. What if she *was* telling the truth? He couldn't let go of the fact that this was a woman who had walked away from a prestigious career for ethical reasons. A woman of strong values and beliefs. She was also a woman who had spent her free time baking goodies for the guys on his team. This was someone who definitely cared about others.

And more than anything, he couldn't forget that she had been celibate for eight years. He had a gut feeling it would have taken more than the promise of her products being sold in a Schuster restaurant for her to go as far with him as she'd gone if she didn't really care for him.

He inhaled deeply. Had he acted irrationally two days ago? Had he been unfair by jumping to conclusions and not listening to her side of things? Had he been wrong to place her in the same category as Iris? The two women were nothing alike. Iris was an unscrupulous taker. Jessica was an extraordinary giver.

He glanced over at the clock on the nightstand. It was almost midnight. He wanted to call Jessica, talk to her. When he returned to Atlanta tomorrow he would listen to what she had to say and not be so quick to judge. No matter what, he still loved her. What happened with the Westmoreland recipes no longer mattered to him. If Jessica was hell-bent on proving her grandfather's innocence then he would help her discover how the recipes got into the wrong hands.

He took a deep breath. More than anything he wanted a future with the woman he loved.

"Listen, Jessica, if he loved you two days ago then he loves you now. Nobody can turn love on and off like a faucet, not if it's the real thing."

Jessica heard her stepmother's words but she still wasn't convinced. She had seen the look of loathing in Chase's eyes just moments before he'd left. But then she couldn't erase the memory of another look as well. It had been the look he'd given her just moments before whispering that he loved her. When he had said those words she had believed in her heart that he had meant them, just like she had meant what she'd said to him. She loved him, too.

"Even after I found out what your father had done," Jennifer was saying, "I couldn't hate him. I was hurt and I put up a wall to protect myself from further pain, but the love was still there for a long time."

"It doesn't matter," Jessica said softly. "Chase let me know things are over between us." After a brief pause she said, "I've made some decisions."

There was a short silence, then Jennifer asked, "What sort of decisions?"

Jessica took a deep breath. "I met with a real estate agent today. I've decided to sell this place and move back to California."

"And return to law?"

"Possibly, but it won't be as a corporate attorney. I'm thinking of becoming a consumer attorney specializing in product safety."

"Do you think running away will solve anything, Jessica?"

"I'm not running away. I'm protecting my heart from further damage."

There was a brief pause again, and then Jennifer said, "Well, I think you and Chase need to sit down and talk things through."

"So do I," Jessica said quietly. "But before he left I got the distinct impression that he doesn't want to see me again. And since our businesses are separated by only one building, there's no way we can avoid seeing each other. One of us will have to leave. It might as well be me." After a brief pause she added, "Hey, I'm a survivor. You know that."

She sighed deeply. She *had* let Chase become too important to her. She had done the one thing she'd always promised herself she wouldn't do, give her heart and soul to a man. That made it harder to walk away. But walk away she would.

* * *

"What do you mean she's selling her place?" Chase asked staring hard at Donna. He had come straight to the restaurant from the airport to find Delicious Cravings closed in the middle of the day with a For Sale sign in the window.

Donna leaned back against his closed office door. "Rumor has it that she's moving back to California."

A chill of fear ripped down his spine. God, he'd been a fool to think the worst about her. He had done a lot of thinking over the past three days, and in his heart he knew Jessica loved him. He had been a complete idiot to accuse her of all those things. Unlike Iris, Jessica couldn't relate to greed.

Donna cleared her throat. "I know this might not be a good time but there's someone here who insists on seeing you."

Chase lifted an eyebrow. "Who?"

"A woman named Darcy Evans."

Chase's brow lifted higher upon remembering the name. He sighed deeply. "Please show her in."

A few minutes later, Darcy Evans walked into his office. Although she had only worked with his grand-father for a short while, no more than six months, he remembered her. She had been quiet and kept to her-self, much as Donna was inclined to do.

Chase crossed the room to shake her hand. "Ms. Evans, it's been years. It's good to see you again. Please have a seat."

When she had taken the chair across from his desk he met her gaze and asked. "What can I do for you?" Chase couldn't help noticing that she appeared nervous.

"I wanted to talk to Ms. Claiborne but her place is closed up. She came to see me a couple of times during the past month."

Chase knew he looked puzzled and confused. "Jessica came to see you?"

"Yes. She didn't believe her grandfather took those recipes from your grandfather and wanted the truth. It's my understanding that she talked to me, Donald Schuster, Paula Meyers and Theodore Henry."

Chase recognized all the names except one. "Theodore Henry?"

"Yes, he was the cook for Schuster at the time I worked for your grandfather." She sighed deeply before saying, "Theodore and I were lovers."

Chase's eyes widened and he leaned forward from his desk. "You were?"

"Yes," she admitted. "We were together for almost a year, but we kept things a secret. He felt his job as a cook with Mr. Schuster was on shaky ground and was desperate. He asked me to find a way to take those recipes. At first I wouldn't do it. I liked Mr. Graham for getting me the job and I thought your grandfather was a nice man, although he could be rather bullheaded at times."

Chase nodded. He knew his grandfather could definitely be that. "But you eventually took them, Ms. Evans?"

She nervously clutched the straps on her purse as tears filled her eyes. "Yes. I'm the one who gave them to Theodore. I got upset that Mr. Westmoreland let Mr.

Graham go and wanted to do something to lash out at him. One day he left his recipe book out on his desk while he was out making deliveries. I made copies and passed them on to Theodore."

Chase was surprised; usually his grandfather had kept the family recipe book under lock and key. The old man must have had a lot on his mind that particular day. "I appreciate you coming and telling me the truth. It's finally put a lot of ill feelings to rest."

"Then it's not too late?" she asked, wiping her tears.

He reached across his desk to hand her a tissue. "Too late for what?"

"You and Ms. Claiborne. She told me that she loved you and wanted to tell you the truth, but had wanted to prove her grandfather's innocence first so that you would believe her."

Chase leaned back in his chair, feeling lower than low. Jessica had tried to tell him the truth but he hadn't listened. A bad feeling erupted in the pit of his stomach. What if she wouldn't forgive him for not believing her? What if she didn't want any part of him?

"Mr. Westmoreland?"

Chase took a deep breath and realized he hadn't answered the woman's question. "No, it's not too late. I love Jessica and together we can work out anything."

He had said the words, and he hoped to God that they were true.

Jessica noticed Chase's sports car the moment she pulled into the parking lot. Her stomach fluttered nervously as she gathered her purse and shopping bag to go inside her shop.

Moments later, barely after she'd gotten inside and closed the door behind her, there was a knock. She opened the door to find an older gentleman standing there. "Flowers for Jessica Claiborne."

Jessica smiled. It would be just like Jennifer to send her flowers to cheer her up, she thought, gazing lovingly at the huge vase of beautiful red roses. There seemed to be two dozen of them. "Thanks," she said. "If you wait a moment I'll get you a tip."

The old man grinned. "No need. It's been taken care of." His grin then widened. "He's never sent a woman flowers before. At least not from our shop."

Jessica lifted a puzzled arched eyebrow. "Who?"

The man chuckled. "I can't say, but he signed the card, and since he's aware of my wife's penchant to gab, I'm sure he knows that word of this delivery will be all over Atlanta before the sun goes down today. But evidently he doesn't care about that. Good day, ma'am." And then the man walked off and Jessica watched him get into a van from Coleman's Florist.

Closing the door behind her, a puzzled Jessica walked over to the counter, put the flowers down and pulled out the card.

> *Love makes you do and say foolish things.*
> *I'm sorry,*
> *Chase*

Jessica didn't move. She barely breathed. Chase had sent the flowers to apologize! Before she could gather

her thoughts there was another knock on her door. She quickly crossed the room to open it and found Donna standing there smiling.

"Hello, Jessica. I have a delivery for you, compliments of Chase's Place," she said, handing Jessica a huge bag. The aroma let Jessica know that whatever was inside would be delicious.

Jessica smiled, accepting the bag. "There's enough food here to feed two people."

Donna chuckled. "I think that's the idea."

Before Jessica could say anything, Donna was gone. Closing the door behind her, Jessica walked over to the counter and placed the bag of food next to the flowers. Before she could take a look inside, there was another knock at the door. For a moment she didn't move. Her heart knew. Her body knew. Her soul knew.

It was Chase.

Taking a deep breath she forced her body to cross the room. She exhaled deeply before gripping the handle to slowly open the door.

He stood there, leaning in the doorway holding a bottle of wine in his hand. He looked sexy, good enough to eat. Out of habit she licked her lips and watched his gaze move to her mouth. Her stomach clenched and her pulse spiked.

He didn't appear angry. That was a good thing. She inhaled deeply, knowing she needed either to ask him in or to ask him to leave. "Would you like to come in?"

"Yes." He hadn't hesitated in responding.

She swallowed hard and stepped aside to let him in. Where was extra oxygen when you needed it? she wondered, closing the door behind him. She leaned against the closed door knowing if she took one step she would fall. Her knees were too weak to support her. At this moment, she thought Chase looked more devastatingly handsome than he'd ever been before.

"Thanks for the flowers," she decided to say. "And for the food."

"You're welcome, and this is for you, too," he said, handing the bottle of wine to her.

She took his offering. "Thanks." It was only then that she forced herself away from the door to walk across the room to place the bottle of wine next to the flowers and delicious food. She slowly turned around and he was there, next to her. She hadn't heard him move. The look in his eyes was filled with regret.

"I'm sorry. I should have listened to you. I should have believed you," he whispered brokenly.

"I'm sorry, too," she said as a lump filled her throat. "I should have told you the truth as soon as I knew who you were."

He took another step to close the distance separating them. "I had three days to think about things. To think about us. And I want there to be an us, Jessica. What happened between our grandfathers is in the past. And you were right. Carlton didn't take the Westmoreland recipes. Darcy Evans came to see me earlier today. She came here first and found the shop closed. She wanted you to know the truth. She was the one who took the recipes. She and Theodore Henry were lovers and she took them to get back at my grandfather for letting your grandfather quit."

Jessica tensed and took a step back. She met his

gaze. "Is that why you're here? Because Darcy's words proved my innocence?"

Chase shook his head. "No. Even before Darcy came to see me I had made up my mind about us. I knew that I loved you. You don't have a deceitful or unethical bone in your body. You're nothing like Iris and I'm sorry I ever thought it. Please forgive me."

She met his gaze. They had both made mistakes. "I'll only forgive you if you forgive me for not being completely honest with you from the beginning. But I was so determined to prove my grandfather's innocence. I promised my grandmother on her deathbed that I would."

"And you did."

Jessica was filled with emotion at the thought that she truly had. She inhaled deeply as Chase covered the distance between them and reached out and lifted her chin with his finger.

"I love you, Jessica. I love you so much." He gathered her into his arms and whispered, "And I want forever with you. I want to put an end to the bitterness between our families. I want to form a new Westmoreland and Graham partnership. Please marry me. I want to give you my babies, love you, protect you, till death do us part and even after that."

"Oh, Chase," she said as tears burned her eyes. "I want all those things, too."

The smile Chase gave her would endear him to her forever. And then she felt herself being lifted into big strong arms. "We'll eat later," he whispered against her lips as he carried her up the stairs.

She shivered with need as he placed her on the bed.

Then he was on the bed with her, kissing her, removing her clothes. She was filled with desire and love; her pulse skittered with need so overbearing it took her breath away.

When she was completely naked he stood to remove his own clothes. But she wanted to do more than watch. She wanted to help. She eased out of bed and helped him take off his sweater. Next was his belt. Then she unzipped his pants so he could strip out of them. When he stood before her wearing nothing but a sexy pair of briefs, she reached out and skimmed her hand down his chest, moving lower to his stomach, needing to touch him to make sure she wasn't dreaming.

And then she eased down on her knees to remove the last piece of clothing that shielded his body. She took her time, easing the briefs down his legs. Then she placed a kiss on his navel before leaning back and meeting his gaze.

"Come here," he whispered hoarsely, holding his hand out to her.

He gently tugged her to her feet, held her close in his arms and she felt his engorged arousal press into her quivering stomach.

She met his gaze. "I wanted to—"

"I know," he said, cutting off her words and pulling her closer. "But had I allowed you to do that, things would have been over before they'd gotten started. You're still new at all of this, and I'm going to enjoy spending the rest of my life exploring things with you."

He grinned down at her. "There will never be a dull

moment at our house. You are and forever will be my most delicious craving."

Jessica's entire body swelled with love. "Make love to me, Chase," she whispered hotly against his lips.

He swept her back into his arms and placed her on the bed and joined her there. She shivered as need, strong and potent, raced through her. He pulled her into his arms, promising her a voyage into ecstasy and she knew that he was right—there would never be a dull moment at their house. And that they would spend the rest of their lives together.

She might be his delicious craving, but he was definitely her most ardent chocolate delight.

Epilogue

Two months later, Christmas Day

Jessica smiled at her sister who was asking questions a mile a minute. It was her wedding day and she couldn't wait to join her life with Chase's. They had decided that since all the Westmorelands came home for the holidays, today would be perfect. And it was.

"Slow down, Savannah, and let me answer your first question," she chuckled. "His name is Durango Westmoreland and he's Chase's cousin. He works as a park ranger in Montana."

She watched the interest in her sister's eyes. It had been there since the rehearsal dinner last night when Durango, whose plane had been late, had arrived at Chase's Place, proving without a doubt that all the Westmoreland men were sexy.

"Now are you going to help me put on my veil or are you going to continue to stand there in a daze?" Jessica asked her sister.

Savannah laughed as she stepped behind Jessica and tugged the veil in place. "You look beautiful, Jess."

Jessica smiled. She actually felt beautiful. She glanced at Savannah's reflection in the mirror. Her sister was beautiful too, with hazel eyes, skin the color of caramel and long, wavy black hair that flowed down her back.

Jessica had also noticed Durango checking her sister out last night, but he'd kept his distance.

"Durango doesn't like city women," she said, turning around to face her sister.

Savannah lifted a brow. "Why?"

Jessica shrugged. "Something to do with an old wound. And sister of mine, you're definitely city."

It was Savannah's turn to shrug. She then smiled. "I guess he'll have to learn to like us. Because after seeing him, I've decided I definitely have a thing for mountain men."

Jessica raised her eyes to the ceiling. She didn't know who would need her prayers more: Durango or Savannah. Deciding she didn't want to dwell on that, she smiled, knowing she only had a few moments left before she became Chase's wife.

She and Chase had wanted a small ceremony, but it seemed the Westmorelands didn't know the meaning of small—three hundred plus guests had been invited. With everyone's help they had pulled things off in two months. Savannah was her maid of honor and Chase's cousin Quade was his best man.

The two sisters hugged. "I'm happy for you, Jess," Savannah whispered brokenly.

"Thanks. Chase is a good man. I'm getting the best." She pulled back and gazed lovingly at her sister. "One day it will be your time."

Savannah chuckled and a mischievous glint appeared in her eyes. "Let's not hold our breath for that to happen."

Oh, God, she's beautiful, Chase thought as he watched Jessica walk down the aisle toward him on her brother's arm. He was filled with emotion and had to fight back the lump in his throat and the mistiness in his eyes.

When she reached his side he saw her tears of joy, lifted her hands to his lips and whispered, "I love you."

He saw her smile through her tears. She was making him the happiest man on earth today by becoming his wife. Together, they turned to face the minister. Before he started speaking, Chase spoke up and said, "I do."

The minister lifted a brow. "You do?"

Chase nodded. "Yes."

The minister, who had known Chase since birth smiled. "I haven't asked any questions yet, Chase."

"Doesn't matter. 'I do' to all of them." At his side, he heard a snort and knew it had come from Quade.

The minister's smile widened. "Nevertheless, we will go through the ceremony as planned."

A short while later the minister said, "I now pronounce you man and wife. You may kiss your bride, Chase."

And he did. He turned and gathered Jessica into his arms. There was nothing gentle about the kiss. He totally ignored the fact that he was standing before three hundred guests as he devoured his wife's mouth.

Durango…or maybe it was Storm…tugged on his tux tails and said, "Leave something for later, will you?"

Chase let go of Jessica's mouth and looked at her, then returned her smile and whispered, "I couldn't help it, sweetheart. You're simply delicious."

* * * * *

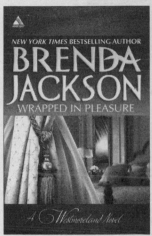

REQUEST YOUR FREE BOOKS!

2 FREE NOVELS PLUS 2 FREE GIFTS!

KIMANI ROMANCE ™

Love's ultimate destination!

YES! Please send me 2 FREE Kimani™ Romance novels and my 2 FREE gifts (gifts are worth about $10). After receiving them, if I don't wish to receive any more books, I can return the shipping statement marked "cancel." If I don't cancel, I will receive 4 brand-new novels every month and be billed just $4.69 per book in the U.S. or $5.24 per book in Canada. That's a saving of at least 16% off the cover price. It's quite a bargain! Shipping and handling is just 50¢ per book in the U.S. and 75¢ per book in Canada.* I understand that accepting the 2 free books and gifts places me under no obligation to buy anything. I can always return a shipment and cancel at any time. Even if I never buy another book, the two free books and gifts are mine to keep forever.

168/368 XDN FDAT

Name _____ (PLEASE PRINT)

Address _____ Apt. #

City _____ State/Prov. _____ Zip/Postal Code

Signature (if under 18, a parent or guardian must sign)

Mail to the **Reader Service**:

IN U.S.A.: P.O. Box 1867, Buffalo, NY 14240-1867
IN CANADA: P.O. Box 609, Fort Erie, Ontario L2A 5X3

Not valid for current subscribers to Kimani Romance books.

**Want to try two free books from another line?
Call 1-800-873-8635 or visit www.ReaderService.com.**

* Terms and prices subject to change without notice. Prices do not include applicable taxes. Sales tax applicable in N.Y. Canadian residents will be charged applicable taxes. Offer not valid in Quebec. This offer is limited to one order per household. All orders subject to credit approval. Credit or debit balances in a customer's account(s) may be offset by any other outstanding balance owed by or to the customer. Please allow 4 to 6 weeks for delivery. Offer available while quantities last.

Your Privacy—The Reader Service is committed to protecting your privacy. Our Privacy Policy is available online at www.ReaderService.com or upon request from the Reader Service.

We make a portion of our mailing list available to reputable third parties that offer products we believe may interest you. If you prefer that we not exchange your name with third parties, or if you wish to clarify or modify your communication preferences, please visit us at www.ReaderService.com/consumerchoice or write to us at Reader Service Preference Service, P.O. Box 9062, Buffalo, NY 14269. Include your complete name and address.

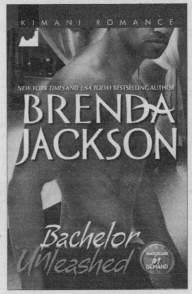

Fru·gal·is·ta [froo-*guh*-lee-stuh] *noun*

1. A person who lives within her means and saves money, but still looks good, eats well and lives *fabulously*

THE TRUE STORY OF HOW ONE TENACIOUS YOUNG WOMAN GOT HERSELF OUT OF DEBT WITHOUT GIVING UP HER FABULOUS LIFESTYLE

NATALIE P. MCNEAL

Natalie McNeal opened her credit card statement in January 2008 to find that she was a staggering five figures—nearly $20,000!—in debt. A young, single, professional woman, Natalie loved her lifestyle of regular mani/pedis, daily takeout and nights on the town with the girls, but she knew she had to trim back to make ends meet. The solution came in the form of her *Miami Herald* blog, "The Frugalista Files." Starting in February 2008, Natalie chronicled her journey as she discovered how to maintain her fabulous, single-girl lifestyle while digging herself out of debt and even saving for the future.

THE *Frugalista* FILES

Available wherever books are sold.

HARLEQUIN®

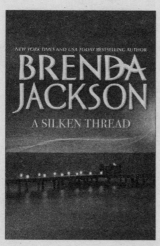